WWP   BHP ✓

P9-COP-542

Also by Mariah Stewart

Last Breath
Last Words
Last Look

Final Truth
Dark Truth
Hard Truth
Cold Truth

Dead End
Dead Even
Dead Certain
Dead Wrong

Until Dark
The President's Daughter

MERCY STREET

MERCY STREET

mariah stewart

STREET

a novel

BALLANTINE BOOKS NEW YORK

Mercy Street is a work of fiction. Names, characters, places, and incidents are the products of the author's imagination or are used fictitiously. Any resemblance to actual events, locales, or persons, living or dead, is entirely coincidental.

Copyright © 2008 by Marti Robb

All rights reserved.

Published in the United States by Ballantine Books, an imprint of The Random House Publishing Group, a division of Random House, Inc., New York.

Ballantine and colophon are registered trademarks of Random House, Inc.

ISBN-13: 978-0-7394-9581-0

Printed in the United States of America

Book design by Susan Turner

For Katie and Mike—
may you live happily ever after.

ACKNOWLEDGMENTS

Once again I've had the good fortune to have a character inspired by a real person who won the right to have her name used in this book via a charity raffle run by the remarkable ladies who gather at the ADWOFF website. This year's winner was Mary Corcoran, a wonderful lady whose true personality is reflected, I hope, in the warmth of the fictional Mary. Many thanks to Phyllis Lannik for inviting me to participate in this once-a-year raffle to raise money to promote literacy.

I'd also like to thank Trula Comfort, a reader who so kindly permitted me to use her wonderful name in this book. I hope she is pleased with the character her name inspired.

Thanks to Joe Drabyak, Chester County Book and Music Company, who is an exceptional bookseller and an all-around terrific guy.

Much love and thanks to my incredible agent, Loretta Barrett, and her terrific staff, Nick Mullendore and Gabriel Davis.

I've been blessed to work with some of the best people in the business: Linda Marrow, Libby McGuire, Scott Shannon, Kim Hovey,

Nancy Delia, Brian McLendon, Signe Pike, and Dana Isaacson. Special thanks, love, and a heartfelt welcome back to Kate Collins, my amazing editor, who is such a joy to work with. Many thanks to all of the hard-working people behind the scenes at Ballantine Books who do such a terrific job getting my books out there. Thanks to Daniel Mallory, who was always so helpful and supportive, and whose humor is greatly missed. New York's loss is Oxford's gain.

Many thanks and love to Chery Griffin for her support and friendship and for cheering me along when I doubt myself.

And last but by no means least, much love to my wonderful, fabulous, and sometimes wacky family—Bill, Katie, and Becca—who make it all worthwhile.

MERCY STREET

From the top of the jetty to the rocks below was roughly twelve feet, give or take. Not enough to break much more than a few limbs, the man standing at the far edge thought wryly. Hardly worth the jump.

Not for the first time, he wished he'd had the jetty built higher.

"Hey! Buddy! You there on the jetty!" a voice called from the beach. "That's private property."

The would-be jumper turned to see a man in an Irish knit sweater and jeans picking his way carefully across the rocks, headed straight for him. As he drew closer, the newcomer said, "Most people aren't aware that the jetty is privately owned. I don't know that the owner wants the liability of having people walking around out here."

"You are."

"I try to keep an eye on the place since the owner doesn't seem to. We're just across the street. Never met the guy who owns it. None of us has. Wouldn't know him if I tripped over him. Realtor says he's a real nice guy, though." He jerked a thumb over his shoulder in the direction of the house. "Imagine building a place like that and never moving in?"

He turned to look back at the house. "Then again, I guess it's understandable. Guy who owns it lost his wife, his only child, too. Disappeared just like that." He snapped his fingers. "Went off to a party or something and never came back."

It was a baby shower. Her cousin's baby shower.

"Yeah, I guess it's something else inside," he continued. "But when you consider who built it . . ." He stopped to watch his brown Lab chasing seagulls along the waterline, then resumed his chatter.

"You probably read about it. Robert Magellan, the gazillionaire? That's his place. Built it for his wife, just before she went missing. Sad as hell, you know? I couldn't imagine that, the wife and kid just, poof. Gone."

Robert stared blankly as the man continued to babble.

He shook his head. "There was some talk early on that maybe he had a hand in it, but no one around here ever bought in to it. You don't do something like *that*"—he pointed to the house—"as a surprise for someone you're planning to get rid of. The money it must have cost aside, I heard he picked out everything himself, didn't even use a decorator. That says something to me about the man, like it must have been real important to him that everything be just right for her, you know?"

"Yes, I know."

"You must have heard about the guy. Hell, you'd have to have been on another planet not to have. The news coverage last year was nonstop for weeks after it happened. We couldn't even park in front of our own house with all the news vans and gawkers. Some days we couldn't even get into our own driveway."

"That must have been a difficult time for all of you."

"It was. It sure was. You have no idea what it was like. Of course, now all the neighbors are wondering what he's going to do with it. We keep watching for a sale sign to go up. Every once in a while, I run into the Realtor—Janice Wilson, if you're looking to buy a place down here." He paused. "You looking to buy a place in Carlson's Beach?"

"I haven't decided what I'm going to do."

"Check in with Janice, Beach Realty, right down there on Bay Avenue. Tell her Ben Miller sent you."

"Maybe I'll do that."

The man whistled for his Lab, but the dog was more interested in the gulls. "Looks like I'm going to have to go after him. Nine years old and he's still nothing but an overgrown pup. Guess I'd better catch up with him." He laughed good-naturedly and took a leash from his back pocket, then looked back at Robert. "So you won't be hanging around here, right? The police do patrol once in a while, try to keep people off the property. Since it is, like I said, private . . ."

"I'll be moving on."

"Okay, well, be careful up there," Ben Miller called over his shoulder as he made his way down the rocks to the sand below. "It's a long way down."

Not long enough.

Robert Magellan watched the man and his frolicking dog until they disappeared over the dune. He took off his dark glasses, rubbed a hand over his face, and tried to decide if he was pleased to know his neighbors believed he'd had nothing to do with Beth and Ian's disappearance, or pissed at the reminder that the investigation had once focused on him.

"Don't take it personally," Joe Drabyak—chief of police of Conroy, Pennsylvania, their hometown—had told him. "The spouse is always a suspect. Because usually, when a person goes missing, someone close to that person is the one who made them disappear."

"You're wasting time," Robert had replied angrily. "While you're sitting here trying to build a case against me, someone else has my wife. My son—"

"Let's get one thing straight, Mr. Magellan." Drabyak's voice had gone ice cold. "I'm not trying to 'build a case' against anyone. I'm only trying to get to the truth. Right now, my only priority is to find your wife and your son and I couldn't care less whose toes I step on to do it. Even yours. So I'll be asking you questions and you'll be answering them. Believe me, everyone is doing everything they can to locate your family. Every cop between here and Gibson Springs is looking for them, okay? Don't think for a second that you're the only person we're talking to. They're all looking out there, looking for your wife and your baby boy, but you are here, in my town, and that makes you mine, got it? Trust me, I'm not going to be the only one questioning you. The boys out in the western part of the state want to talk to you, the state wants to talk to you, and the FBI is waiting in the wings. The longer you and I play this game, the longer it will be before we get out of here, so let's get on with this, shall we?"

Robert may not have liked it, but he couldn't deny that the police had pulled out every stop to find Beth and the baby. Even he had to admit that the fact that they'd failed was no reflection on the effort. He'd personally witnessed Drabyak's growing frustration that neither his force, the state police, the FBI, nor any of the private investigators Robert had hired had been able to pin down any real clues to his missing family.

How was it possible that a woman, a baby, and a Jeep Cherokee could disappear into thin air?

He glanced once more at the dark water swirling around the rocks below and pulled up the collar of his jacket. A brisk breeze blew in off the ocean, and clouds were starting to gather overhead. As the sky darkened, Robert walked back along the jetty toward the house. The man-made wall of rock extended along the entire line of his property on one side, gradually diminishing in height until it reached the road out front. He checked to make sure the outbuildings—the guesthouse, the garage, and the playhouse—were all securely locked before going up the back steps and into the main house.

He made his way through the silent rooms, trying not to think about the countless hours he'd spent designing this home. So many times, Robert had tried to imagine Beth's reaction when he brought her here for the first time. He knew she would have loved the fact that he'd bought the weathered shingles from a house that had been demolished in Maine, and that he'd had a guesthouse specially designed where Beth's sister, Pam, and her husband, Rick, and their children could stay. There was a walled yard where the kids could play safely, and a playhouse that Robert had sketched out for the architect, his own childhood fantasies come to life in clapboard and brick. The master bedroom in the magnificent main house had a balcony with an expansive view of the ocean where he and Beth could watch the sun rise over the water every morning.

He'd just about given up on the dream of sharing that view with her.

His plan today included a stop at the Realtor's office to tell her he was putting the place on the market, but after having spent the better part of the afternoon here, he realized he wasn't up to having that conversation today. Tomorrow he'd have Susanna, his assistant, call Janice Wilson and tell her he'd like her to handle the sale of 1217 Heron Place.

Robert walked through the empty rooms, his footsteps echoing on the hardwood floors, and reset the alarm before leaving by the front door just as the first fat drops of rain began to fall. Once outside, he turned the key in the lock and slipped it into his pocket for what he knew would be the last time.

The decision to sell had not been made easily. In Robert's heart, it felt like a betrayal, because it meant he'd given up on ever seeing Beth and Ian again. But coming here was nothing short of torture for him. It was just one more reminder of that day when his entire world tilted and everything that mattered to him vanished.

"Fuck it," he said aloud. "Just . . . fuck it."

He turned his back on the house, got into his car, and drove home through the rain, the wipers slapping against the glass.

Hours later he found himself seated in his car, the engine turned

off, in front of the wide iron gates outside his house. He had no rec-
ollection of having driven the five hours from the beach house near
Stone Harbor, New Jersey, to his home in Conroy, Pennsylvania, and
started to tune back in now only because he had to key in the code to
open the gates. That morning, he'd taken the first of the cars that he'd
come to when he walked outside. It was the only vehicle that didn't
have the remote for the gates built in.

See how easy it is for something like that to happen? he told himself
as he tapped the numbers on the keypad. *You take the wrong vehicle
and it's a minor inconvenience. Beth borrowed a car and we lost her forever.*

Don't say forever, a voice inside his head pleaded. *Maybe it's not
forever . . .*

He drove around to the back of his house and parked near the
brick walk that led to the kitchen.

"Good. You beat the worst of the storm home." Trula Comfort,
Robert's housekeeper and his late grandmother's best friend, greeted
him as he came in through the back door. "You look like you need
something warm. I have fresh coffee made, just put the pot on for Father Kevin. He's in the den. Been waiting for you for an hour or so. If
you'd told me he was coming, I'd have planned one of his favorites
for dinner."

"I didn't know he was coming," Robert told her as he accepted
the mug she held out to him. He stole a glance at it. BLOOM WHERE
YOU ARE PLANTED was apparently the message of the day. "And what
about having one of my favorites?"

"You're here every day. Father Kevin hasn't been here in two
weeks."

"So what you're saying is I have to leave to get special treatment."

"Well, dessert should make you both happy. I picked up some
strawberries—the first of the season—from that nice young Amish
couple who bought the Turners' farm. You probably don't remember
the Turners—the family owned that land for, good Lord, must be a

hundred years or so." She fixed her gaze on him to let him know she was not oblivious to the fact that he was inching toward the door. "But now that you bring it up, a nice vacation away would do you good. Be a vacation for me, too, a few weeks without you around. And you could use a little color in your face. Here it is, almost summer, and you're as pale now as you were in February." Trula was winding up, Robert could feel it. If he didn't move quickly, she'd be at full blast and he'd be stuck in here for way longer than he'd like.

"And I'll probably be just as pale next month."

"You make a joke, but you could use the vitamin D you get from the sun."

"I thought those vitamins you make me take every day had lots of D in them."

"There's no pill that's as good as getting it right from the source." She pushed open the kitchen door and pointed down the hall in the general direction of the den. "Go, make sure Father Kevin doesn't try to sneak out before dinner."

"Yes, sir." Robert followed the pointed finger.

"Funny man," Trula muttered as he passed.

Robert opened the half-closed door to his den and stepped inside the large well-lit room.

"Trula wants you to stay for dinner," he said by way of greeting.

"She already invited me," Father Kevin Burch replied without looking up from the book he was engrossed in. "She tempted me with fresh sea bass. How could I say no?"

"I thought priests weren't supposed to give in to temptation." Robert took a chair near the windows opposite his cousin. It occurred to him that when either of them had something on his mind that he wanted to discuss, somehow they both always ended up here, in the den, in these chairs, facing each other.

"We're also supposed to honor our elders." Kevin smiled. "You know many people more elderly than Trula?"

"Good point."

"And the last thing Gramma asked was that we take care of her, Trula being on her own and not having any family and all."

"Trula can take care of herself," Robert noted. "But I like having her here. Like having her in charge."

"You like not having to deal with the house," Kevin pointed out. "Even if she weren't as efficient as she is, you'd still let her run things. Between her running the house, and Susanna running your life, do you have to make any decisions at all anymore?"

"Not if I can help it." Robert pulled a small table closer and placed his mug on a coaster. "So to what do we owe the honor?"

Kevin closed the book he'd been reading without marking the place—uncharacteristic for him—and Robert knew there was something on his mind.

"We have . . . a situation in Conroy." Kevin cleared his throat. "You've heard about the two boys who were shot and killed at the playground a couple of weeks back, I'm sure."

"I may have heard something about it." Robert tried to think back to the last news report he'd heard. He paid so little attention these days, rarely turning on the television and rarer still opening a newspaper. The events of last year had pretty much cured him of seeking out the reports of the latest local, national, or international tragedies. These past few days, all the talk had been about a sniper on the loose. After the initial story, Robert had pretty much tuned it out. "Refresh me."

"Four teenagers—three boys, one girl, all seniors at our school, by the way—went to the playground on Dexter Street around ten PM two Fridays ago. The next morning, two of the boys were found shot to death. One shot each to the back of the head."

"And the other two?"

Kevin held out his hands in a gesture of hopelessness. "No one knows what happened to them. They just seem to have vanished."

There was an awkward pause. Both men had spent the past year dealing with the uncertainties of unexplained disappearances.

"And this involves me how?" Robert asked flatly.

"The boy who disappeared—he's Mary Corcoran's grandson."

"Mary Corcoran . . . your Mary Corcoran who works in the rectory?"

Kevin nodded slowly. "She's raised the boy since he was a baby. His mother, Kathleen, was Mary's only child. She would have been about thirty-five if she hadn't died when Ryan—that's the boy's name, Ryan—was two. Some kids found Kathleen in an abandoned building in Philly, the needle still in her arm, Ryan curled up next to her on the floor."

"Jesus."

"Oh, He must have been there for the boy, when you consider what could have happened to him. The police turned him over to social services, who tracked down the boy's father, some punk who had no interest whatsoever in the kid. The father suggested they contact Kathleen's mother, which was the best thing that could have happened. Mary dedicated her life to raising that boy right. I've known them—him and Courtney, the girl who went missing with him—since they were in grade school. They're good kids, Rob. There's no way they had a hand in what happened to their friends."

"So what were four 'good kids' doing in that park after dark on a Friday night? Dexter Street isn't in the best part of the city."

"That's the far end of my parish." Kevin bristled slightly. "I know the neighborhood has seen better days, but it isn't exactly a slum. It's strictly working class, Rob. The whole city is pretty much blue collar these days."

"So how much do you want?" Robert asked. "I'm assuming you want me to put up the reward money."

"It's not reward money I'm asking for."

"Then what?"

Kevin took a deep breath. "One of the two dead boys had taken money out of his savings account the day before, almost a thousand dollars. He'd looked at a car that afternoon but decided he didn't want it. According to his mother, he still had the money in his pocket when he left the house that night, but the police report indicates there was no money found on either of the bodies. The current thinking is that Ryan—and possibly Courtney, they're not sure what her involvement is at this point—killed the other two and took off with the cash." Kevin stood and walked to the window. "Mary believes her grandson is innocent. And frankly, so do I. But in the absence of any other suspects . . ."

"The police have locked in on him as the shooter."

Kevin nodded. "They keep coming back to the fact that if Ryan and/or Courtney had nothing to do with the murders, at the very least they would have contacted their families by now."

"Maybe they're dead," Robert said bluntly. "Maybe the killers took them along with them and killed them elsewhere."

"That's definitely a possibility. Or maybe they were taken and are being held hostage for some reason."

"Has there been a ransom demand?"

"Not yet." Kevin paced from the windows to the fireplace and back again.

"Well, as we both learned, if there's no ransom demand within the first forty-eight hours, there isn't likely to be one, so kidnapping is probably not what you're looking at here. What else is on your list of possible scenarios?"

"They could have run when the shooting started, but that doesn't explain why they haven't come back or at least contacted someone," Kevin admitted. "The only thing we know for certain is that they are gone and the police have already decided their guilt."

"Go back to the part about why you're telling me this."

"Mary's ready to mortgage her house to hire an investigator to find her grandson. She can't afford to do that. This is a woman who worked two jobs for almost thirty years to pay for that house and raise her daughter's child. She shouldn't have to strap herself with another loan at this stage of her life." Kevin leaned over the back of the chair he'd been sitting in. "I want you to hire an investigator to find out what happened that night, to find Ryan and Courtney."

"You may have noticed that I haven't had particularly good luck with private investigators over the past year. I've lost track of how many I hired. Not one of them was worth shit."

"Maybe there's someone else . . . someone you didn't speak with."

"Are you kidding?" Robert laughed hoarsely. "Every PI on the East Coast descended on this house after Beth and Ian disappeared. And I shouldn't have to remind you, of all people, not one of them found a damned thing. Five firms, no leads. Every damned one of them spent weeks spinning their wheels and running up exorbitant fees. Sharks circling a bleeding swimmer, Susanna called them. Sorry, but I don't have much faith in PIs, pal."

"How about if we try someone for a week and just see if—"

"No."

"Rob, Mary is going to hire someone whether you help her out or not. You not helping her means she'll be taking on a financial burden she really can't afford."

"Sorry, Kev, but no."

"Then make a loan to me, and I'll hire someone."

"Because you believe in the kid, or because you'll feel guilty if you don't help the grandmother?"

"Both," Kevin answered without hesitation. "I do believe Ryan is innocent, and I'd never be able to look myself in the face again if I didn't do everything I could to help Mary now."

Robert tapped his fingers on the arm of the chair, annoyed. He'd do just about anything for Kevin. As close as brothers, they'd grown up together—born on the same day to sisters who entered the hospital at the same time, delivered by the same doctor, with Robert three hours older. *People* magazine, a fledgling publication the year they were born, had covered the story. For Christmas one year, Robert had gotten his hands on the photo the magazine had printed of the two pretty former Malone sisters holding their infant sons in front of

St. Francis Hospital and had a copy made for Kevin. Robert had never hesitated when Kevin asked for something—a new roof for the parish hall, a new gymnasium for the elementary school, a tennis court, pool, a new track for the high school; he'd never asked for anything for himself—and Robert had always been happy to help. But this hit too close to home, and he wanted no part of it. He'd had his fill of private investigators.

"Maybe if we hired a lawyer instead," Robert suggested, "someone with a lot of muscle who could put some pressure on the police department to . . ."

Kevin waved away the suggestion. "We have an attorney at the church who's been trying that for the past ten days."

"Maybe you need a better lawyer." Robert stood and took his cell phone from his pocket. "Let me give you the number of someone I think highly of. Here, write this down . . ."

"She wants an independent investigation, Rob. The police don't even seem to be looking for anyone else. They think they have good suspects in Ryan and Courtney, and with this sniper shooting up the highway, no one seems to have the time or the inclination to look beyond them. You know what that's like, right?"

Ignoring the pointed reminder, Robert walked to the desk and took out a piece of paper. He found a pen under a stack of mail and wrote on it.

"Here. Matthew Day. Give him a call, tell him I referred you and to send his bill to me." Robert passed the slip of paper to the priest, who took it without looking at it.

"He's going to need a lawyer sooner or later, Kev," Robert reminded him.

"We have to find him first."

The words hung between them for a long moment.

"All right." Robert caved. "If you can find someone who's not a thief, hire him."

"Thank you. I'll get on this first thing in the morning." Kevin put the slip of paper with the lawyer's information on it into his pocket.

"I'll have Susanna give you a list of agencies not to call."

"I'd appreciate that."

Trula's voice over the intercom surprised them both. "Boys, dinner is in five minutes. Don't make me come down there to get you." Static transmitted loudly as she fumbled with the switch in the kitchen.

"Has she ever actually come down here to get you?"

"She has. She does. Whenever she thinks I'm ignoring her."

"God forbid." Kevin drained the rest of the coffee from his cup and started for the door. He'd only taken a few steps before turning and asking, "Rob, remember when we were kids and we used to talk about how someday, when we grew up, we'd be really, really rich and how we'd spend our fortunes helping people who couldn't help themselves?"

"Your point?" Robert brushed aside the image of the idealistic boy he'd once been.

"Just that now you are, that's all." Kevin's smile recalled that long-ago time wistfully. "And now you can . . ."

TWO

Morning, Trula." Susanna Jones rapped her knuckles on the back door seconds before she entered the kitchen.

"Good morning, Susy." Trula looked up from her newspaper. "Have you had breakfast?"

"Sort of." Susanna dropped her handbag and a sweater on one of the chairs in the cozy blue-and-yellow breakfast room. Robert Magellan's house may have been a mansion, but thanks to Trula it was not without its homey corners.

" 'Sort of' means you stopped at one of those doughnut places again, didn't you?" Trula's eyes narrowed.

Susanna felt the finger of disapproval poking her, right between the shoulder blades.

"Guilty." Susanna nodded and held up the paper bag. "But I did get a muffin."

"Made with God knows what." Trula waved an agitated hand in the direction of her employer's personal assistant. "There's coffee there on the counter."

"Free trade, organic, no doubt." Susanna reached for one of the mugs Trula had set out. She grabbed the blue one, a favorite of hers, with WHEN ALL ELSE FAILS, READ THE DIRECTIONS written in hot-pink script.

"No doubt." Trula's smile had the look of satisfaction. "And decaffeinated. You and Robert have both been revved up enough lately."

Susanna made a face. "Some of us like a little revving on Monday morning."

"Go to bed earlier on Sunday night and you won't need anything to kick-start your week." Trula turned to the op-ed page.

"Oooh, a little testy this morning, aren't we?" Susanna added some sweetener to the mug and a little cream. As much as she liked to tease Trula, she couldn't deny the woman made excellent coffee. Free trade, organic, decaffeinated, or otherwise.

"So how was your weekend?" Susanna rested both elbows on the counter.

The question was, as both women knew, more about Robert's weekend than Trula's.

"Quiet. Robert drove to the beach house yesterday."

"Will he be back this morning?"

"He came back last night."

"He drove both ways in one day?" Susanna frowned. Ten hours on the road? "What time did he leave?"

"Long before I got up, so it must have been around four or five." Trula lowered her voice. "Father Kevin was here when Robert came in around seven, and he stayed for dinner. They sat up talking for a while."

"He's going to want the high-test this morning, Trula."

"Then he's going to have to make it himself. All the stress he's been under this past year, he doesn't need to bring heart problems on himself."

Susanna could have noted that the problems Robert had with his heart had nothing to do with the level of caffeine in his bloodstream.

"So did he say why he went to the beach house?" Susanna sipped her coffee thoughtfully.

"No, but you know Robert. He probably went there to mourn." She shook her head from side to side. "That big place standing there empty, all the money he spent on it, all the time it took to build, just to surprise her . . ."

Before Susanna could remind Trula that the money he'd spent was a mere drop in his personal bucket, Trula added, "Nothing good is going to come from his hanging on to that place, you mark my words."

The clock in the front hall chimed eight.

"And how did you spend your weekend?" Trula asked.

"Oh, you know. The usual." Susanna smiled. "I need to get to my office. Thanks for the coffee." She grabbed her bag and draped the strap over her shoulder, stopped at the counter long enough to top off the mug, then headed for the door. "If you need me, you know where to find me."

She pushed open the kitchen door with her foot and entered a long, wide hall that had glossy hardwood floors under thick Oriental runners and landscape paintings on the walls. Beth Magellan had picked out most of the art that adorned the house. Susanna found it all too dark and depressing for her taste—but then again, she rationalized, her taste was more plebeian than Robert's former-debutante wife's had been.

A pile of mail from Saturday had been placed in the middle of her desk in the sitting-room-turned-office at the end of the hall. The room overlooked a shady courtyard on one side and a sunny garden on the other.

Susanna turned on the overhead light and draped her sweater over the back of her chair. Robert liked the house cool, and some days it bordered on cold. Susanna thought it was almost as if he thought that if he kept the temperature low enough, he could preserve all the memories the house held. A silly thought on her part, she knew, but then again she was one of the very few people who understood just how despondent Robert had become. The more time that passed, the more withdrawn he grew.

It was killing her.

"Hey," he said from the doorway, the same greeting he'd given every morning since that first day they'd worked together, more than eight years ago.

"Hey yourself." She forced a smile and studied his face while pretending not to. "How was the weekend?"

Ignoring the question, Robert came into the room and pulled a chair up to her desk. "Anything important there?" He nodded in the general direction of the mail.

"I haven't had time to look through it. If you want, I can take a minute now and . . ." She reached for the stack.

"It can wait." He rested his elbows on the desk and gazed out the window. On the courtyard side, a large holly grew up close to the pane. In early spring, a pair of mockingbirds had built their nest there.

"I guess they're gone now," he said.

"I'm sorry?" Susanna tilted her head to one side.

"The baby birds. I guess they're gone."

"They're still there, but I doubt they will be for much longer. I saw them on Friday. You have to get up really close to the glass to see down. They're jumping out of the nest and onto the branches these days."

Robert made no effort to move to the window.

They sat in silence for a few more moments, Susanna waiting patiently.

Finally, he said, "I drove down to the beach house yesterday. I couldn't sleep on Saturday night, thinking about the place."

"Did you sleep better last night for having made the trip?"

He shook his head. "I want you to call the Realtor this morning and tell her I'd like to put the house on the market. She can draw up the listing agreement and send it here and I'll sign it. I want to be done with it."

He spoke without looking at Susanna, a sign, she knew, that he wasn't saying what he was really thinking.

"Are you sure that's what you want to do, Rob?"

"I don't know what else to do." He steepled his fingers and asked, "What if she comes back, Suse? Will she think that I gave up?"

"Selling that house doesn't mean you've given up." She reached across the desk and took his hands in hers. She chose her words carefully. "But it's a very tangible reminder of a dream that hasn't come true, and it's clearly eating you up inside. Besides, if Beth comes back, you're going to have more to talk about than a beach house that you built and sold."

She watched his face for a moment, then added, "Unless you're referring to the fact that you're giving up on yourself."

He turned his head so as to not meet her eyes.

"Don't do anything foolish or stupid, Rob," she said very softly. She knew this man so well. "Don't do anything that can't be undone."

"I think about it a lot, you know?" he said flatly, not bothering to explain, knowing she understood the unspoken.

She knew, but didn't say so.

"Some days I feel like I have nothing to live for, but then I think maybe one day we'll find them. The thought that Beth could come back, that I could get my son back . . . If they're going to come back, I need to be here for them." He blew out a long breath. "And if I . . . if I wasn't here . . . what would she think of me? What would she think when she realized I'd given up without knowing the truth? Would she think I didn't think she was worth waiting for?"

"She'd think you were a coward," Susanna said matter-of-factly. "That you were thinking only of yourself. And she'd be right."

"You never pull punches, do you?" He turned to face her.

"I wouldn't be much of a friend if I did."

"You and Trula and Kevin are the only people I really trust to tell me the truth, you know that, don't you?"

"You'd have been an idiot to have hired me a third time if you didn't trust me to watch your back. Once, maybe. Twice . . . questionable. Three times . . ." She shook her head. "That would make you really stupid. And you are far from stupid, Rob."

"We've come a long way together since those days at Tanner Intel, haven't we?" He looked out the window at the holly again.

"A very long way." Susanna nodded in agreement.

At Tanner, he'd hired her as administrative assistant to the group he headed up. She'd worked for him and five other techs for three years; impressed with her organizational skills and common sense, Robert brought her along when he and Colin Bressler left to start up their own company. When they'd sold their Internet search engine for an unbelievable amount of money eighteen months later, Robert kept Susanna on as his right hand. Since Beth's disappearance, she'd run his life pretty much the way she'd helped run his company.

"I need you to prepare a list of the PIs that we used." He changed the topic abruptly. "Kevin's going to need it."

"Kevin needs a PI?" She frowned.

"Someone in his parish does. I told him we'd give him a list of the ones we'd hired."

"Well, who would you suggest we put at the top of the list?" Susanna said, scowling. "The one who convinced you that a woman and baby matching Beth and Ian's descriptions had been sighted in the Bahamas so that we would send him—all expenses paid, of course—to check it out? Or maybe the one who . . ."

Robert held up a hand. "I want Kevin to know who *not* to hire. Which would be any one of the ones we had working for us, so it doesn't matter which order you put them in."

"Sorry." She turned on the laptop on the right side of her desk. "I just get so angry when I think of those bastards. Not one of them gave a shit about you or Beth or Ian or finding them. They were merely milking a cash cow."

"Thank you for the reminder."

"Sorry. Sorry." She flushed. Of course he didn't need to be reminded.

"I told him I'd pay for an investigator if he could find an honest one. So if he asks you to pay a bill, just write the check. Not that I expect he'll be able to locate one who isn't above robbing a priest blind." Robert stood up and rolled his head as if working out a kink in his neck, then went to the fish tank that stood along one wall and peered inside. "I also told him I'd fund the new front steps for the church, so he'll be getting bids and giving them to you. You know the drill."

"The usual anonymous gift?"

Robert nodded and walked toward the door. "I'll be in my office for a while if anything comes up. Make the call to the Realtor first thing, though. I want to get moving on that." He got as far as the door before he turned around and asked, "You really think she'd be okay about me selling the house?"

"Frankly, I think the only thing she wouldn't be okay about is you." Susanna turned her back, opened the computer file, and printed out the list for Kevin.

"Well, I guess it's like the lawyers say," he told her from the doorway. "Never ask a question you don't already know the answer to."

THREE

L et me get this straight, Father Burch." Joe Drabyak's eyebrows rose almost to his hairline. "You want me to help you find an investigator to second-guess an ongoing investigation that's being conducted by my department on a high-profile case."

"No, no. I'm not trying to second-guess anyone." Kevin shook his head and smiled his most reassuring smile. "But I remember what you'd said before—when Beth and Ian first went missing—about your department having only so much manpower, so many resources. About how this wasn't like TV, where all the cases are solved before you move on to the next one. I know that your people have their hands full now with that sniper who started shooting at the highway over the weekend. And since this does involve members of my parish, I thought the only right thing to do would be to try to help out."

"Nicely said, Father. But I'm afraid I can't think of one PI that Robert Magellan didn't hire—and subsequently fire—over the past year." The police chief shook his head. "And even if I knew of someone, I don't know how it would play with the mayor if it got out that I was helping to build a case for our prime suspect."

"If it should turn out that Ryan Corcoran had anything to do with these senseless murders, I'd be the last person to defend him." The priest smiled kindly. "But right now, no one really knows what happened in that playground, isn't that correct?"

"Yes, unfortunately, that's true. We have our suspicions, though. . . ."

"But no hard facts."

Drabyak nodded reluctantly.

"Look, we both want the same things, don't we? To find the truth? Justice for the victims? To find the missing boy and girl? Their families are beyond frantic, all this time and not a word. They're thinking the worst and trying to hope for the best. Put yourself in their places. This is nothing short of a nightmare for the people who love these kids."

"Don't think this hasn't been a nightmare for the city too, Father Burch. A public relations nightmare. We're under a lot of pressure because we have no leads, no evidence. Just two dead bodies and two missing kids."

"And because they're missing, they're the prime suspects." Kevin rubbed the back of his neck. "Let me ask you something, Chief. Are you looking at other suspects?"

Drabyak sent a dark glance in the priest's direction. "We've interviewed everyone we could think of. We haven't found any indication that anyone would have wanted the two boys dead. Robbery appears to have been the primary motive, but there's been no word on the street that anyone's been walking around with a few extra bucks in his pocket. We don't have a whole lot to go on."

"My point exactly." Kevin nodded. "So what would it hurt if we were able to help you out here, maybe find the two kids who disappeared, maybe find out what really happened that night?"

The unspoken *Maybe find the real killers* hung in the air between them.

"I don't have a problem with you hiring someone to look into it—obviously, I can't stop you. If someone else is responsible for these killings, we'd love to know who." Chief Drabyak ran a hand through thinning brown hair. "Father, I have no personal agenda here. I'm not out to hang innocent kids. And of course I want the truth. It's my job to find the truth. We've canvassed the neighborhood, we've spoken with everyone we could find who would talk to us—but we haven't been able to find a witness that would lead us in any other direction. You have to admit, the facts are not lining up in the Corcoran kid's favor."

"But the fact that he and Courtney have disappeared . . ."

"Doesn't make them innocent, Father. Two witnesses saw those four kids—and those four kids only—enter the park. There is simply no evidence that would lead us to believe anyone else was on that playground that night."

"But conversely, no evidence to suggest that others were *not* there."

"If you think you can find something that we missed, or find a witness that we've been unable to find, go for it." Drabyak was clearly exasperated.

"I intend to. All I need is a name. I was hoping you could give me one. I don't know who else to ask."

The chief stared out the window, a thoughtful look on his face. Finally, he said, "I might know someone who could help you."

"So there really is a PI that Robert missed?"

"No. A former cop."

"Someone in business for himself now?"

"Not exactly. *She's* writing a book about the Preston murder-suicide case that happened here in town about six years ago."

"The coal heiress who was murdered by her husband, who then turned the gun on himself?"

Drabyak nodded. "Apparently, true crime pays. At least, she's hoping it will. Anyway, she was a good cop. A really good investigator. A few months before she quit, she'd been promoted to lead detective."

"She got promoted, then quit?"

The detective hesitated for a moment. "Let's just say she'd made a name for herself within the force, and it wasn't a complimentary one."

"What did she do?"

"It wasn't what she'd done, but the perception of what she'd done."

Drabyak apparently wasn't inclined to go into greater detail.

"How long has she been gone?"

"Six, seven months."

"And you still think she's good?"

"As good as they come, yes."

"You think she'd be interested if she's already working on this book you mentioned?"

The cop shrugged. "I have no idea. All you can do is ask."

"I'll do that, thanks. Where do I find her?"

Drabyak took a small black book from the inside pocket of his jacket and thumbed through it, then made some notes on the back of a piece of paper he tore from a WHILE YOU WERE OUT pad. He handed the slip to Kevin.

"Mallory Russo. That's her phone number. Call her, tell her I gave you her name and I'd appreciate it if she heard you out. No guarantees she'll be interested. But there's no harm in trying. The worst that can happen, she says no."

"Right. Thanks." Kevin folded the paper and tucked it into his jacket pocket. He'd call the former cop as soon as he left the station. It was the first bit of encouragement he'd had since he'd agreed to help Mary Corcoran find her grandson. Maybe with luck, by the end of the day he'd have something positive to tell her.

"Have you lost your mind, Joe?" Mallory Russo started in on her former boss before he'd had time to say hello. "Giving out my name to a priest who wants to hire me as a PI? Jesus, Joe."

"Did you hear him out?" The chief leaned around his desk to close his office door lest the call be overheard. Mallory Russo was not exactly missed by her former coworkers.

"Yes, I heard him out. But—"

"Then you know this is one high-profile case."

"I've followed it, of course I have. But there's no way I can get involved. Besides, I've had my fill of law enforcement. I'll never go back."

"So you let the bastards win, eh?"

"It's not a matter of letting anyone win," she snapped. "I just don't want to be involved anymore. I can't imagine what you were thinking when you gave him my name."

"I was thinking that you were the best detective I had and it's a sin and a shame to waste your talent. And I was thinking that if, in fact, someone other than Ryan Corcoran or Courtney Bauer killed those two boys, I don't want to be the last to know." Joe paused. "Besides, I thought maybe you could use the money. How are your savings holding up?"

"They're holding up. I'm good for a while," she said. "But back to the issue, Joe. You have three other detectives on your staff, if memory serves me. Why aren't they looking for another suspect?"

"*Had* three," Drabyak said tersely. "We're a little shorthanded right now."

"Right. The sniper."

"All available hands are on that deck right now. Christ, if one more old lady gets shot at while walking out of a store on Congress Avenue . . . It's a miracle no one's been hurt. We need to get this bloke before he actually hits someone." He blew out an exasperated breath.

"Plus, one of my best detectives, Catherine Pawley, left on maternity leave three weeks ago, so I'm down to two and right now they're both a bit busy. I got a new hire, but he isn't starting for another week yet."

"Guess the number of candidates for promotion from the ranks is pretty slim."

"Not funny, Mal."

"It wasn't meant to be." Mallory chewed a cuticle. "It could be a challenge for me just to get my hands on a copy of the police report, depending on who's working the desk when I make the request."

"I can get that for you."

"Oh, swell, let's start that talk up all over again, shall we?"

"No one who knows you—no one who matters—believed any of that crap."

"Enough believed it to make my life a living hell."

When he didn't respond, she added, "I know you mean well, and I appreciate your thinking of me. But no one in that department will give me the time of day."

"I'll put the request for copies of the reports and the statements in Father Burch's name."

"And won't that give him confidence in me? That his private investigator can't even get a report from the same department she worked for for nine years?"

"It would if you told him what really happened."

"I'd appreciate it if you'd put that story to bed once and for all. I've tried to put it all behind me, thank you very much. I don't see any reason to relive what was the worst time in my life."

"How 'bout we do this: I'll get everything you'll need and I'll drop it off at your house on my way home from work. You can meet with the priest after you've reviewed the file."

"I'm sorry, did I say I was going to do this? I don't remember saying that I would do this."

"Just look over the material, Mal. Just take a look and if you don't want to take on the job, give Father Burch a call and let him know."

Joe paused. "Though I'd really be interested in hearing your take on the case. I think once you start looking into it, you're going to be hooked."

"I'm not licensed to work as a PI, Joe. I couldn't take this if I wanted to."

"Getting a license is not going to be a problem for you. Nine distinguished years as a detective—"

She snorted.

Joe ignored her. "—and you know your references will be the highest. Me, the DA . . . hell, even the mayor. You had a lot of admirers, Mal."

"And some who didn't admire me at all," she reminded him.

"So don't ask them for a reference. I think you only need five."

"I have no idea what I need."

"So you'll find out."

"I cannot think of one good reason why I should do this."

"I can think of two." Joe sounded unexpectedly cheerful. "One, because it's a really complicated case, and that always gets you going. It's what you do best. And two, because until you sell that book on the Preston case, you probably need the income."

"Income didn't come up. We didn't talk about money, but I'm sure I'm not likely to get rich off what this priest is going to be able to pay."

"Didn't he tell you?" Now Drabyak sounded flat-out amused.

"Tell me what?"

"Father Burch isn't footing the bill. His cousin is."

"And his cousin is what, the monsignor?"

"Robert Magellan."

There was a notable pause.

"Robert Magellan, super-rich guy? Mogul? The one whose wife and baby disappeared last year? That Robert Magellan?"

"Yes."

"What's his connection?"

"Magellan and Father Burch are more like brothers than cousins. And I'm sure he told you that the boy is his parish secretary's grandson."

"Not hard to connect those dots."

"So why don't you think about it and let Father Burch know by tomorrow afternoon if you're going to take the job or if he should look for someone else."

"All right." Mallory sighed. "But I'll come into the station today and get the report myself."

"Are you sure you want to do that?"

"I'm not a coward, Joe. Some might say a less-than-beloved cop, but no one's ever called me a coward." Mallory disconnected the call and slid her cell phone back into her pocket.

Father Burch hadn't mentioned Robert Magellan, but now that Joe brought it up, she remembered seeing him along with a priest in Joe's office about a year ago. Joe had brought Magellan in to interview him following the disappearance of his family. He would have made a great suspect if he hadn't had an airtight alibi and an endless string of people who'd testify that the man was totally devoted to his wife and baby son. Oh, and there was that matter of a lack of motive, and the fact that the series of events leading up to Beth Magellan's disappearance could not have been foreseen.

Mallory had been one of two detectives who had not worked on the Magellan case. Because it had been so high-profile and the FBI had been called in, once they realized who and what they were dealing with, Joe had handled it himself. Mallory and her partner, Cal Whitman, had been assigned to two homicides back-to-back. Joe's immersion in the Magellan case had left the door open for her to fill the role of lead detective that he had vacated when he was promoted to chief. It had also put her in a position to have a jealous partner crank up the rumor mill.

She crossed her arms over her chest, walked to the back door of her small town house, and stepped out onto what passed as a patio in her complex. Large enough only for two plastic chairs and a wooden table she'd found at a yard sale and painted red, the concrete rectangle provided a change of scenery from the tiny second bedroom she used as an office. She sat on one of the chairs and stretched her legs out in front of her, wiggled her feet out of her shoes, put her head all the way back, and closed her eyes.

She couldn't deny she'd been intrigued, even before Robert Magellan's name came into the conversation.

Of course she'd seen the news stories about the double homicide on TV. For the first week, all the local stations covered the story daily, keeping it right out in front, and why not? It had everything that the media loved, though over the past few days the local sniper had taken over page one. The two young men who'd been shot to death on the playground were already fading into the background. For their sake, if for no other reason, Mallory had to admit she was interested.

Joe was right, of course. This was just the kind of case that got her going.

Before she could talk herself out of it, Mallory went into the kitchen and grabbed her bag from the counter. She slid her sunglasses onto her face and walked outside through the front door, locking it behind her.

"I need my head examined," she grumbled under her breath as she got into her car and started the engine. "I need to deal with those assholes again like I need a hole in my head."

She backed out of her parking space and took the familiar route that led into the center of town, all the while reminding herself that Daniel had survived the lion's den and that there were people who swam in shark-infested waters all the time and were never attacked. She tried to think of other analogies to her situation, but she arrived at the station before any others came to mind. Force of habit had her pulling into a reserved parking place, but she caught herself before she'd driven all the way to the end. She put the car in reverse and headed for the visitor spots closer to the back door, then went up the steps leading into the back of the building. As she'd told Joe, she wasn't a coward, but there was no point in looking for trouble.

"Well, well. Look who's returning to the scene of the crime." Frank Toricelli stood two steps up, his beefy hands on his hips.

The dark glasses half covering her face were apparently insufficient as a disguise.

"Nice to see you again, too, Frank." Mallory tried to go past him, but he sidestepped to block her way.

"Not so fast, Blondie." His smirk turned her stomach. "You just missed your old partner. Of course, I could always call him back if you have something to say to him." He stepped closer to the close the gap between them. "You got something to say to Cal, Blondie, or did you say it all to IA?"

"Get out of my way, asshole." Mallory shoved him to one side.

"Careful, Blondie. I can arrest you for assaulting a police officer." His eyes narrowed behind his dark lenses. "Just the thought of you behind bars gets my blood pumping, you know what I mean? I'll bet you look really hot in orange."

She shook her head in disgust and pushed past him, praying he wouldn't follow her inside the building. She opened the door at the top of the steps and turned slightly to glance over her shoulder as she entered. Toricelli still stood where she'd left him. Knowing he'd watched her climb the stairs sent a chill up her spine.

"Bastard," Mallory whispered under her breath as she closed the door behind her and walked to the information desk.

Relieved to find no one she knew working the desk at that hour, she filled out the request forms and handed over the required cash.

"You're lucky things are slow this afternoon," the pert young officer behind the counter said with a smile. "This shouldn't take too long. You can have a seat over there." She gestured in the direction of the plastic chairs on the opposite wall of the counter.

"Thanks." Mallory nodded and took a seat. Apparently her fame hadn't spread quite as far as she'd feared. There'd been no apparent recognition of her name. Must be one of the new recruits.

So I'm batting five hundred, she told herself. *Could be a lot worse.*

After ten minutes passed, she searched for a couple of quarters to buy a newspaper from the metal stand at the front of the lobby.

Fifteen more minutes passed before Mallory's name was called.

"I can only give you the preliminary report." The officer—OFFICER P. CROMWELL, Mallory noted the name tag this time—held out several stapled sheets of paper. "The case is still active, and some of the reports are classified at this time. You can stop back in a few weeks to see if that's changed."

"I'll do that. Thanks again." Mallory folded the papers and tucked them into her bag. If she ran into any of her other former co-workers, she'd rather not advertise her purpose in being there.

With a knot in her stomach, Mallory started toward the door, almost afraid to step outside. But Toricelli must have been on his way to a call—or meeting one of his several girlfriends—as it appeared he hadn't hung around. She took a deep breath and started down the stairs. She'd almost made it to her car, her hand stretched out toward the driver's-side door, when she realized her visit hadn't gone unnoticed after all.

Along the drive leading to the exit stood half a dozen or so of her former colleagues, their arms crossed over their chests as they watched her approach.

She debated whether to leave through another exit and pretend she didn't see them, or to drive directly past. She took her time starting her car, her head down as if she hadn't noticed their disapproving stares, while she deliberated. On the one hand, the thought of facing their cold condemnation yet again made her physically ill. On the other, running just wasn't her style. She took a deep breath, slid her sunglasses down from the top of her head, and backed out of the parking space.

Through her dark glasses, she saw the unsmiling faces of people she'd once counted among her friends. At least, she'd *thought* they were friends. She shook her head imperceptibly. How could any one of them ever have thought she'd lied, that she'd wanted a promotion so badly that she'd make up a story to cast a fellow officer in a bad light?

Not that Cal Whitman had needed any help in that regard. He'd done more than his share of stupid things in the three years they'd been partners. She'd often wondered if matching him up with her had been the powers-that-be's way of trying to keep him out of trouble until he was able to retire. After all, she did have the well-earned reputation of being levelheaded, while his rep was somewhat less complimentary.

Since it was easier to not make eye contact with anyone, she stared straight ahead as she passed from the parking lot onto the street. In the rearview mirror, she could see them turn their backs and walk back toward the building.

If she said it didn't sting, she'd be lying.

On the way home, she stopped at a fast-food drive-through at the edge of a strip mall for a cold drink. The all-brick strip had once been home to a somewhat fashionable clothing store, a florist, a pet shop, and a bookstore. Now those same storefronts housed a Laundromat, a pizza parlor, a nail salon, and one boarded-up newsstand.

She drank the soda as she drove, hoping to push back the lump in her throat. Inside her house, she forced the incident behind her, behind that wall she'd thrown up a long time ago, where she tossed everything she wanted to hide or push from her mind, and settled down to read the file.

By the time she was finished reading, the events of the day were behind her, and she was, as Joe had predicted, hooked.

FOUR

Mallory pulled up a chair to her small kitchen table, typed "magellanexpress.com" into her laptop's browser, and wondered how many other people had used the mechanism named for the man to follow the story that had, by all accounts, destroyed his life.

Many thousands, at the very least, she figured.

She stuck a straw into the can of Diet Pepsi she'd just opened, and read through several accounts regarding the disappearance of the mogul's wife, along with their six-month-old son, in March of the previous year. The results page had brought up countless articles describing how Beth Magellan had driven herself halfway across Pennsylvania to her sister's home in Gibson Springs to attend a baby shower for their cousin, how she'd left for home in a hurry the next morning.

"Beth said there was something Robert had wanted to do on Sunday afternoon, and she had to get home," Pamela

Clement, sister of the missing woman, said in an early interview.

"When Beth arrived here on Saturday," Clement continued, "she parked her car—a Land Rover—up near the garage. When she came out to leave the next morning, she found that my husband, Rick, had parked behind her when he came in late Saturday afternoon. By the time Beth was ready to leave for home, Rick had left for an early golf game, and I couldn't find the spare keys for his car. She was in a big hurry to leave, so she borrowed our old Jeep. The plan was that I'd drive down on Monday or Tuesday in her car to make the exchange."

At this point in the story, Pamela Clement broke down. "If she'd taken her own car, we'd know where she is. We'd have been able to track her, but the Jeep doesn't have GPS."

Clement added that Mrs. Magellan had left her cell phone in her car when she arrived at the Gibson Spring home and had neglected to retrieve it before leaving on Sunday.

"I'm sure she forgot she left it on the seat," Clement said. "She hadn't needed it while she was at the house, and I think Beth just assumed it was in her purse. Ian had been fussy when they were leaving, and Beth was distracted."

The article, like many others that appeared as the result of her search, was accompanied by photos of the happy family. Several had the same photo of a grave Robert Magellan walking side by side with Father Kevin Burch.

Interesting, Mallory thought as she tapped a pen on the tabletop, recalling her conversation with Joe Drabyak. The two men certainly did look more like brothers than cousins. Both tall—though Robert appeared to have a few inches on the priest—both lean, dark-haired, and good-looking. She'd read that they were the same age—had she read something about them having been born on the same day?—

but Robert looked older. Could be due to the stress he'd been under for the past fifteen months.

She returned to the results page and clicked on the link to the next article. WHERE IS ELIZABETH MAGELLAN? the headline asked, and below it, in smaller type, WHERE IS BABY IAN?

Mallory studied the accompanying pictures of Beth Magellan, from a college yearbook photo to one taken just days before she disappeared. In the first, she was shown taking part in a charity run hosted by her sorority. In the other, she stood shoulder-to-shoulder with her husband, and while Mallory assumed that Beth Magellan had been wearing high-heeled shoes to the charity bash where they'd been photographed, she was clearly a tall woman. Tall and very pretty, with long dark hair that cascaded over trim shoulders and was clipped high on one side with what Mallory thought looked like a diamond-encrusted clip. A sapphire necklace that circled her neck surely had been chosen to match the designer gown of the same color. She clung to the arm of her husband and wore a very wide smile.

Well, duh. Mallory snorted. *Young and gorgeous and married to one of the wealthiest men in the country. What's not to smile about?*

Stylishly dressed, stylishly coiffed. Stylishly young.

Mallory followed the article to the next page, where she found pictures of Ian Magellan's chubby-cheeked face. The baby had been darling, there was no question of that, she thought, then chided herself for thinking of the child in the past tense. He could very well be alive. Robert Magellan still held to that possibility, if his cousin was to be believed.

She read online for another hour or so, then used Magellan Express to locate articles on the playground shooting. The story was familiar: four kids from Our Lady of Angels High—James Tilton, Adam Stevens, Ryan Corcoran, and Courtney Bauer—had arranged to meet at the playground around ten on Friday night, the twenty-fifth of

April. The four had been close friends since kindergarten and spent a good deal of time together outside school. On that particular night, they'd gotten together to commiserate with Courtney over her rejection by Penn State, her first-choice college. According to her mother, while Courtney had applied knowing it was her "stretch" school, she had been very upset by the rejection. She'd called Ryan as soon as she'd opened the letter, Mrs. Bauer told reporters, and they made arrangements to meet the others later that night, after Courtney dropped her younger sister and two of her friends off at a community center dance.

"It was all she talked about in the car," Courtney's fifteen-year-old sister, Misty, told police. "She'd been accepted at a couple of other schools, but she decided late that she wanted to go to Penn State and I guess by then they'd filled all their places. At least, that was what Courtney was saying. She was really mad at herself for not applying earlier."

There were interviews with the families of both of the murdered boys, and Mallory read every one of them trying to get to know the victims. Adam had been accepted at Rowan University in New Jersey, where he'd play saxophone in the band. He'd auditioned several times, and had been holding his breath until his acceptance arrived. James—Jamey—was going to Pitt on a full scholarship and hoped to write for the university newspaper, as he'd done at Our Lady of Angels. His dream was to one day write for one of the big newspapers— *The Washington Post,* the *LA* or *New York Times, The Boston Globe.*

Ryan had been offered a full ride to Temple in Philadelphia to study film.

"He is going to be a famous producer," his grandmother, Mary Corcoran, was quoted as having said. "He likes making documentaries that examine social issues. He submitted a film about religious prejudice as his senior project, and he recently shot one about the Underground Railroad stops in the area. His teacher thinks he has a lot of promise."

Mallory sat back against the hard wood of the kitchen chair and absentmindedly began to chew on the end of the straw. These were all bright kids, focused kids, kids who had plans for their lives. Who the hell would have wanted to kill them?

Courtney and Ryan? That didn't work for her. These didn't seem like kids who would have hurt anyone, least of all two of their closest friends. For what? A thousand dollars?

While Mallory knew that people had been murdered for far less than that, she didn't think these two college-bound kids with great futures were so shortsighted that they'd kill for one thousand dollars.

She got up and began to pace. It had to have been a robbery. Random. Some thugs coming across the kids in the playground and robbing them, killing them because they could. But the two missing kids? What were the chances that Ryan and Courtney could have been taken by the killers and killed somewhere else? Or maybe Ryan had been killed and Courtney kept alive to be abused by the abductors? Or had one of them been the shooter, forcing the other to leave the park at gunpoint only to shoot him—or her—somewhere else? Her mind raced through every conceivable possibility, but none felt right.

She tried, but she just couldn't see Courtney or Ryan as the shooter.

Then again, she'd been around long enough to know that sometimes there was just no rhyme or reason to murder. As unlikely as she thought it that either of the two missing kids could have pulled the trigger, she knew it couldn't be ruled out. She couldn't blame the police for taking a long hard look at these two—especially since they'd gone missing. But at the same time, it just didn't ring true to her.

It didn't ring true to Joe Drabyak, either, she realized, or he wouldn't have asked her to take the job.

She reached for the phone to call Father Burch to let him know he'd found his investigator, but turned the phone off after dialing the first five numbers. There was one more thing she needed to do before she committed. She stuck the straw back into the can and tossed them both into the trash on her way out the door.

Mallory kicked aside the remnants of the yellow crime scene tape that had marked off the entrance to the park not so very long ago. A path led from the gate to the playground equipment near a chain-link fence that trapped empty potato chip bags, candy wrappers, and soda cans tossed by passing cars or kids on their way home from school. She followed the path slowly, taking in her surroundings, very much aware that she was the only person in the park. Odd, she thought, for seven o'clock on a warm spring night. Could be that recent events accounted for the fact that the playground was deserted. She couldn't blame the neighborhood mothers if they were keeping their children safely inside, even in the daylight. If she had kids, she probably wouldn't permit them to play here, either, at least until the killer or killers were arrested.

The grass along the path hadn't seen a lawn mower in weeks, and the long green leaves spilled onto the concrete sidewalk in several places. The overhead lights had yet to switch on, and her left foot turned on a couple of chunks of mulch that had been kicked up from the playground area just ahead. As she drew closer, she was surprised to find the equipment somewhat antiquated, the slide, swing set, and old-fashioned merry-go-round all made of heavy dark gray metal and rusted in spots.

Thirty years old if it's a day, she thought as she ran her hand along the rough side of the slide.

The climbing apparatus made in the shape of a fire truck appeared to be of more recent design, and the sandbox looked newly constructed—it couldn't be more than a month or so old. The sand looked clean and new. Plastic cars, abandoned by their young owners, lay scattered about, and here and there small paw prints marched across the sand's surface.

She noticed that the chains holding the seats to the crossbar of the swing set were missing, along with the seats themselves—taken, no doubt, by the crime scene techs the night of the shootings. Both Adam and James had been seated on the swings when they were shot in the back of the head.

Who shoots a kid in the back of the head, then walks away? Surely not a best friend.

Mallory walked around the swing set and stood where the shooter—or shooters—had stood. Had the boys seen them coming? Did they know they were about to die? Or had they been laughing and talking and unaware of the danger that was coming at them through the dark? She stared until she could almost see the two boys, first on the swings, then crumpled on the ground where they lay after falling. The vision sent a shudder through her, then disappeared.

She tried to picture Ryan pulling a gun—where would he have gotten a gun?—and approaching his friends from behind the swings. Pressing it to the back of Adam's head—Adam, with whom he'd been best friends since kindergarten!—and pulling the trigger. How had Ryan been able to get James to remain seated on his swing after he'd shot Adam? Surely Courtney's presence alone wouldn't have been enough of a threat to keep James still.

Bang! Bang! Mallory tried to imagine the scenario, tried to hear the gunshots, tried to see Courtney standing by while Ryan killed the two others, but she just didn't see it happening that way. She couldn't accept either Courtney or Ryan as the shooter. It just didn't fit. There had to have been someone else there that night.

So if neither Courtney nor Ryan was the shooter, where were they when Adam and James were murdered?

According to the police report, the shooting had occurred sometime after ten PM, so it would have been dark. Assuming that on the night of the shooting there had been a bulb in the lamppost at the end of the walk, just as there was now, what, Mallory wondered, could be seen from where the shooter stood?

She did a 360-degree scan, and when she came back to where she'd started she had a pretty good idea of where the missing teenagers might have been when the shooting began.

Straight ahead—in direct line with the swings—stood the slide. In her mind's eye, Mallory could almost see how it could have happened. She walked toward the slide, playing out the possibilities in her head. Supposing one of them—Courtney, more likely—had been at the top of the slide, just sitting there, maybe, or maybe about to go down, when the shots that killed the boys on the swings rang out. Might she have screamed, drawing attention to herself? Might she have frozen there, at the top of the steps, where she easily could have been seen by the shooter?

She saw the shooter, the shooter saw her.

Where would Ryan have been? At the foot of the slide or behind her on the ladder—either could work.

What would Courtney or Ryan—or both—have done?

They'd have run like hell, wouldn't they? Wouldn't they have looked for a way out of the park, or at the very least a place to hide?

Sure they would. They wouldn't have stood there, waiting to be shot like Adam and James had been. They'd have looked for a way out. And since their bodies hadn't been found, perhaps they'd found one.

Or maybe the shooter forced Courtney and Ryan to leave the park at gunpoint, killed them somewhere else. They'd already fired twice, enough to attract attention. Maybe the shooter feared the police had already been summoned by someone who'd heard those first two shots.

Possible, Mallory acknowledged. But why hadn't their bodies turned up by now?

The first scenario sounded more likely to her than the second; it felt right. And if she was right, the missing kids were most likely still alive.

Mallory walked back to the slide and stood at the bottom of the ladder, wondering if it had been dusted for prints. She climbed the steep steps without grasping the sides, just in case. Once at the top, she stood as someone might before heading down the slide, and looked over at the swing set. She was right in line with the swings where the two boys had been shot. If, in fact, the lamppost had been working that night and Courtney had been standing where Mallory was, she would have been very visible.

So the next logical question would be: Where did they go from there?

Mallory walked around the slide board once, twice, trying to imagine the scene.

Where could they have hidden? No place that Mallory could see.

It was growing darker, so she returned to her car for the flashlight she always kept in the trunk. She walked back through the silent park to the playground and sat on the bottom of the slide. Logistically, she couldn't figure it out. She took the police report from her handbag, opened it on her lap, and studied it again.

Hey, dummy, it's right under your nose. Literally.

The sketch that had been made by one of the investigating officers the night of the shooting clearly showed a small Dumpster in the parking area off to the right of the slide. Courtney walked to where the Dumpster should have stood according to the drawing. There on the macadam were marks left when the bin was hauled away, possibly by the police department for processing of its contents.

Mallory walked it off. Courtney and Ryan could have made it to the Dumpster without being seen, since the light from the lamppost didn't extend much beyond the shrubs to the right of the slide. So they could have cut across the grass to the Dumpster and hidden inside.

She frowned. Too obvious to hide there. The shooter could have figured that out and would most likely have shot them in the Dumpster.

She walked the area anyway. When she found nothing, she expanded her search to the fence, thinking it was too much to hope that there'd be a break in the mesh where the kids could have slipped through.

With the flashlight, Mallory went over every foot of link, but found no break. *So they didn't go through it,* she thought as she stepped back to judge its height. *But what are the chances they went over it?*

She read the descriptions of the missing kids. Courtney was five foot four; Ryan, six three. She went back and stared at the fence. Could he have lifted her over it, then vaulted over behind her without being seen? Could it have happened that way?

Maybe. Maybe . . .

By now it was too dark, and her flashlight battery too weak, to continue. She was annoyed with herself that she hadn't come to the park earlier; she'd have to return tomorrow if she wanted to take a closer look at the fence. *Both sides of the fence,* she told herself. And she'd bring her camera, get some shots of the layout.

In the meantime, she had a phone call to make. She hoped Father Burch was back from whatever meeting he'd told her he'd be at that night. There was always voice mail, she was thinking as she stepped onto the walk that would take her back to the gate. As she passed the broken-down benches, she looked up and her heart all but stopped beating in her chest. A man in a dark coat stood smack in the middle of the park entrance, his hands in his pockets, his feet planted apart, his features indistinguishable in the dark. All she could tell from the distance was that he was tall and looked very menacing.

And he was watching her.

Force of habit sent her right hand to her waistband, but there was nothing where her gun used to be holstered. It wasn't the first time since she'd left the force that she'd reached for it.

Mallory continued to walk purposefully toward the entrance.

As she approached, he called to her. "Are you all right?"

"Why wouldn't I be?" Her fingers closed around the handle of the flashlight, just in case.

"Maybe you haven't heard. Two kids were shot and killed here a couple of weeks ago."

As she drew closer, Mallory tried to gauge how much room there was to either side of him, just in case she had to make a run for her car.

"I heard." Three feet on either side. Close enough for him to reach out and grab her, if that was what he had in mind.

"So you might think it's not a good idea to go walking around alone in the dark," he said as the distance between them narrowed. "You never know who you're going to meet in a place like this."

"Right. You never do," she said as she passed him, never breaking stride, her gaze level and straight ahead. "So you be sure to be careful out there, okay?"

She unlocked the car with the remote while she was still ten feet away, but never looked back. Once she was safely behind the wheel, she glanced over to where he'd stood, but he'd already disappeared into the night. With a shiver, she started the car and drove off, vowing that first thing in the morning she'd get her handgun out of its box in the bedroom closet and apply for the license necessary to carry it as a concealed weapon. And while she was in the courthouse, she'd pick up an application for her PI license.

FIVE

The drive to Robert Magellan's home took Mallory down meandering roads she normally wouldn't have cause to travel. Once outside Conroy's city limits, beyond the deserted factories and the paper mill, all long since closed, the road widened slightly and the scenery vastly improved. Gone were the rows of brownstone houses that, once fashionable, now were home to several families on each floor. The downtown area where boarded-up storefronts were commonplace gave way to farms whose crops were just starting to come in. Fields of summer wheat and newly sprouted corn lined the road on either side. Long lanes led to farmhouses that had been standing for more than a century. Mallory opened all the windows in the car and let the warm, fresh country air blow through until she reached her destination.

She turned off the road and followed the short two-lane drive until she reached the gated entry. When she'd met with Father Burch the previous night, he'd given her a passkey that would open the gate when she arrived. She slid it into the slot and removed it once the gate began to swing open. She drove through, then stopped along the side of the road and dialed the priest's cell phone as the gates closed behind her.

"I'm here, Father," she told him when he answered.

"Great. Just come on up to the house. I'll meet you outside the front door."

Well, he sounds chipper, she thought as she put the car in gear and continued up the driveway. Once she was past a big bend to the right, the house came into view.

"Holy shit," she muttered.

There were bigger houses in this world, she was sure, probably some much bigger right here in Pennsylvania, but to Mallory, the Magellan home was more than impressive. Built sometime in the 1920s, she guessed, judging by its Tudor architecture, its wings sprawled both to the right and to the left from a very large rectangular center stucco and half-timber structure. She parked her car and got out, taking it all in while pretending not to in case someone was watching. Before she rang the bell, she reached out with her right hand to touch the smooth coolness of the heavy front door—at least she hoped it was the front door; she'd passed several others, but they'd looked less significant.

"Good morning." A cheerful Father Burch opened the door almost immediately. "I forgot how short the drive is from the gate. Come in, please. Susanna is waiting for you." He gestured for her to follow him.

"Susanna?" She tried not to appear knocked out by her surroundings, as if walking through sumptuous mansion halls was an everyday thing for her.

"Rob's right hand. She's worked with him forever," he explained. "She takes care of things like this for him."

"Oh," she replied, disappointed. Would she not be meeting with the man himself? So much for her plans to try to make an in with him. Bye-bye, authorized biography.

"Right in here." Father Burch ushered Mallory into a spacious corner room that had tall, wide windows on two sides. Behind an antique wooden desk sat a very attractive woman with dark brown hair and deep blue eyes who smiled when Mallory and the priest entered.

"Mallory Russo, meet Susanna Jones." Father Kevin stood to one side while he made the introductions.

Susanna Jones rose from her seat and walked around the desk to offer her hand to Mallory. She was slim and dressed in a stylishly casual boat-neck dress of a teal knit fabric that came just to her knees. She wore fashionably flat shoes and chunky silver jewelry, and next to her, Mallory felt underdressed in her plain black suit and white cotton shirt.

"Mallory, thanks for coming in this morning."

Mallory wasn't sure how to respond. Somehow, *I really wasn't given a choice* didn't seem appropriate.

"I was under the impression that Mr. Magellan wanted to meet me," she said, opting for a more innocuous reply.

"Please, take a seat, either chair is fine." Susanna brushed off her remark. "Kevin? You're staying?"

He shook his head. "I've got to be at the school by ten thirty. There's an awards assembly that I shouldn't miss. If I leave now, I'll just make it." He turned to Mallory. "Suse will answer any questions you might have, but don't ever hesitate to call me if you need me for anything. You have the list I gave you yesterday of the names and numbers of people from the neighborhood you might want to talk to. I'll let everyone know they can expect to hear from you. Anything else, just give me a shout." He patted Mallory on the shoulder and said, "Good luck."

And with that, the priest vanished into the hall and closed the door.

"I was under the impression I'd be interviewing with Mr. Magellan." Mallory turned to Susanna and tried again.

"He might stop by, might not." Susanna's eyes appeared to assess Mallory from head to toe. "Actually, I do the hiring."

"I like to see who I'm working for."

"Well, once again, that would be me." Susanna smiled not unkindly, but clearly marking her territory. "You'll give a weekly report to Kevin, with a copy to me when you hand in your expenses. If Robert's interested, he'll take a look at it. If not . . ." She shrugged and slid a file across the desk. "Before we go any further, however, I'd like you to take a minute to read this."

Mallory leaned forward, opened the file, and scanned the one-page document.

"Are you serious?" she asked when she'd reached the bottom of the page.

"Absolutely," Susanna assured her.

"I'm not to discuss my employment with anyone? Not to talk to the press . . . well, that's a no-brainer. I don't do press." She glanced across the desk where Susanna sat, no doubt studying Mallory's reaction. "Why all the secrecy?"

"You're well aware of what happened to Robert's family last year. Even if you hadn't been a member of the police department at the time, you'd have heard about it. I'm sure Kevin told you about the efforts Robert made to find his wife and son."

"He told me that a number of private investigators had been hired."

"Hired and fired," Susanna said, heavy emphasis on the latter. "Not one of them worth a damn, frankly. To them, this tragedy was just one big endless gravy train."

"Father Burch told me that Mr. Magellan had been taken advantage of."

"That's putting it mildly." Susanna's smile held no warmth as she added, "It won't happen again. I assure you, I intend to be much more vigilant this time around."

"Ms. Jones . . ."

"Susanna."

"Susanna, I can appreciate your concern, but I would remind you that this was not my idea. I did not seek out this job. Father Burch came to me. I have no intention of taking advantage of anyone."

"Good." The smile was more genuine this time. "Then we understand each other."

"It appears we do." Mallory met Susanna's gaze but did not look away. Best to lay that card on the table right up front. Mallory did not intimidate easily, and wasn't one to back down under pressure.

Susanna was the first to break the lock when she reached for the phone and entered two numbers. After several seconds had passed, she spoke softly into the receiver.

"I know you're busy, but I'd like you to meet Mallory Russo." Pause. "The investigator Kevin hired to look for Ryan Corcoran." Another pause. "Yes, I do think it's necessary." Pause again, then, "For heaven's sake, Robert, it will only take you a minute." She hung up, shaking her head.

Mallory waited for her to offer some explanation, but she did not, and before Mallory could ask, the door swung open. She turned in her chair just as Robert Magellan entered the room.

"Robert, this is Mallory Russo." Susanna made the introductions. "Mallory, Robert Magellan."

Mallory rose to face him. He was taller than she'd expected, and much better looking. He'd have been even handsome, she thought, if he wasn't scowling.

"Good to meet you," she said, offering her hand.

He took it and gave it a perfunctory shake. "So you're going to find Mary Corcoran's grandson and his friend and prove they didn't kill these two other kids, and peace will prevail at Our Lady of the Angels once again and Kevin can get back to tending his flock and I can get back to whatever it was I was doing."

"That's the plan, sir. I'll do my best," Mallory told him.

"Good." Robert looked back at Susanna as if to say, *Okay, I met your new person. May I leave now?*

Susanna nodded, her eyes following Robert as he headed for the door. "Nice to meet you," he said on his way out.

Before Mallory could respond, he turned back. "Oh. One thing. Don't call me sir."

"Sorry, Mr. Magellan," a slightly taken-aback Mallory replied.

"Robert. It's just Robert," he corrected before leaving the room and closing the door behind him.

"So that's Robert Magellan" was the only thing Mallory could think of to say after he'd left the room.

Susanna laughed, the first sign of real warmth she'd shown since Mallory arrived. Except when her boss had entered the room. There had been more than warmth in her eyes as she'd watched him.

"Yes, that's Robert. He isn't always so . . ." The smile still on her face, she fished for a word.

"So rude? So obviously disinterested?"

"Either will do nicely, yes."

"You'd think he'd be a little more interested in the investigation since it's his money that's paying for it."

"Money isn't very important to him anymore," Susanna explained. "It was, once upon a time, when he was first learning how to make it. Now it's . . ." She shrugged.

"It's not consolation for what he's lost." Mallory finished the thought for her.

"That's as good a way to put it as any, I suppose." Susanna reached for the file, suddenly all business again, the light gone from her eyes. "I'm going to insist that you sign the agreement, Ms. Russo, or there isn't going to be an investigation. At least, not one conducted by you."

"I don't have a problem with not discussing the details of my employment." Mallory reached for the pen that Susanna held in her hand. "The object is to find out what really happened that night. No one needs to know that Mr. Magell—Robert is involved in any way."

"Good." Susanna handed her the pen, and Mallory signed the document. "Did Kevin tell you how we'll work this? At the end of the week, you'll give me your hours, receipts for whatever expenses you incurred—meals, gas . . ." She paused, then asked, "Will you need a car? We have several available."

"I have a car, thank you."

"Any expenses connected to the case will be reimbursed by me on Friday morning or early afternoon. Though I usually leave around three on Fridays, so anytime up until then, just stop in with your documentation and I'll write the check."

"How do I document my hours?" Mallory asked.

"You just keep track on a daily basis and add them up at the end of the week." Susanna appeared somewhat confused by the question. "Surely you're familiar with time sheets?"

"I meant, how will you know if I actually worked that number of hours?"

"I guess I'm just going to have to trust you on that." Susanna stood to indicate the meeting had concluded. "But of course, if after several sixty-hour weeks you've nothing to report, I might start to wonder just what you were doing all that time."

Before Mallory could respond, Susanna walked around the desk and said, "You can find your way out, I trust?"

"I wouldn't be much of an investigator if I couldn't," Mallory said drily as she rose and swung her bag over her shoulder, "since it's a straight shot down the hall from here to the front door."

"I'll see you on Friday, then." Susanna leaned back against her desk, her arms folded over her chest.

"Not this Friday, I'm afraid," Mallory told her. "Until I'm licensed, I can't charge for my services. I can start my investigation as a friend of the family, but I can't do the work 'for hire.' "

"Who would know if you did?"

"I would."

"I see." Susanna raised an eyebrow. "Will there be a problem . . . ?"

"I don't anticipate one. The license comes from the county, and I'm well known there."

"How long will this take?"

"I'm not sure. I'll let you know when I know."

"Then you'll save your hours and bill them when the time comes."

"We'll see. A lot can happen between then and now." Mallory walked to the door. "You should know one thing about me. I'm a good investigator. I can't find evidence where there isn't any, but I will find whatever is there. And if there comes a point when I feel I can't do any more on this case, you will be the first to know. So you won't have to worry about firing me for dragging out an investigation that's going nowhere. I'll have quit long before that."

Mallory left the office and walked down the silent hall toward the door, her footfalls little more than whispers on the thick carpets. She passed no one on her way out, and wondered if Robert and Susanna were the only souls in the house. *Someone must clean this place,* she was thinking as she let herself out. *Someone must cook and take care of all the details of everyday life.* She was pretty certain that someone wasn't Susanna Jones.

She got into her car and left the way she came, following the lane to the gate, which opened on its own at her approach. Off to her right, a landscaping crew worked on extensive flower beds that lined the drive on either side. She drove slowly, noting the lush swaths of peonies and roses that appeared to be newly planted, some flowering shrubs she didn't recognize, and dozens and dozens of perennials already in bloom.

Whose idea was that? she wondered.

Not Robert Magellan's, certainly. The man didn't appear to have much of an interest in anything. And probably not Susanna's, either.

She didn't strike Mallory as the type to concern herself with such tasks, though Mal could be wrong about that.

What Susanna did strike Mallory as was distrustful. Cool. Detached. Except, she suspected, when it came to Robert.

The gates closed behind her, and Mallory headed back toward Conroy. At first, she hadn't been sure she liked the idea of having to sign what amounted to a confidentiality agreement, but she saw no harm in it. After all Robert Magellan had been through, it was probably a good idea, though she was pretty certain the idea had been Susanna's rather than Robert's. Mallory smiled and turned on the radio. It had been a very revealing morning. Trained observation and well-honed instincts had led her to three compelling realizations in a very short amount of time.

One was that she'd probably never get close enough to Robert Magellan to write the authorized book on the disappearance of his wife and child. She doubted he'd ever entrust that part of himself to anyone. That was okay, though; she didn't blame the man. She could live with that.

Two, it was clear to Mallory that Susanna was in love with Robert—probably had been for years.

And three—and possibly even more intriguing—was that Robert appeared to be absolutely oblivious to Susanna's feelings.

If nothing else, Mallory mused as she slid back her sunroof, this had all the makings of a really interesting ride.

SIX

A t promptly eight on the following morning, Mallory walked up the steps of the Conroy Diner and smiled at the elderly man who held open the door for her.

"Thank you," she said, looking past him into the diner.

"My privilege, beautiful." He half bowed, and she laughed, shaking her head.

Only a man of a certain age could get away with something like that these days, she was thinking as she entered the diner and looked for a familiar face.

She was still smiling when she slid into the booth next to Father Burch.

"Good morning, Father," she said, adding to the woman seated opposite her, "You must be Mary Corcoran. I'm pleased to meet you."

"God bless you, Miss Russo, for doing this." Mary Corcoran's eyes filled. "Father told me you're going to help us find Ryan."

Mallory held up a hand.

"One thing at a time. First of all, I agreed to look into the case, but you have to understand that there are no guarantees here. Ryan and Courtney have been missing for more than two weeks. That's a long time, Mary. If they're hiding someplace, they've done a damned good job of it. It's going to be very hard for anyone to find them if they don't want to be found."

"I understand, I do." Mary nodded a little too quickly. "But knowing that someone other than the police is looking for them makes me think they're more likely to be found."

"I was a member of that police force for a long time. I'm sure they're doing their best."

"They're only trying to find them to arrest them. They're not doing anything to find the real killers." Mary lowered her voice and leaned across the table. "Detective . . ."

"Not anymore," Mallory corrected her. "Or maybe I should say *not yet.* I have applied for a license, but right now, I can't legally refer to myself as an investigator. So just call me Mallory."

"I don't know what that means." Mary frowned and looked at Father Burch. "I thought you said . . ."

"Don't worry, Mary, she's come highly recommended by none other than the chief of police. What she means by not legally being a detective is that she can't charge for services as a private investigator until she has a license, isn't that how you phrased it, Mallory?"

"Basically, yes. So until I have my license in my hand, I'd like to keep this all pretty much low-key. It's going to take me a while to talk to everyone Father Burch thinks I should, and hopefully by the time I've finished, the paperwork will have gone through."

"And in the meantime, I'm just telling people that Mallory is a friend of mine who's agreed to help us out. Which is the truth." The priest smiled. "A new friend, but a friend all the same."

"I don't care about any of that official stuff." Mary waved a dismissive hand. "I'm only interested in the fact that you're going to try to find Ryan."

The waitress stopped by the table to take their orders, and Mallory took the opportunity to study the woman who sat across from her. There was no question that the uncertainty and fear following her grandson's disappearance had taken a heavy toll on Mary. Her pale blue eyes were rimmed in red, and the dark circles beneath them were a likely testament to the many sleepless nights she'd spent since Ryan went missing.

After they ordered, Mary tapped on the table with an index finger to get Mallory's attention.

"My grandson is innocent, Mallory. He could not have done this thing." Mary removed a stack of photographs from her purse and started to place them on the table. "Does this look like a murderer? Look, here he is at his prom . . ."

Mallory didn't have the heart to tell the worried grandmother that murderers don't have any particular look.

"He's very handsome, Mary." Mallory took the photo of tall, good-looking Ryan in a tuxedo next to a pretty blond girl in a pale pink gown on the front steps of what appeared to be a red-brick twin home. "And Courtney is a very pretty girl."

"Oh, that's not Courtney," Mary told her. "That's Ryan's girlfriend."

"Courtney isn't his girlfriend?"

"No, no. See, that's another thing the police got wrong and even though I told them—and Courtney's mother told them, too—they're making this big thing, like these two kids are Bonnie and Clyde." She shook her head. "Ryan's been going out with Shelby for almost two years now."

"Shelby Keeler," Father Burch supplied the last name. "She's a junior at Our Lady of Angels."

"The newspeople make it sound like Ryan and Courtney have some big romance going on, but they're just good friends. Have been since kindergarten." Mary passed several other pictures to Mallory.

"Same with these boys, Adam and Jamey. The four were pretty much inseparable most of their lives. There is no way either Ryan or Courtney could have hurt Adam or Jamey.

"Don't think I don't know what you're thinking," she went on, searching her purse for a tissue. "You're thinking, *Of course she has to say that, this is her flesh and blood.*" She blew her nose softly. "I want you to understand that this isn't Ryan's grandmother blindly defending her grandson. This is God's truth. Ryan could never have pulled a gun, pulled the trigger, on either of his friends. Or on anyone else, for that matter. It isn't in him."

"Mary, do you know why the kids went to the park that night?"

"Courtney was bothered about something or other, something she wanted to talk to the boys about."

"Did Ryan tell you what it was?"

"No." Mary shook her head. "He just said she needed to talk about something important and they were going to get together at the park. It was something they'd done a lot over the years, just got together to talk from time to time. I didn't think anything of it."

"Did they always meet in that park?"

"Pretty much, yes. It was where they used to play when they were little, you know? It used to be so much nicer than it is now, but they never got out of the habit of meeting there. I used to ask Ryan, 'Can't you find another place to hang out?' It's maybe not so nice there after dark anymore, but he always just said it was their place."

"Did you see Courtney that night, Mary?"

Mary nodded. "She came to the house and went upstairs to get Ryan. They were up there for a while, then they left to meet up with Adam and Jamey." Mary looked down at the napkin she'd been shredding. "Maybe I should have talked to her. Asked her what was bothering her. Maybe I could have helped. Then maybe they wouldn't have gone to the park at all that night."

Mary began to weep.

"Mary, is there a gun in your house?"

"No."

"Was there? Ever?"

"No, I just told you . . ." Mary dropped her hands to the table and stared at Mallory.

"Ever? At any time, did you have . . ."

"No. No. No. You're not listening to me." Mary's voice rose slightly in obvious frustration, and she slapped a palm on the table, surprising even herself. Mallory guessed that Mary Corcoran was not a woman who generally made a scene or raised her voice, but she did so now. "We had no guns in the house. Ryan had no gun. Courtney had no gun. No. Gun."

Father Burch reached across the table to pat her hands. "Shhhh, Mary. We're not back at the parish hall in your office."

"I have to ask," Mallory said softly, hoping to calm Mary down a bit. "You have to understand, if I'm going to work with you, there are certain questions I have to ask."

Mary nodded, her head down. She was about to speak when the waitress arrived with their order, sandwiches for Mary and Father Burch, coffee for Mallory. After they'd been served, Mallory looked up at Mary.

"Tell me about Shelby, Ryan's girlfriend."

"She's lovely. Wants to be a nurse. She's upset about Ryan graduating and going off to college. She's afraid he'll forget about her." Mary shrugged. "It happens. Maybe he will, I tell her, maybe not. They're both too young to worry about such things."

"Do you know her family?"

"Joe and Shirl, sure. I've known them forever. Even before Shelby was born, before Ryan came to live with me. They're great people. They're trying to stand behind Ryan now, and I know it's hard for them, with all the publicity and everything."

"And Courtney, she has a boyfriend?"

"She had been going out with someone, but I think that was sort of casual. I only met him a few times."

"Do you know his name?" Mallory sipped her coffee, but found it too hot to drink. She added some ice from her water glass and tried again.

"Joe something. He didn't go to school here. But Linda would know. Courtney's mother. Or Misty, her sister."

"How about Jamey and Adam? Did they have steady girlfriends?"

Mary shook her head. "Not that I know of."

"If I wanted to talk to someone at their school, who would I want to see?" Mallory asked.

"Stop in the principal's office tomorrow after school—around four or so—and I'll have everyone available to you that I think you'll need to talk to. To start, anyway," Father Burch told her.

"Thanks," Mallory said. "How about extracurricular activities?"

"Ryan played football, you probably saw that in the papers. That terrible headline." Mary shivered, and Mallory recalled the article referred to. The one that started out, FOOTBALL STAR SUSPECT IN DOU-BLE SHOOTING. "That and film club were the only things he really was involved in. He had a lot of AP classes. He worked really hard, got straight A's . . ."

Mary held half her sandwich in her right hand, but hadn't taken a bite.

"And Courtney . . ." Mary's eyes filled with tears again. "She didn't have time for a lot of extracurriculars. She's worked part-time at Hazel's for the past couple of years."

"Hazel's Market, the mom-and-pop over on Appleton?" Mallory asked.

"Right. She's been saving for college. She'll be the first in her family to go."

She placed her sandwich back on her plate. "You know this city, Mallory, you've worked here for how many years?"

"Nine."

"You know about the mills closing, about how everything in town sort of went downhill. Things have gotten a little better with that new mall between here and Toby Falls. That town has money, always has. A lot of people from Conroy have found work in those stores. They sure can't afford to shop there. Conroy's strictly blue collar these days." She smiled ruefully. "Some might say we're lucky to have any collar at all. But I guess you know that."

Mallory nodded. She'd seen with her own eyes how, block by block, downtown Conroy's shops had been boarded up as one small family-owned business after another found itself unable to compete with the big chain stores and closed its doors. Nights found more and more kids gathering on the dark corners. When she'd worked patrol, she'd hauled in her share of underage drinkers, many of whom later were picked up on drug charges, sales as well as possession. The flip side of poverty was crime, and over the past few years Conroy had had more than its fair share of both.

"If you know the town, you know how important it is for some of these families to send a child to college. Ryan would have been our first too. Temple University. Big-time for us, you know? They wanted him to come out for football. One of the assistant coaches came here to watch him play last fall, called the house a couple of times, too." Her eyes flashed angrily, and she clenched her fists. "This is Ryan's golden opportunity to go places no one in his family has gone, understand? Smart, handsome, athletic, talented—the sky's the limit for a kid like him." Mary shook her head adamantly. "No way would he have thrown away his future for a thousand dollars. No way . . ."

"I've thought the same thing, Mary," Mallory said thoughtfully. "There just doesn't seem to be a motive for either Courtney or Ryan to have been the shooter."

"That's what I'm telling you. Just like I told that detective they sent over to talk to me, but all he was interested in was where did I think Ryan would go if he was running for his life."

"*Is* there a place he'd go? To hide? A relative? A friend or a friend of the family?" Mallory asked.

"No one that I can think of, and I have tried. I haven't much family. My only sister died five years ago. My husband died in 1987. My daughter . . ." Mary's eyes clouded with pain. "I lost my only child shortly after that."

"I'm sorry, I'm confused," Mallory said. "I thought your daughter was Ryan's mother."

"She was. When I say 'lost,' I mean lost to me. Before her father died, Kathleen was hard to handle. After his death, she became impossible to control."

"How did he die?"

"Car accident. He was working the night shift at the paper mill and was driving home in a storm. A tree uprooted and fell just as he was passing under it. He died a few days later."

"I'm so sorry," Mallory said.

Mary shrugged. "It had to have been God's will. Otherwise, the tree would have fallen on someone else, you know?"

"A lot of kids have problems after losing a parent," Mallory told her.

"Kathleen had problems since the day she was born. She wasn't an easy baby, never liked to be held much. The terrible twos? Doesn't even begin to tell the story. Fussed all the time, cried, threw tantrums to get what she wanted. As soon as she learned to talk, she was talking back. She was always very strong-willed and contrary." Mary blew out a long breath, her eyes sad. "The truth is, she wasn't a particularly likable child. Some kids just aren't."

"That's true, Mary," Father Burch agreed. "Some children are more of a challenge than others."

"Well, I'm afraid I wasn't always up to that challenge, that's the God's truth. I never knew how to handle her on the best of days, but after John died, things more or less fell apart. I fell apart," she told them, "and Kathleen, well, she just fell. Unfortunately, with her father gone, there was no one there to catch her. She caught up with a bad crowd, moved out of the house on her sixteenth birthday, and I didn't see her again for almost two years."

"That must have been very hard on you," Mallory said.

"It was harder after she came back." Mary smiled ruefully. "She had Ryan when she was seventeen. Stopped at the house with him when he was just a couple of months old. She never even told me who his father was. Well, of course, I wanted her to stay, told her I'd send her back to school to finish up, I'd take care of the baby. For a while, she might have even thought about it. But one morning I woke up and they were both gone. Last I heard of her until the detectives from Philadelphia rang my doorbell one day to tell me they'd found her dead of an overdose and not to worry about my grandson because he was in foster care but the baby's father said they should look for me, maybe I'd want him. Foster care! As if I'd let my flesh and blood grow up in foster care! Father Whalen—God rest his soul—got on the phone and talked to some people in the city, and the next day I had Ryan in my arms."

She looked up at Mallory and added, "I was determined that he was not going to grow up to be anything like his mother, and as God is my witness, he is not."

Mary grabbed Mallory's wrist and gave it a tug. "I have lost everyone I have ever loved, you understand? You have to find my grandson and bring him home, and let him get on with the wonderful life he's supposed to have. You have to find him before something terrible happens to him, and I lose him forever, too."

SEVEN

Mallory took the steps leading from the county courthouse at a brisk pace, grateful to have completed her business without having run into anyone she knew but not wanting to push her luck. Though it pissed her off that after nine years on the force, she had to submit fingerprints and references and sign a consent form for a background check, she paid her two hundred dollars and tied up all the loose ends that had been required to apply for her private investigator's license. If Mary Corcoran hadn't grabbed her heart when she'd grabbed her wrist yesterday, Mallory might have said the hell with it all and told Father Burch to find someone else. But she knew there was no one else who would approach this case the way she would; no one else better at ferreting out the fine points and following up on the details. It had been a source of pride for as long as she'd been a cop, and while at first the thought of becoming a PI felt like a huge step down, after meeting with Mary, Mallory realized something very important: It didn't matter what she called herself. She would search for the truth until she found it. Period. She'd never approached a case with lesser resolve and she wouldn't do so now. Ryan Corcoran mattered. Courtney Bauer mattered. Chances are they were somewhere in or nearby the city, and she was determined to track them down.

Hopefully, they'd both still be alive when she found them.

The streets surrounding the square upon which the courthouse stood were narrow and one-way. Mallory's low heels clicked on the concrete as she hurried to her car. Completing the paperwork had set her back by more than an hour after she'd left the diner, and she wanted to go back to the playground and finish the walk-through that had been cut short the other evening.

And there was that matter of checking out the other side of the fence, the side facing the alley that ran behind the last row of town houses before Kelly Creek cut through. While the police report had indicated that the neighborhood had been canvassed the day after the shooting, Mallory knew that *how thoroughly* would have depended on who was doing the canvassing. She knew, too, that if she'd been assigned to this case, it wouldn't have mattered to her who had done the preliminary investigation. She'd have gone over the area with a fine-tooth comb, and would have personally spoken to every resident who admitted to having been home from eight o'clock on the night of the shooting until the following afternoon. There was no telling who might have seen or heard something they weren't aware could have been connected to the shootings. Getting the right answers more often than not depended on asking the right questions. When she was with the department, she was the one who usually did the asking, but who did they have now who was as thorough? No one that she could think of. Which was, of course, why Joe Drabyak was so quick to offer her name to Father Burch. He knew if he had to depend on his current staff to solve the case, it would go cold and stay cold, especially since the sniper gave no indication of turning himself in anytime soon.

Joe had mentioned that he had someone new starting next week,

Mallory recalled as she got into her car and started the engine. Must be someone with some experience, if he or she was coming in at detective level, and he or she must be good or Joe wouldn't have bothered. She drove away wondering where Joe had found his new hire.

Ten minutes later, she was standing behind the swings where Adam Stevens and Jamey Tilton had met their deaths, her digital camera in hand, lining up the shot from the swing to the slide. She took the picture from several angles, then went to the slide and climbed the ladder. She raised the camera to capture a photo to the swings from the top of the slide, just where she thought Courtney could have been standing when she heard the shots and looked up to see the killer or killers. Mallory got off several frames before a shadow edged into the picture. She hesitated then took the last shot, slid the camera back into her pocket, and looked out over the playground.

To the right of the swing set stood a man wearing dark glasses and a blue baseball cap. Mallory was pretty sure he was the same man she'd seen the other night. She hadn't seen his face, but the stance was the same.

Military background, maybe.

He was definitely watching her, so on a whim she took the camera back out of her pocket and snapped his picture, then looked at him for his reaction. There was none that she could see.

Definitely military.

Could be a member of one of the victim's families, she thought as she climbed down the ladder. Could be a reporter. Or he could be the killer, returned to the scene of the crime because he couldn't stay away. She knew that many killers did exactly that: came back again and again to relive the moment. Some did their best to involve themselves in the investigation, to stay close to it. Force of habit sent her right hand inside her jacket, seeking the weapon that was no longer there. *Must be something like phantom pain,* she was thinking, wondering how long it would take for that reflex to go away.

With luck, she'd have her license to carry concealed before then.

"Hello," Mallory called out to him as she rounded the slide. Might as well take the initiative, she decided, since he made no attempt to disguise the fact that he was watching her. "Nice day."

"Very."

He stood between her and the path, his thumbs hooked in his belt loops, but made no move toward her.

"You the park inspector?" he asked as she drew closer.

"What?" She almost laughed.

"You were here the other night, and now I see that you're back and taking pictures of the playground equipment," he said with a touch of sarcasm. "I figured you must be inspecting it."

She continued walking.

"Or you could be a reporter. Or maybe the parent of a kid who fell from the top of the slide." He crossed his arms over his chest. "So I'm wondering, which is it?"

Mallory forced a smile. "None of the above."

He stepped into her path.

"I'm guessing you're with one of those tabloids, maybe, since the more legitimate papers have run their stories without photographing the scene of the crime from every conceivable angle." He took off his glasses. "And don't try to pretend you don't know that a couple of kids were shot and killed here."

"I'm not a reporter," she told him, close enough now to study his face while he studied hers. He was almost handsome, she thought, nice features and neatly trimmed sandy brown hair. Dark blue eyes. Wary eyes.

Cop's eyes.

"You're a cop," she said, watching his face. He was too casually dressed to be FBI; not spit-and-polish enough to be state.

"Technically, not until Monday," he told her.

Joe's new hire.

"You're going to inherit the case, the shooting case," she said.

"Ah, I get it. You're a psychic."

She shook her head. "Just someone who's interested in the case."

"May I ask why?"

"I'm a friend of the Corcoran family."

"The missing boy. The one believed to be the shooter."

"He wasn't."

"I'd expect a member of the family to stick up for him."

"I'm not a member of the family," she corrected him. "I said I was a *friend* of the family."

"A friend of the family who likes to take photographs of the crime scene. Interesting." His eyes narrowed. "What exactly are you doing here?"

She hesitated.

"Mary Corcoran asked me to help find her grandson."

"And why would she do that?"

"Because I used to be a detective."

"That explains the reaching for the gun that isn't there." He raised one eyebrow. "So what are you now, a PI?"

"No." She shook her head. "Just a—"

"Right. A friend of the family." He looked annoyed. "What's your name?"

"Mallory Russo." She watched his face, but her name didn't appear to register with him. Might as well throw it out there. "I used to be with the department here in Conroy."

"Charlie Wanamaker." He did not offer to shake her hand.

"There's a Wanamaker family that lives over on Fourth Street," Mallory said. "Any relation?"

"My mother and sister," he told her.

"So that was your brother who was killed two years ago in Iraq?" She could have added, *And your mother that I picked up, oh, about a dozen times for public drunkenness back when I was on patrol?*

"Yes."

"I'm sorry. I never met him, but I heard Dan was a great guy."

"The best." His face seemed to harden. He changed the subject abruptly. "So you're trying to help Mrs. Corcoran find her grandson. Any leads?"

"Not really." She shrugged. "You have any thoughts on it?"

"Not really." He mimicked her shrug. "I haven't finished reading through the entire file yet."

"Joe gave you the file before you even started the job?" Her interest was piqued.

"He's been letting me read through it in the conference room down at the station when I can find a minute here and there to stop in, thought he'd give me something to think about until next week."

"Who are the statements from?"

"Different people."

"I can't believe he's given you access to the file."

"Sounds as if you know him well."

"Like I said, I used to be a detective here in Conroy."

"Used to be? You quit?"

"Moved on to other things." She had no intention of going into details with this stranger. The stranger who'd been hired to replace her, so it would seem. "Joe must be eager to get you on the case."

"He wanted me to start a couple of weeks ago. I had some things I had to take care of, but he didn't want to wait that long for me to become acquainted with the case. He wanted me to be able to move right into the investigation. This seemed to be the most expedient way to do that."

"But you're technically a civilian," she pointed out.

"Technically, I suppose you're right."

"Well, it's been nice chatting." She extended her hand, and he took it. "I should be getting along."

"So how do you see it?" he said, holding on to her hand a few moments longer than necessary and ignoring her attempt to leave.

"What do you think really happened that night? You obviously don't think the Corcoran kid or his girlfriend was the shooter."

"No, I don't"—she slid her hand from his light grasp—"and Courtney wasn't his girlfriend. They and the two boys who were killed were all really close friends and had been since kindergarten."

"Any thoughts on who the killer was, then? Or what happened to the kids who are missing?"

She shrugged again.

"Oh, come on." He laughed. "This is the second time I've seen you here. You know you have some thoughts on what went down that night."

"Assuming I had thoughts, why would I share them with you?"

"Because there might be some things I could share in return. Like statements from witnesses, that sort of thing."

"What makes you think I can't get those on my own?"

"Oh, please." He laughed again, and she liked the sound of it. "Your eyes got a hungry look in them when I mentioned having read them. The minute you leave here, you're going to call Joe Drabyak and ask him why he allowed a civilian to look at the investigative reports."

He had her there.

"Why would I share my theories with you? And why would you even be interested in what I think?"

"A, because we both want to get to the bottom of this, and B, because I'm thinking you're the detective Drabyak said was going to be real tough to replace."

"What else have you heard about me?" she asked, prepared for the worst.

"What should I have heard?"

Mallory bit the inside of her cheek and ignored the question, thinking about the offer to share. It was tempting. It would certainly be to her advantage to have access to the information she normally wouldn't be able to get, unless she went directly to Joe and asked for it. She hoped she'd never be desperate enough to have to do that, which would not only make her feel inept but also kick-start the rumor mill all over again if anyone ever found out.

And if Charlie didn't actually start full-time until Monday, that would give her five days to get as much information as she could before Frank and some others started filling the new guy's head with garbage about her. Not that she cared about his opinion of her, but once they got to talking, chances are Charlie wouldn't be as interested in sharing much of anything with her.

She took her phone from her pocket, speed-dialed a number, and waited.

"Joe, it's Mallory. Talk to me about Charlie Wanamaker . . ." She walked past Charlie and continued toward the gates so that he could not overhear the conversation.

"How do you know about Charlie?" Joe did not sound surprised that she was asking.

"We more or less ran into each other at the playground."

"Thirteen years on the job in Philly, the last few as a detective. Came highly recommended. He's from the area, and local is always good. He knows Conroy, he knows a lot of the folks around here. He was by far the best candidate for the job. We were damned lucky to get him." Joe paused, then added, "It wasn't easy to replace you, Mal."

"I appreciate that. Why'd he come back, if he was doing so great in Philly."

"Family obligations."

Interesting.

She wondered how Joe would react to the idea, so she decided to just lay it out there. "Listen, what are the chances we can more or less make a sort of deal here? Information for information, theory for theory. Totally off the record, of course . . ."

"So you want an open dialogue with my soon-to-be detective," Joe said. "You think you have insights that could help solve the case?"

"Maybe."

Joe laughed. "Technically, I can't tell Charlie what to do, since, technically, he doesn't work for me yet."

"You've given him access to the case files."

"True. Originally, he was to have started two weeks ago, but he had to delay his starting date twice. I can't spare any officers right now because of this damned sniper, but Charlie did mention he would have some free time, on and off, so we agreed he'd become familiar with the case before Monday so that he'd already be into it when we gave him his badge and his gun."

"No point in wasting any time."

"That's how I look at it. And he was more than willing to get a head start on it, so I figured hey, why not. I couldn't think of one good reason not to."

"So you're okay with this? Us pooling our info?"

"As long as this is kept between you, me, and Wanamaker."

"That would have been one of my stipulations."

"Then we're on the same wavelength. And between you and me, I can't say it bothers me to have your fingers in this pie. You know how much I respect you. You were a damned good detective. Charlie's coming on board with a fine reputation: They were really upset about losing him down in Philly. I have high hopes for him."

"One thing, Joe." Mallory turned and started back down the path toward the bench where Charlie was waiting. "I had to sign an agreement not to discuss my employment with anyone, so I'd appreciate it if you didn't mention it to anyone."

"Magellan made you sign an agreement not to let anyone know he's involved?"

"Yes. Of course, you know, since Father Burch had already spoken with you, but I'd appreciate it if it didn't go beyond you and me."

"It's not something I need to discuss with anyone, Mal, don't worry about it. But what did you tell Charlie? You tell him you're a PI? Who does he think your client is?"

"It will be a few more weeks before I'll have my license, so I'm not pretending to be something I'm not. I told Charlie I was a friend of Mary Corcoran's." Mallory paused. "Which after yesterday isn't really a lie."

"You learn anything from her?" he asked a little too quickly. "Has she heard from the grandson?"

"Nothing yet."

"I guess that's one of those things you'll talk to Charlie about if it happens, right?"

When Mallory didn't respond, Joe said, "Well, I'm just as happy to keep this arrangement we're talking about under wraps as well. The last thing I want is for the press to get the idea that you're working undercover on this. It could lead to a lot of shit that neither of us needs to deal with."

"I couldn't agree more," she said. "Now, why don't you discuss that part of the arrangement with Charlie . . ."

Mallory sat on a bench and watched Charlie pace as his soon-to-be boss reiterated what he and Mallory had discussed. She'd known Joe would jump at the proposition, and why not? He'd want to be kept in her personal loop, to know what she knew when she knew it. It was like getting an extra detective for free. His person would be in on anything she dug up—and Joe had to know she'd dig up something before too long—and his department could take the credit for it. Between her inability to discuss her employment, and the fact that she wasn't yet licensed, Mallory couldn't act publicly even if she wanted to. Joe had nothing to lose and everything to gain.

"It's fine with me as long as you're clearing it," Charlie was saying as he walked back to Mallory. "Did you want to talk to Mallory again? Mallory, did you need . . . ?"

Mallory shook her head and stood up and reached for the phone after he disconnected the call.

"Joe explained that this arrangement will work as long as no one—I mean, no one—in the department or anyone else knows about it, right?" she said as she dropped the phone into her pocket. "One person finds out and we're done. Agreed? Questions?"

"You mean, as in, why would you not want anyone in the department—or anyone else—to know we'll be sharing our thoughts on this case?" He smiled. "You and Drabyak have your reasons, I'm sure. So no, as of right now, I have no questions."

"Good." She nodded. "Now, tell me about the statements that you read."

"Theory first." He sat next to her on the bench.

"Uh-uh. Statements first."

He took a nickel from his pocket. "Call it."

"Heads."

He flipped the coin onto the walk. "Tails." He leaned over and re-trieved the nickel. "You first."

Mallory sighed, then related her theory about the killer standing behind the boys on the swings and looking up to see Courtney at the top of the slide.

"That's why you were photographing the sight line," he said, nodding. "Makes sense. So what do you think went down here? You think this was a crime of opportunity? You got the two guys sitting there on the swings, just talking. Someone comes through the park, sees them sitting there, randomly decides to rob them?"

Mallory shook her head. "That doesn't feel right."

"So how about this: Maybe someone knew about the thousand dollars, maybe heard the kid talking about it in school, how he was going to take this money out of the bank and go buy a car. Sees the boys heading for the park, decides to follow them, see if the grand is still in the kid's pocket."

"Better," she said, "but I'm still not feeling it."

"Do we know what brought the four of them here that night?" He looked around at the park. "There have to be nicer places in Con-roy where kids can hang out."

"According to Ryan's grandmother, they often got together here to talk. Mary said that something was bothering Courtney and she wanted to get together to talk it over with the guys."

"Could she have known about the money?" Charlie asked thoughtfully. "Maybe set the other two up to be robbed?"

"If she was setting it up for someone else to rob them, why would she have had Ryan come along with her? Wouldn't she have told Adam and Jamey to meet her there at a specific time, and just have the robber show up instead of bringing Ryan along with her?"

Charlie thought that over for a moment, then said, "Let's just say we don't know if the robbery was random or premeditated, and move on."

"Okay. So after the shooting, you have the two boys on the ground where they'd fallen after they'd been shot. Where did the other two go?"

"The police report showed a Dumpster was over there"—she pointed toward the fence—"the night of the shooting. They could have run there to hide but . . ."

"Too obvious, to hide in or behind the Dumpster." Charlie shook his head. "The killer would have caught up with them, and more likely than not shot them right there. But there was no blood on the Dumpster and no blood on the ground over there."

"You've seen the Dumpster?"

"Photos. No blood," he told her. "So where did they go?"

"I think they went over the fence."

"Over the fence?"

"As far as I can see, it's the only thing they could have done." She gestured with her head. "Come on, let me show you . . ."

Mallory led him across the parking lot.

"Here's where the Dumpster was." She pointed to the spot along the fence. "I think they may have made a run for it, but maybe they were being chased. So they're cornered here, right?"

She pointed next to the fence.

"It's tall enough to keep most people out," she said, "but Ryan was a big boy. Six three, two hundred twenty pounds. Played on the football team, might have played in college. We're talking a big strong boy here, right?"

"So you think he was able to jump the fence. . . ."

Mallory nodded. "After he lifted Courtney and got her over, yes, I think he was able to go over it."

"Sure, he could have done it, but there's no way of knowing for sure." Charlie approached the metal fence and studied the top links. "You look on the other side yet?"

"No. I was going to do that today."

"Let's walk around and take a look."

There was heavy traffic on the main road outside the fence, but once they turned the corner onto the one-way side street, there was none. Cars were parked on either side of the narrow road, which made a sharp turn to the right. A row of old, three-story brick homes faced the street, and an alley ran along behind them. Charlie and Mallory walked along the park fence as far as the alley, then stopped to take in their surroundings. Across the alley from the houses, a heavily wooded area led down to a creek.

"If they got over the fence, they probably got away clean." Charlie said. "They could have run down the alley and hidden behind cars, they could have hidden in the woods over there, or they could have gone across the creek and disappeared."

"I don't suppose those reports you've been privy to mention whether or not the fence has been dusted for prints."

"None I've run across. I'll check, and if not, once I have the equipment, I'll run back out and see if there's anything worth lifting. In the meantime, let's see what we've got here."

Mallory went right for the fence, and began to scrutinize it while Charlie walked down toward the woods.

When he came back up, she was on her knees, staring at the fence.

"Did any of the reports mention what Courtney or Ryan was wearing that night?" she asked.

"If one did, it's one I haven't gotten to yet." He leaned over her shoulder to see what she was looking at.

"There's a bit of yellow fabric caught right there." She pointed at a fence link with her index finger.

He came in closer to get a better look.

"Oh, yeah, we want that," he told her. "Do you have anything to put it in?"

"Not on me." She stood up and straightened her back as she searched her bag, pulled out her camera, and began to take pictures of the fabric in situ.

"I have some bags in my car," he told her. "I'll be right back. . . ."

Mallory took seven shots, then put the camera back in her bag and got out her phone. She searched her pockets for the card upon which she'd earlier written down Mary Corcoran's home and office numbers. She dialed the office number first.

"Mary, it's Mallory Russo. Sorry to bother you at work, but I have just one quick question. Do you happen to know what Ryan and Courtney were wearing the night they disappeared? Do you remember?"

Mallory watched Charlie as he came around the corner and walked toward her, several brown paper bags in his hand. He certainly was easy on the eyes.

"Are you sure? You're certain?" Mallory smiled at Charlie. "Thank you, Mary. We'll talk again soon. . . ."

"You're looking smug." Charlie's eyes narrowed as he came closer. "Why are you looking smug?"

"According to his grandmother, on the night of the shooting, when Ryan left home, he was wearing jeans and a red T-shirt."

"Red is not yellow, so why are you looking so smug?" he repeated, but he smiled as if he knew what was coming next.

"Courtney Bauer stopped at the Corcoran house on her way to the park. Guess what she was wearing?"

"A yellow something."

"A yellow knit shirt." She watched Charlie coax the bit of fabric from the broken link where it had been caught. He tucked the prize into one of the bags and sealed it. "Mary remembered because she had yellow roses in a vase in the dining room and she commented on the fact that they matched Courtney's top."

"So we'll see about getting this to the lab, see if there's anything interesting they can tell us about it."

"Don't hold your breath till that comes back," she told him as he tucked the folded bag into his back pocket. "This isn't Philly. One small lab, three lab techs—that's all you get here. It's going to take awhile. Unless Joe wants to use the state lab, which really isn't much faster."

"So how do you know about Philly?" Charlie asked.

"Joe mentioned you'd come highly recommended from there," she admitted.

"So, the deal is, I can't ask about you but you can ask about me?" He made a face. "Doesn't sound like a very equitable deal to me."

"I didn't ask about you, he told me. And you can ask me anything you want." She folded her arms across her chest. "Go ahead. Anything."

"Who are you really working for?"

"Anything," she told him as she turned heel and walked toward her car, "but that."

EIGHT

*S*o *that's Mallory Russo.*

Charlie watched her drive away with a wave and a smile. Interesting to put the name and the face together. Very interesting.

Even in the faint light at the park the other night, he'd recognized her as the pretty cop with the pale blond hair and the long legs who'd come to his brother's funeral along with several others from the force. She hadn't known Danny, she'd told him, yet she'd come to pay her respects to his mother anyway. He hadn't spoken with her at the funeral home, but he'd seen her and remembered her face. Eighteen months ago, he hadn't gotten close enough to see her eyes. Today he had, and he'd found them to be an odd shade of light green, a nice contrast with her hair.

He wondered why she hadn't mentioned that she'd been to the funeral home.

And of course he'd heard the rumors: that she'd ratted out her partner for some very minor infraction and he'd been busted back to patrol, his life ruined. What that minor infraction was, he didn't know. He'd asked, but it had been glossed over in the telling, which made Charlie pretty sure the infraction probably hadn't been so minor. He'd listened to the telling because there had been no way to avoid it. He'd been in the conference room three days ago reading through the playground murder files when the door opened and a tall man with a marine-style buzz cut stepped in and introduced himself.

"Hey. You're the new guy," he'd said, offering his hand. "Frank Toricelli. I'm one of your fellow detectives. Hear you're coming on board soon. Just wanted to stop in and say hi."

Charlie stood and leaned across two chairs to shake the proffered hand.

"Thanks. Yes, I start next week."

"I see the boss is getting you tuned up." Toricelli had nodded his head in the file's direction.

"Yeah, he thought it would be a good idea if I got up to speed quickly on this case, since you're apparently shorthanded right now."

"Got ourselves a sniper." Toricelli smiled as if that was a good thing. "Bastard's keeping us busy, lots of OT, you know? We're at least one man down, since we got one out on maternity leave and we were already a man down before that. So we're short at least one man on this sniper case—this bastard is all over the place, man, he's been a bitch to try to catch—but there's still that playground mess. So yeah, we're in need of some help here. Old Joe sure as hell took his sweet time finding someone." The detective had leaned closer to Charlie, lowered his voice, and added, "We think he was kind of hoping the other one would come back, but she's too smart for that. She knows her days would be numbered, no one watching her back, know what I mean?"

"Ah, no, not really." Charlie had shrugged. He'd never been one for gossip; had seen firsthand what careless words could do to someone's feelings or reputation.

"A call for backup that goes unanswered, maybe a stray bullet here or there, come on, you know the drill, man." Toricelli had smirked. "She was smart to get out on her own when she did."

"I don't know who she is."

"Russo, man. Mallory Russo." He stared at Charlie as if the name was supposed to mean something. "Ex-detective? You mean you haven't heard about her yet?"

"I haven't really talked to anyone," Charlie told him. "This is only the third time I've been in the building for anything more than an interview or preemployment talks, so I don't know who or what you're talking about."

"I'm surprised he didn't mention her." His head jerked in the direction of Joe Drabyak's office. "Shit, everyone knows he has the hots for her, and she sure as hell took advantage of that, you know? Hot chick, ambitious detective, older guy who just happens to be the lead detective. He brings her in, he pushes her up through the ranks. Then the old chief retires, he gets the nod to fill that job, moves his girl up to lead. You know how it goes. Happens every day."

Charlie debated whether or not to tell Toricelli to save his breath, he wasn't interested in hearing the scuttlebutt on his soon-to-be boss and some woman he had a fling with, but it would have been like trying to stop a moving train. Toricelli barely took a breath.

"Yeah, this chick, Russo, is real ambitious, you know the type. There's one guy—one detective—between her and the promotion to lead. So what does she do? She rats him out for some stupid little thing, gets Drabyak to write the guy up—did I mention the guy was her partner for Christ's sake?—gets him bounced back down to patrol. Figured she'd skate right into the top slot." He laughed derisively. "Like the rest of us were going to let that happen. That bitch didn't know what hit her, trust me. Not a soul on the force—except for the old man there, of course—no one had a word to say to her."

"You mean you shunned her?" Charlie asked.

"Yeah, we all just stopped talking to her, wouldn't have anything to do with her. Worst thing that can happen to a cop, you know? Not knowing if anyone would respond to a call for backup. Never knowing if anyone had her back. Made her life a fucking hell. She finally quit. Good riddance. She wasn't that good anyway. Stupid bitch."

"What exactly had she told Drabyak?" Charlie had asked.

"What difference does it make? What kind of cop rats out her own partner? You tell me that."

Charlie had opened his mouth to speak at the same time the door opened and Joe Drabyak stuck his head in.

"Toricelli, I need you in my office." The chief had glanced from one man to the other. "If you're done bending Wanamaker's ear."

"Yeah, I'm done." Toricelli had nodded. "Good to meet you. Looking forward to working with you."

"Thanks, me too," Charlie had replied.

He hadn't really given the incident much thought until this afternoon, when he'd realized that the woman in the park was the much-maligned former Detective Russo.

From the little he'd already observed, he'd put his money on Russo any day. Interesting that Drabyak had so readily agreed to having him share information with her. That had to be a bit off the books, even for a small city force like Conroy's.

Charlie turned the key in the ignition of his BMW, thinking Drabyak didn't look like the type of guy a woman like Mallory Russo would be interested in. *I could be all wrong on that, God knows I've been wrong in the past when it comes to reading women. But somehow . . . her and Drabyak . . . uh-uh. Don't see it.* So if that part of the tale was wrong, what did that say about the rest of it?

He wondered if he'd ever get the chance to ask.

Then again, maybe having Mallory involved was Drabyak's way of covering his ass should Charlie turn out to be a bad decision on his part.

Not that that could happen, Charlie told himself. He'd been damned good in Philly, and he'd be damned good here as well.

Drabyak's faith in Mallory didn't seem to be misplaced, though, Charlie'd give her that. He liked the way she'd walked the crime scene and played it out in her head, piecing it together. And finding that bit of fabric on the other side of the fence, well, that was heads-up work. While he believed that, on his own, he'd have checked both sides of the fence for evidence, he had to give her credit for having thought of it first. He was impressed by her quick mind and her focus on the case. Obviously she still had it in her blood or she wouldn't be putting so much of her time and energy into the case. A case, he reminded himself, she wasn't even getting paid to work.

Or was she? He'd asked her who she was working for on a whim, and she'd slammed that door unexpectedly fast, surprising him. He wasn't even sure why he'd asked; he hadn't thought about it before the question came out of his mouth. After years on the job, you just develop a sixth sense about things, he rationalized. But once it was out there, he'd expected any answer other than the one she gave. He hadn't consciously thought she was on someone's payroll, but if she was, why wouldn't she just say so?

Doesn't matter, he told himself. She's good at what she did, and let's face it, she's damned easy on the eyes. He'd have to be blind not to notice the woman was exceptionally well put together. He'd always been a sucker for a pretty blonde, and Mallory was more than just pretty, with those pale green eyes and bow-shaped mouth. She'd be even prettier if she smiled more, he thought, and found himself wondering what it would take to make her face light up, what would make her throw her head back and laugh out loud.

He parked in front of the one-level masonry house on Fourth Street where his family had lived since 1997, when his father died and the family circumstances changed drastically. His father had lost his job just months earlier, and with his job had gone his benefits, including the only life insurance policy he'd had. The death of Charlie Senior had taken the family from their lovely brick colonial in Toby Falls to the tired little ranch in this tired neighborhood. Charlie had been three years out of college and still working off his obligation to the navy—tuition, room, and board in return for four years of service after graduation—and though he'd come home to help with the move from one house to the other, he'd never really felt the full impact of that move. Chances were he still wouldn't have if his mother's next-door neighbor, Lena Woods, hadn't called him six weeks ago to tell him just how bad things had gotten and ask him when he was going to do something about it.

Charlie had never lived in this small house, which even all these years later he thought of as the "new" house. He'd grown up in their old home, and all of his childhood memories had been made there. He'd come here for occasional visits, holidays and special family event days, but he hadn't stayed. On those visits, he'd slept on the sleeper sofa in the basement recreation room, since this house had three bedrooms, and all of them were occupied. He'd never really minded sleeping in the basement, though. It gave his visit more of a transitory flavor, and for years that was fine with him.

Not anymore, he reminded himself as he grabbed the morning paper from the lawn where it had been tossed and forgotten, and unlocked the front door.

The house was dark, as it generally was these days, and quiet—also normal—so much so that upon entering the tiny space that served as a front foyer, Charlie could hear water dripping from the spigot in the kitchen sink. He turned on the hall light and followed the sound of the drip.

"Charlie's home! Charlie's home! Charlie's home!" The whirlwind that was his sister flashed into the kitchen. "I drew a picture for you! Come see! Come see! Come see!"

Ah, he thought. *Today everything comes in threes.*

"I'm coming, Jilly," he told her as she grabbed on to his arm and tugged him along with her to her room. "Show me what you did today."

"See see see," she said as she dragged him to the small table in the corner of her bedroom. "A bird! A bird! A bird!"

"I do see," he replied, studying the picture at the same time he glanced around. He could always tell what kind of a day Jilly'd had by the state of her bedroom. On a good day, the room was tidy, everything put away neatly if not compulsively. On a bad day, the room reflected the chaos that sometimes stirred in Jilly's mind, and on those days anything could—and often did—happen. Today Jilly's desk was neat as a pin. So far, so good.

It was one of the two reasons Charlie came back to Conroy.

"You drew a great bird, Jilly. A beautiful bird," he told her.

"More." She pointed to him gravely. "More more."

"A beautiful bird," he repeated. Then because today was a *three* day, he said it again. "A beautiful bird."

Jilly smiled broadly, and he reached for the picture she held out to him just as his cell phone rang. His sister clapped her hands over her ears and moaned, falling to the floor in a heap, a look of intense pain on her face. He fumbled with the phone in his pocket to turn it off.

"Jesus, Charlie!" his mother called from the next room. "Damn it, how many times have I told you to turn that damned thing off before you come into the house? You know what it does to her."

Without responding, Charlie sank to the floor next to his sister and held her, rocked her, until the pain stopped. It happened every time she heard a bell or a siren or a car horn. It was one of those things that parents of autistic kids had to learn to deal with.

Unfortunately, his mother's way of dealing was to drink herself into a near stupor by late afternoon every day. Which meant the skills that Jilly had acquired during all those years at Riverside had fallen by the wayside. Her teachers had stressed the importance of consistency and routine, but it was apparent that there'd been precious little of either in Jilly's life over the past several years. Now, at twenty, it seemed she had regressed. She looked like a typical pretty young woman, with her strawberry-blond ponytail and pert face, but she had the social skills of a child. Something had to change, for both his mother's and his sister's sakes.

Mary Jo Wanamaker stood in the doorway, her light brown hair pulled back into a bun that earlier in the day might have been neat. She wore a short-sleeved yellow sweatshirt, brown capri-length leggings, and white flip-flops. She was fifty-seven years old and dressed as if she were thirty years younger. Charlie wasn't sure what he felt when he looked at her. Love, certainly, and equal amounts of sympathy and confusion.

"You set her off, you can calm her down," his mother said, her words slightly slurred.

"She's calm, Mom, she's fine," he said softly, Jilly's head still resting on his shoulder.

"Fine?" His mother rolled her eyes. "Right. Fine."

"Jilly, will you draw another bird for me?" Charlie helped his sister to her feet. "Will you draw one more with blue feathers for me?"

"Blue." Jilly repeated the word. Blue was Jilly's favorite color. "Blue. Blue."

He guided her to her table and pulled out the chair for her. She sat and searched her crayon box for just the right shade.

"Blue. Blue. Blue."

Charlie turned to his mother. "I think we need to talk, Mom."

"Not tonight, Charlie." His mother left the room. "I'm going down to Everett's with Gail. They've got a band on Thursday night and . . ."

"Not tonight." He repeated her words back to her. "Tonight, we are going to talk."

"But Gail . . . ," she protested.

"Gail can find someone else to warm that bar stool next to hers."

He took his mother gently by the arm and steered her in the

direction of the kitchen. He'd find something to fix for dinner, put on a pot of coffee, and then he and his mother would have a long-overdue conversation about Jilly's future, as well as her own. It was time she understood she had few options as far as her daughter's well-being was concerned, and it would be up to Charlie to explain to her exactly what those options were.

NINE

"What?" Robert stood in the doorway of Susanna's office. "You've got that look on your face."

"Which look is that?" Susanna's hand was still on the receiver, even though she'd already hung up the phone.

"The one that says, *Huh?*"

She waved her hand dismissively. "I just finished talking to Mallory."

"Who?" Robert pulled an armchair closer to her desk and plunked into it.

"Mallory Russo? The PI that Kevin . . ." She sighed. She'd thought he hadn't been paying the least bit attention when Mallory was in the office the other day; now he'd confirmed it.

"Oh, right. Right." He nodded and, obviously disinterested, got up and went over to the fish tank. "So what about her?"

"I told her to drop off her hours on Fridays before two. So today, being Friday, I expected to see her well before now, even though she only had a few days to bill. When she didn't show up, I called her." Susanna frowned.

"And . . . ?" He shook food into the top of the tank, something he did every week at this time. Every other day, Susanna looked after the fish. But for some reason, on Friday it occurred to him to feed them.

"And she said she wasn't billing any hours this week."

"Not billing?" Robert snorted. "A PI that misses an opportunity to bill? What's up with that?"

"Well, see, that's just it. She isn't licensed to work as a PI. . . ."

"Oh, swell. You're just finding this out?"

"Well, no, she did tell me that when she was here the other day, but . . ."

"Why'd you hire her, then? I thought that was the point. Kevin wanted a PI." He put the container of food back on the shelf and returned to the chair, sitting on the arm this time rather than the seat.

"She did tell me that she'd applied for a license, but it hasn't come through yet. She doesn't expect any problems in obtaining it; she was a cop for nine years. And she did tell me that technically, she couldn't charge for her services until she was licensed."

"So if she told you this the other day, why are you surprised now?"

"I guess I didn't think she was serious. As you just said, when was the last time someone declined to bill us for anything?" Susanna leaned back in her chair. "I mean, I figured she'd bill me anyway. I even told her she could call it something else. You know, consulting on the landscaping or flower arranging, whatever. But she said no. She said when she could go on the clock, she'd let me know."

Robert made a face. "So she'll pad her bills and slip the hours from this week in somewhere else."

"I don't think she will."

"Oh, come on." He laughed. "What are the odds of that happening?"

"I'm betting she doesn't."

"You're too trusting."

"You're too cynical."

"So what do you want to bet?"

"I don't know. Something I can afford to lose."

"Dinner at the top of the Eiffel Tower."

Surprised, Susanna laughed. "I said something I could afford to lose. That eliminates fuel for that bird of yours. Try again."

"The flight will be on me, but if you lose, you pick up the tab for dinner."

She studied his face for a moment, then looked away. Sometimes it was just too hard to look for too long.

"All right," she said. "You're on."

"Great." He stood. "I haven't been to Paris in a long time. Beth and I always talked about going." His demeanor changed in the blink of an eye. "I always thought there'd be time."

"I've never been," she said, disappointed that his mood had changed so suddenly. She was pretty sure he hadn't heard her.

Robert started toward the door as Susanna logged off her computer and pushed back from her desk. The clock chimed three.

"Well, I guess I'll be heading out." She slipped her bag off the back of her chair, then pushed the chair under the desk.

"So what are your plans for the weekend?" he asked from the doorway.

"Oh, you know." She shrugged, sensing that the question had been an afterthought, the type of thing you figured you should ask a coworker when they were leaving the office for the weekend. "The usual. You?"

Robert shrugged. "No plans."

"I thought Doug and Karen were in town this weekend?" Old friends of his from college.

"I don't really feel like company." He shrugged again. "I told them I wasn't available."

"I hope you never give me the brush-off like that." She turned off the lamp on her desk.

"I never have to. You always understand. I never have to explain myself to you." He patted her on the back when she reached the door. "You're my best friend, Suse. One of my two best, anyway."

She forced a smile. "Well, if you change your mind about having company, give me a call," she said, knowing he wouldn't.

"Will do." He stepped aside to let her pass. "See you on Monday. Have fun."

Susanna smiled again and left the office. At the front door, she turned around to wave, but he'd already disappeared. She went through the kitchen to say good-bye to Trula, but she wasn't there. Outside, Susanna got into her car and tossed her bag on the passenger seat.

"Fun," she muttered as she started the engine. "Yeah, I'm going to have a ball."

She drove out through the gates and pulled into her own drive less than five minutes later. While not palatial, her home on one of the side roads was situated on a nice piece of ground that had plenty of room for her gardens. It had been built from plans originally intended for an English cottage, but the architect who'd designed it had enlarged the room sizes and added modern amenities, making it the perfect house for her: a romantic cottage with all the comforts of contemporary life. She'd fallen in love with it the first time she laid eyes on it, driving around the area one day shortly after Robert had bought the estate. She'd been secretly thrilled when he asked her to stay on as his personal assistant after the sale of Magellan Express.

"Don't make me break in someone new," he'd pleaded. "Not after all these years. Please, Suse—have a heart . . ."

She often wondered whether she'd have taken the job if she'd known how things would work out. It was less than six months later that he'd met Beth and married her after a whirlwind courtship.

Sometimes it was tough being his best friend.

Over the years, she'd amassed a nice little stash of Magellan stock, and when Robert sold the company, it went sky-high. Susanna had sold her shares high—high enough to buy the house outright and still have plenty to invest. That, plus money she'd saved from a lifetime ago, meant she was as financially secure as she'd ever need to be. She could easily retire tomorrow and never have to worry about money. But money wasn't what kept her returning to the Magellan home five mornings out of every week.

She glanced at the clock and debated on the best time to leave. If she left now—right now—she'd miss the rush-hour surge of cars onto the highways around here, but would run into traffic later on her journey. Fridays were always bad anyway, she reminded herself as she flipped through the mail she'd gathered from the mailbox at the end of the driveway. All those people heading to their banks with their paychecks, all the singles on their way to meet their friends for a night out and a little time to put the stresses of the workweek behind them.

She decided she'd leave now, while it was still light enough to admire the scenery on her way west. Her bag was already packed, her reservation at the small motel already made, so all she had to do was change her clothes. From casual office attire to jeans and a light sweater took less than five minutes. Another few minutes to set the timers on her lamps downstairs and the outside lights—not that this was a particularly high-crime neighborhood, but no place was crime-free these days, so there was no point in tempting fate by declaring NO ONE'S HOME over the weekend.

She grabbed one of the magazines that had come in the mail that afternoon and checked her tote bag to make certain the maps she'd printed off the Internet the night before were there. Finding she did, in fact, have everything she'd need for the weekend, she headed off for her weekly trip to Gibson Springs.

TEN

Father Kevin Burch opened the door to the small conference room and leaned in.

"How's it going?" he asked before stepping inside.

"Okay, I suppose." Mallory frowned. "I'd hoped to hear something about one of these kids that I hadn't heard before, but so far there haven't been any surprises. Everything you told me has been reiterated by the teachers I spoke with. Four good kids, no discipline problems, great students. Just as you said."

"Trust me, if there'd been anything negative, I'd have told you up front." He leaned over the back of the nearest chair. "It's getting late. I was wondering if you'd rather come back on Monday to finish up."

Mallory glanced at the clock on the wall. It was almost six o'clock.

"I didn't realize how late it was." She picked up the sheet of paper listing the names he'd given her earlier and waved it. "I only have two others to speak with. Ryan's football coach and the guidance counselor." She looked up at him. "I'd really rather finish this up now than have it go into next week."

"The football coach is also the golf coach, and they have their banquet tonight, so he had to leave at five. He told me to tell you he'd be happy to speak with you." Burch took a card from his jacket pocket and walked over to where she sat. "Sorry. I almost forgot. He said to feel free to call him anytime."

"Thanks. I'll try to catch up with him tomorrow." Mallory put the card in her wallet. "So that just leaves the guidance counselor, Sister Rosalie Clark. I'm sorry to have made her wait so long."

"She said she'd be in her office working anyway," he told her. "She's the third door down from here on the left."

"I'll walk down." Mallory gathered her notes and tucked them into a leather folder. "Thanks for your help in organizing everyone for me."

"You're welcome. Whatever we can do to help, of course we will." He pulled back her chair for her, and she stood. "I had spoken with many of the teachers and some of the students a week or so ago myself, but nothing popped out at me. Still, I'm not trained to ask the right questions. I was hoping you'd be able to dig out something that would help."

"If there was something there—if one of the teachers knew something—I think they'd volunteer that information, don't you, instead of waiting to be asked?"

"One would hope." He escorted her to the door, pausing to turn the light off. "No, actually, I'm sure if someone knew something that would lead us to understand what happened that night, I would have heard about it by now. Then again, sometimes you could probably know something that you aren't aware you know, if that makes sense."

"Perfect sense." Mallory nodded as they walked toward the guidance counselor's office. At the door, they stopped. "Thank you again for all your help."

"Make sure you call me if you need anything else." He knocked softly on the door.

"Thanks. I will."

"Come in, Father Burch," a voice from within called.

"I'm just the escort, Rosalie," he called back. "I'm sending Mallory Russo back to see you."

"Straight on down the hall," the counselor told Mallory. "First door . . ."

Mallory waved to the priest, then followed the voice to the first door.

"I apologize for not getting up," the woman behind the desk told Mallory before she'd reached the door. "Twisted my ankle in the parking lot on Monday and it still hurts like hell."

She smiled at Mallory and pointed to a hard plastic chair. "Sorry I don't have something more comfortable to offer."

"That's quite all right," Mallory told her as she took the indicated seat. "Sorry about your accident."

"That pothole had my name all over it. And I knew the damned thing was there, too. Momentary lapse, stepped right into it. Talk about the flying nun. What can you do?" She shrugged. "So I understand you want to talk about the kids."

"I do. I'm sure as their counselor you got to know them fairly well over the past year, with college applications and such." Mallory sat back in her chair, immediately comfortable with the slightly overweight, sixtyish woman behind the desk.

"I knew them well before that," Sister Rosalie told her. "This is a small school. We start to get to know the kids as freshmen, follow them through their sophomore years, start thinking ahead to what schools might be a good match for each of them. I usually know by mid–sophomore year where everyone will end up."

"You must be very good at what you do."

"Lots of experience helps. And frankly, if we had more students, I wouldn't be able to operate like that on my own. But with a limited number of students, I have the luxury of making sure everyone makes the right choice."

"These four kids—Jamey, Adam, Ryan, Courtney—they all made the right choices, in your opinion?"

Sister Rosalie hesitated, then said, "For the most part, yes. Courtney had been accepted at two state universities—Bloomsburg and Millersville—either of which would have been a great fit for her. Then, all of a sudden, out of the blue, she decided she really wanted to go to Penn State, main campus."

"You didn't think that was a good fit for her?"

"No, I did not. For one thing, it's too big a school for her. She'd get lost there. Those huge universities aren't for everyone. Some people thrive. Others can't handle it. I didn't think it was the place for her, and frankly, her sudden interest took me completely by surprise." She made a face. "I wouldn't have recommended it to her even if she'd wanted to apply back in August, but to apply so late, she had zero chance to get in."

"I thought she was a good student."

"Courtney was an excellent student, but they get a ridiculous number of applicants who are excellent students, and they fill their spots early with the best kids who apply. As good as Courtney was, there was nothing that stood out about her. She was a good athlete, but she wasn't great, so she hadn't been recruited. She would have needed something spectacular to have caught their eye at that late date. Like all-state in field hockey, or winning the state science fair."

"Why was she so focused on Penn State?"

"Who knows? She just came in one day and said that she wanted to apply. I thought it was a waste of money, given that most of their acceptances had already been mailed, but she insisted."

"And she never said why?"

"Just that she wanted to go farther away. That's the most I ever got out of her. That she wanted to go away."

"Any reason for that, that you knew of?" Mallory's interest was piqued. "Problems at home? A boyfriend, maybe, who was influencing her?"

"Again, not that I know of. It's just her and her mother and her sister, and they are really tight. Dad walked out when the sister was about six months old; Mom has done a bang-up job raising both girls. I think Courtney just got the bug, thought she was missing something, and decided Penn State was the place to go. I've seen it happen a hundred times, Detective Russo. The kid applies to a number of schools, gets accepted, then decides at the last minute that the one they *didn't* apply to is the one they really want to go to. The old grass-is-greener thing. It generally isn't more than that."

Mallory caught the "detective" but didn't correct her.

"Was there any change in her behavior over the past year? Had she made friends with a new group of people, or had she lost interest in things she'd previously liked to do?"

Sister Rosalie thought for a moment, then said, "No, nothing over the past year. Like I said, Courtney comes from a pretty solid background, there's a good safety net there. This class was really close. Most of the kids have been together since the early grades, if not from kindergarten. She's had her ups and downs, like all kids do, but nothing really seems to throw her off course."

"How about that last week, maybe even that last Friday before they disappeared. Did you see her then?"

Sister nodded. "I saw her early in the day."

"Did she seem upset about anything?"

"Not that I noticed. Courtney was a pretty laid-back kid." She paused, then added, "The only time I ever saw her shaken up about anything was that shooting at Hazel's year before last."

Mallory's head shot up. "Was Courtney working at Hazel's at the time?"

"Yes, but she wasn't in the front of the store when the robbery took place. She said she was on break at the time, in the back, so she wasn't right there when the boy was shot."

"The boy was eighteen," Mallory recalled. "Hazel's nephew. There had been a suspect, the case almost went to trial, but the DA pulled it because he didn't have strong enough evidence, if I recall correctly. I didn't work that case, but I think I would have remembered Courtney's name if she'd been a witness."

"I don't think she was. She said she hadn't heard anything before she heard the gunshots, and she didn't see anyone in the front of the store when she came out front to investigate, so she couldn't have testified to anything."

"She called it in?"

"No, a customer who'd dropped down to hide behind a display when he heard the shouting by the register called 911 on his cell when the killer left the store. Courtney said when she came out from the back, the police were already there. I imagine that would shake up a kid, though, knowing how close she came to being the one on the register when the robber came into the store."

"It would, yes," Mallory said thoughtfully. "You said that Courtney had changed after that incident. How so?"

"She became very quiet for a while, spent more time at home, I think. And that marking period, her grades slipped a little. Nothing terrible, but enough so that I noticed."

"You spoke with her about it?"

"She just said she was having a lot of trouble sleeping, but she was hoping it would pass."

"Any chance she might have tried taking something for it?" Mallory asked.

"If you're suggesting that she turned to drugs, the answer is no. I told her that her family doctor might be able to help, but she thought she'd be okay. I offered to counsel her—told her she was welcome to come in whenever she felt she needed to talk."

"Did she take you up on that?"

"No. She said she'd work it out on her own, and apparently she did. By the end of the next marking period, her grades were back up, and everything seemed fine."

"How about the boys? Anything similar there?"

"No." She shook her head. "Like I said, these are all good, solid kids. No drugs, as you were suggesting. Someone would have noticed."

Mallory raised a skeptical eyebrow.

"Someone would have noticed, Detective," Rosalie insisted. "If one of our kids is into something he or she shouldn't be, we'd have found out about it."

"How can you be so sure?"

"Because we always do." Rosalie smiled. "Yes, over the years we've had a few kids veer from the straight and narrow, but we've always found out, one way or another."

"And you are confident that nothing was going on with any of these kids?"

"One hundred percent confident." The counselor folded her hands on the desktop. "I'd bet my life on it."

The first thing Mallory did when she got into her car was dial Charlie Wanamaker's cell phone. She'd hesitated only briefly before deciding to share what she'd learned with him. Something was nagging at her, and she thought that by talking things out she might get a better idea of what that something was.

His voice mail picked up, and she left a message for him to call her back. She'd been driving for less than a minute when her phone rang.

"Mallory, hi. It's Charlie. What's up?"

"That was quick—thanks for getting back to me so soon. Listen, I just left Our Lady of Angels after spending the last several hours talking to teachers and a few students and the guidance counselor. I'd like to run something past you. Any chance you could meet me for . . ." She looked at the clock. It was after seven. "Well, dinner or coffee or a drink or something?"

"I'm sorry, but I'm afraid I can't make it tonight."

She mentally slapped her forehead. Duh. Friday night. Dinner hour. He probably had a date.

"Oh, that's okay. I just thought that while I was on the way home . . . ," she said, slightly embarrassed.

"But I'd like to sit down with you and catch up tomorrow. What's your day look like?"

"I might have some time." *Like all the time in the world.*

"I have something I have to do first thing," he told her, "but I don't know how long I'll be tied up. Can I give you a call, maybe sometime around noon, one o'clock, see what your schedule is?"

"Sure. That would be fine. I'll talk to you then."

Mallory disconnected the call and tossed the phone into her bag. Wherever Charlie had been, whatever he'd been doing, he obviously wasn't alone. In the background, she thought she'd heard the sound of a woman weeping.

Well, of course he'd have someone in his life. Maybe that's what brought him back here to the town where he'd grown up, she thought as she drove toward home. Maybe he wanted to . . .

To what? Marry his hometown sweetheart? Mallory frowned, realizing that she didn't know that he wasn't already married.

Not for you, she told herself. *You've done a lot of things in your life, but you've never gone after another woman's man. Now is not the time to start. Use Charlie for the information he can share just as he's surely going to use you for the same purpose. Find the kids, collect your fee, and skedaddle back on into your own little life.*

Yeah. She nodded as she parked in front of her town house. *That's the plan.*

She turned the key in the front door and walked in just as a message was being recorded on her answering machine. She reached for the phone, then stopped, her hand frozen in midair, when she recognized the voice.

"Say, I was in court today with an old friend of yours from the DA's office. Steve Mooney, you remember him? He sure remembers you. Says you used him on more than one occasion to get charges upped or lowered, depending on whatever it was you wanted at the time. Yeah, that Steve Mooney." Frank Toricelli coughed into the phone. "Anyway, he says to me, So, I see where your favorite girl is gonna be a PI now. Well, I got a lot of favorite girls, your name never made it to that list, so you can imagine my surprise when he tells me, Yeah, I see where Mallory Russo's name is posted on the list of people who applied for a license."

He coughed again rudely into the phone, and she knew he was doing it to be as annoying as possible.

"So I says, Where'd you see that? And Steve says, They have to post the name of everyone who applies, the list is right outside on the wall. So when my case is over, I go out and look, and sure enough, there it is. Mallory B. Russo. We know what the *B* stands for, don't we? Heh, heh. Anyway, I'm thinking how hurt I am, you didn't put me down as a reference. How 'bout Cal, you put him down?" His laugh was harsh and without humor. "Gonna be some fun, the first time you and I cross paths out there, know what I mean? So I hope you get lots of criminal work, because your ass isn't going to be worth . . ."

"Asshole." She hit DELETE, wondering why she'd listened for as long as she had.

Annoyed, Mallory went straight on to the kitchen and tossed her bag on the table. Her grumbling stomach reminded her that it had been hours since she'd eaten, but Toricelli's message had left her with little appetite. She checked the refrigerator and found a container of yogurt that had expired the previous week and a bottle of iced tea. She plucked a spoon from the dishwasher and sat at the table looking out at the backyard, mindlessly eating the yogurt. Surprised when she found she'd finished it, she went back to the refrigerator for more and found one last container stashed behind the bottle of pomegranate juice that she'd bought because she'd heard it was healthy but had forgotten once she'd stuck it in the fridge.

She unlocked the back door and walked out onto the tiny patio. The parrot on the deck next door began to squawk.

"Hello, beautiful," the parrot called, his customary greeting to any woman. Men, on the other hand, were always greeted with, "Who goes there?"

"Hello, Leroy," Mallory called to the bird, whose cage hung over the deck rail and was a mere ten feet from her door. "Did Jacky go out and leave you outside again?"

"Jacky's a bad, bad boy!" the parrot said, climbing along the side of his cage as if to engage Mallory in conversation.

"There are lots of bad boys out there, Leroy."

Mallory stepped off the concrete onto the grass and walked to the back of the property. Her town house was located at the very end of the development, the last row of houses before a dense wood. She stopped halfway to the trees and inhaled deeply, recognizing the scent of spring rain and damp earth. The sun was setting over the woods, as it had been the day she'd first seen the house. She'd liked the view enough to make an offer the next day. For the most part, she'd been relatively comfortable here and had never thought twice about her decision to buy it. It was the right size for one person and an occasional guest—should she ever want to have one—and required little maintenance, so all in all she figured it had been a good choice.

She took a few more deep breaths of fresh air before turning back. It was quiet except for the birds chattering in the hedge that ran past her next-door neighbor's unit. As the last one in the row, Jacky had a bit of a side yard, a narrow strip of grass between the dark green of the hedge and the white brick outside wall of his house. Sometimes on summer nights, he set up the posts for games of horseshoes, and if her bedroom windows were open, she could hear the metal shoes clanging well into the night. She'd never complained, though the sound had kept her awake on more than one occasion. It reminded her of summer evenings in the house where she'd grown up, when all the boys in the family would play outside after she'd been tucked in, and she'd lay in the dark, listening to their voices and their laughter, envying their camaraderie, knowing that they were separated by more than age and gender.

"Who's your daddy?" Leroy squawked merrily at her approach.

"Ah, now that is one of life's great mysteries, Leroy," Mallory said under her breath as she went back inside.

She made a pot of coffee and, while it brewed, went upstairs to her den and turned on her computer. Opening a new file, she began to type up notes from that day's interviews. There was little of substance until she got to her meeting with Sister Rosalie, and her fingers began to move over the keyboard more quickly, then she stopped and reread the last two sentences she'd typed.

> *Why the change in Courtney's college choice—significant or not?*
>
> *Courtney in Hazel's during shooting.*

The first, Mallory knew, could very well have been nothing more than a teenager changing her mind.

But the second set off that buzz in her head. Tomorrow she'd talk to Charlie, have him get a copy of the police file relating to the shooting. While she hated to rely on someone else, hated the thought that she'd be dependent on a man she didn't know well enough to trust to get information she needed, she was just going to have to live with it.

For a moment, she wished she were still with the force so that she could sit down and read all the reports herself, talk to the officers who had investigated, read all the witness statements. Then she thought about the harassment she'd endured until her patience wore out and remembered why she'd left.

"Not for all the money in the world," she murmured as she read over her notes.

Her arrangement with Conroy's newest detective was just going to have to work out. She'd have to watch her own back—she couldn't depend even on Joe for that, because when it came down to helping her or protecting his department, she knew there'd be no choice—but she could live with that, too. It was just one case, she reminded herself.

One case, then she would go back to writing her book, and get on with her life.

ELEVEN

Charlie locked his hands behind his head and finished his last set of sit-ups. It was barely six AM, but he'd been awake most of the night. He'd slept—or tried to—in his late brother's bed, the only one available, and in retrospect Charlie thought he'd have been more comfortable on the sofa. Except for the fact that his mother had sat up half the night watching old movies and infomercials. Twice he'd heard her placing orders over the phone. He couldn't imagine what she'd been buying.

Across the hall, his sister was still softly singing the same song she'd been singing since about one. He'd peeked in on her once and found her on the floor, fixated on the spinning arms of a pinwheel, singing "Tiny Dancer" and wiggling her toes. At four, she was still singing, though the pinwheel had been forgotten, her feet tapping up and down on the carpet.

Charlie rested his head back against the side of the bed, trying to figure out what the hell had happened to his family in the two short years since Dan died.

Whatever the cause, Charlie couldn't help but feel he was responsible, at least in part, for his sister's deterioration and his mother's drinking problem. He should have come home more frequently and stayed longer than he had. He should have realized how hard his mother was taking Danny's death. He should have realized that in her state, she wasn't going to give Jilly the attention she needed. He should have, he should have, he should have . . .

He rubbed the back of his neck, overwhelmed by a sense of guilt. His mother had needed help, and he'd failed to see it, choosing to immerse himself in his cases—street shootings of school-aged children, housewives with the backs of their heads bashed in, prostitutes disappearing from their corners, whatever the hot case of the week might have been—which somehow always seemed more important, more urgent, than a weekend trip back home.

Would he be here now if his mother's next-door neighbor hadn't called him? The honest answer was probably not. The truth of it was that he didn't want to deal with Danny's death any more now than he had when they'd first been notified. His mother probably didn't want to deal with it, either, he reminded himself. God knew, in her life, she'd had more to bear than he had. She sure as hell had not had an easy life.

Mary Jo Wanamaker had buried her husband at too young an age and had lost the home she'd loved. She'd had five miscarriages, two between Charlie and Danny, three more before Jilly had been born. It wouldn't have taken a genius to figure out that Danny's death would be Mary Jo's last straw. Intellectually, Charlie supposed he'd been aware, but emotionally, he'd been clueless, which in the long run had made things easier for him. But his last trip home had made it apparent that he could no longer ignore the situation in Conroy, that something needed to be done, that it was up to him to figure out what that something was and to make sure it happened.

It had taken him a while, but he'd finally come up with a plan to get the Wanamaker family back on its feet. He'd taken the necessary steps, made all the arrangements. By the end of the week, the only thing left to do was to break it to his mother, and he'd had that discussion with her the other night.

He'd steeled himself for her reaction, and as he'd anticipated, she hadn't liked a bit of what he'd had to say.

"You don't know how hard this has been for me since we had to leave Toby Falls, Charlie," she'd said accusingly after he'd laid out his plan. "I loved my old life. My pretty house. My friends. I didn't want to give it up, not any of it."

Her eyes had misted, and her face had grown softer. "When you were little, we'd walk to the park—I don't suppose you remember, you were so little then, but there was a lovely park across the street. We used to have picnics there, just the two of us—this was before Danny was born. I'd pack up our food and take a blanket and spread it out on the grass . . . Oh, it was just like a movie scene. Then when you started school, and Danny came along, I used to picnic with him." She'd looked up at him with round sad eyes. "I had such a pretty life back then. . . ."

"I know, Mom. I'm sorry that things turned out the way they did for you."

She hadn't seemed to have heard him.

"Then it was time for Danny to go to school and for a long time, I didn't have anyone to picnic with. Until I had Jilly. My perfect baby girl." She smiled wryly. "Well, perfect for a while, anyway."

Charlie remembered Jilly's birth, and how sweet she was, what a good baby she was, up until she was almost two and her symptoms became more and more pronounced. He'd been in high school then, and had been as confused as his parents and brother as gradually, Jilly began to change. Her increasing lack of responsiveness, her inconsolable crying, her singsong speech patterns, her increasing sensitivity to light and sound, her constant movement, and her zoning out of the present and retreating into a place that was hers alone—all classic symptoms of the disorder they would come to know well over the next few years.

Charlie had been getting set to leave home for college when Jilly was diagnosed. No one in the family really understood what autism was, and what it would mean for Jilly, what it would mean for the entire family, what her special needs would be. The private schooling they were able to afford while Charlie Senior was still employed as vice president of Conroy Mills went the way of their big house when the mill closed.

"Jilly did fine when she was in private school," his mother had wept two nights ago.

"She did fine when she was in Riverside, too," he'd reminded her. Riverside was the facility Jilly had attended after they'd moved to Conroy. "It wasn't as fancy as her old school, but she did well there."

"Structure." His mother had nodded, sniffling and blowing her nose in a tissue she'd dug out from her pocket. "Structure and consistency. That's what they told us she needed."

"The two things she needs most, neither of which she's getting now," he'd said softly.

"You can't imagine how hard it is." His mother had started to cry again.

"Mom, we have a problem here." He corrected himself. "Two problems. Your drinking and Jilly's total lack of structure, and there's a definite connection between the two. When you drink, no one's there to take care of Jilly."

"I can't stay in this house twenty-four hours a day, Charlie. I'd go insane. And I can't bring anyone in to stay with her because she gets upset when strangers are around and I—"

"Mom," he said firmly, "you can't keep on going out at night and leaving Jilly home alone. Really bad things could happen to her."

"But now you're here, and you could stay with her."

"No, I can't. There will be a lot of nights when I will have to work, or times I get called out in the middle of the night." He hadn't told her yet that his plan for their living arrangements did not include his staying with them. "Lena told me she found Jilly walking through the backyards, eleven thirty at night, dressed only in her nightgown. You know what could have happened to her, don't you, Mom, a pretty young girl like Jilly roaming around in the dark alone at night?"

"I don't want anything bad to happen to her," his mother had sobbed, "but I can't do it all for her anymore."

"I know you can't, Mom. And that's why we have an appointment at ten on Saturday morning with the doctors at Riverside."

"For God's sake, Charlie, that place is for kids. She's not a child." The sobbing stopped abruptly.

"They've expanded their facilities, Mom. They're taking a few select adults. They're willing to evaluate Jilly."

"She's not going to want to go." His mother got up and began pacing nervously. "And I can't afford it anyway, even if she agreed to go, which she wouldn't do."

"She's not going to be given a choice, and I'm going to pay for it."

"You are?" She'd stopped pacing.

He nodded. "But only if you agree to stop drinking."

"Sure, Charlie."

He'd almost smiled, she'd acquiesced so quickly.

"No, Mom. This is serious. If you don't kill yourself, you're sure as hell going to kill Jilly. I can't let that happen." He took her hand gently. "So here's the deal. Jilly is going to Riverside, and you go to Sharon Heights."

"Don't be ridiculous." She pulled her hand away angrily. "To hear you talk, you'd think I was an alcoholic."

"You are, Mom." There. He'd said it, said it as gently as he could, but the words were still out there. She reacted exactly as he'd known she would.

"That's a terrible, horrible thing to say to your mother." Her voice rose in righteous indignation. "I can stop drinking whenever I want to."

"Then why haven't you?"

"Because . . . because . . . ," she sputtered. "Because I'm not an alcoholic, Charlie. Because it's not a problem."

"Mom, just stop. Riverside for Jilly, Sharon Heights for you."

"I won't do it." She drew up archly. "I won't go to a place like that."

"That's the deal, Mom. Jilly gets the best care possible if you admit yourself to Sharon Heights and complete the program."

It had taken another hour and a half of denials and pleading and crying, but she'd finally agreed to go with him on Saturday to take Jilly to Riverside for an evaluation, and to admit herself to Sharon Heights as soon as Jilly was admitted to the residential facility. Both Charlie and his mother were exhausted when they'd said good night, but he wondered how much sleep either of them had gotten that night, or the next.

Getting an uncooperative Jilly ready to go to meet with the doctors earlier that morning, and leaving her there where she'd remain for the next forty-eight hours for observation and evaluation, was more of an ordeal than he'd imagined. Jilly was crying and shaking and pleading with him not to leave her there. He knew in the long run it was the best thing for her, but at that moment he felt like the worst person in the world. He was saved at the last minute from breaking down and taking her home when the therapist appeared and miraculously managed to calm his sister and talk her into the next room.

He left then, ushering his mother out through the front door before either of them lost their nerve. They barely spoke in the car, and as soon as he dropped her off at the house, he found Mallory's card and dialed her number.

"I'll be at the Conroy Diner by around one," he said on her voice mail, "so if you want to join me, that's where I'll be . . ."

When he arrived at the diner, he took a booth at the end of the row. He ordered a cup of coffee and tried to work past the guilt he felt for putting his sister in a live-in school and forcing his mother into rehab. Making decisions for other people's lives and hoping he'd made the right ones. Guilty for doing it now, guilty for not having done it sooner. Either way he looked at it, he hadn't taken very good care of his family, and right now they were all paying the price for his neglect. He was going to have one hell of a time making it all right.

Mallory parked her car across the street from the two-story clap-board twin house that looked identical to every other one on either side of the street. She had decided not to wait to hear from Charlie, who apparently had better things to do, judging from last night's phone conversation. She needed to get on with her investigation, and if he wanted to be part of it, fine. If not, she didn't mind going it alone. This morning she had two people to talk to, with or without him, and she needed to get to them early. People often made plans for Saturdays. She wanted to hit the Bauer home before anyone had a chance to get on with theirs.

She rang the doorbell and waited. On the porch sat two dark green plastic lawn chairs that were identical to the ones Mallory had on her patio, and a pot of struggling red geraniums. She rang the bell again just as the door opened by a crack.

"Yes?" The woman stood behind the door.

"Linda Bauer?"

"Yes?"

"My name is Mallory Russo. I'm . . ."

"Father Kevin's detective." The door opened, and on the other side stood a stocky woman in her early forties with blond hair cut short. "He told me you'd be stopping by to talk about Courtney. Please, come in."

Mallory stepped inside the dark living room. The shades were drawn, giving the place a claustrophobic feel.

"Come into the kitchen and have some coffee." Linda Bauer led the way. "I have to be at work by noon, so we can talk while I get myself together."

"I apologize for coming by, unannounced—," Mallory started, but the woman cut her off.

"We're talking about my daughter here, right? You're trying to find her? I don't care if you show up at three in the morning, if you can help find Courtney." She turned on the kitchen light and pointed to a chair at the kitchen table. "Have a seat. We can talk while I get the coffee on."

"Mrs. Bauer, let me start by saying that I cannot guarantee that I will find your daughter, but I can promise I'll do my best."

Linda nodded and turned her back. She stood at the sink, filling the coffeepot with water.

"I may ask you questions that you don't like, but I want you to understand that I'm only asking because—"

"I know, I know. There are things you have to ask. It's okay. Whatever you need. Just . . . go ahead. Start." The woman's voice was shaky.

"Is there any way Courtney could have gotten her hands on a gun? Do you keep guns in the house?"

"No. Not ever. I'm scared to death of them and so are both my kids. And even if she wasn't afraid, even if she had one, she'd never use it on a friend. She just isn't capable of that. Next question."

"Was Courtney having any problems that you know of?"

"Only that she didn't get into Penn State. Crazy." She shook her head. "She had an offer for a partial scholarship at Bloomsburg. She could play lacrosse there, they have a good program. All of a sudden, she has to go to Penn State. Sister Rosalie told her it was too late to apply and expect to get in, but Courtney had to try anyway." She turned to face Mallory. "So other than the fact that she didn't get into the number-one college on her list, I can't think of a damned thing that was bothering her."

"When did you last see her?"

"Friday morning, before school."

"How did she seem to you?"

Linda shrugged. "Normal. Cranky because she is not a morning person. Never wants breakfast so we have that argument. Perfectly normal. If anything, she seemed like she was in a better-than-normal mood."

"How about a boyfriend? Was she seeing anyone?"

"Not recently. Over the winter she had been dating a boy, Joe Slivinsky, but that wasn't a serious thing, on either of their parts. They really were just friends. She wasn't interested in him as anything more than a friend."

"She told you that?"

"Oh, no. She wouldn't have." Linda smiled. "She told her sister. A most reliable source. She confided a lot in Misty."

"Her younger sister."

"Right."

"So as far as you know, there was nothing bothering Courtney? Nothing upsetting her."

"Just Penn State."

"Sister Rosalie mentioned that Courtney had been working at Hazel's the night of the robbery—"

"—when Chris Jackson was killed right there at the register." Linda visibly shuddered. "Good God, that was a nightmare."

"What did she tell you about that night?"

"Just that she was on break, in the back of the building. She had a soda and some chips or something, she'd called one of her friends on the phone and stepped out back, so she hadn't heard anything or seen anything. She said when she went back to work out in the front of the store, she found all this commotion—the police were coming through the front door and Chris was on the floor behind the counter and there was just chaos."

"But she hadn't seen or heard a thing?"

"Nothing. Scary, isn't it? That a kid could be gunned down like that? Even scarier when you think that it could have been *your* kid."

"Sister said that Courtney had a rough time after that." Mallory's ears picked up the barely perceptible sound from directly overhead. That would be Misty, she guessed.

"Nightmares like you wouldn't believe." Linda nodded as she opened the refrigerator door. "You take milk in your coffee?"

"Yes, thank you. Linda, what else can you tell me about that time? Did Courtney's behavior change?"

"Yeah, some. For a while, she didn't like going out at night, and she had a hard time sleeping. Hazel had given her a few weeks off after that, but when it was time to go back, she really didn't want to go. Of course, she did, but she didn't want to. I told her she could quit, but she wouldn't because the prom was coming up and she'd bought a dress that she was still paying for, so she needed the job. After a while, she seemed okay."

"Were you present when the police questioned her?"

"Oh, sure."

"And they asked her just what I've asked you?"

"Yes, and she answered just like I've said."

"Did they ask her anything else?"

"No. Should they have?"

Mallory smiled. "Did she say who she was talking to on the phone while she was on break?"

Linda nodded. "Callie Henderson."

"Do you know if the police spoke with Callie to verify that?"

"I don't think they did. I'm pretty sure I would have heard. Callie's mom is a good friend, and she didn't mention it." Linda had filled two cups and set them on the table. "What are you getting at?"

"I'm not getting at anything. I'm just asking the questions I would have asked if I'd handled the investigation in the first place." Mallory opened her bag and took out a small pad of paper. "I think I'd like to write down her name, though. I might want to talk to her." She continued to rummage through her bag. "Well, I would write it down, if I could find a pen. You wouldn't happen to have one I could borrow . . . ?"

"Sure." Linda opened a drawer near the refrigerator, took out a ballpoint pen, and handed it to Mallory.

"Thanks," Mallory said as she began to make a note on the paper. "You said the girl's name was Callie . . . ?"

"Henderson."

"Right. Henderson. You wouldn't happen to know where she lives?"

"Over on Crawford, I forget the number. She goes to Our Lady of Angels, though, so Father Kevin can probably help you there."

"Thanks." Mallory slipped the paper and the pen into her pocket.

"You used to be a detective here in town." Linda sat opposite from Mallory and pushed the milk carton across the table. "Why'd you leave?"

"It was time to move on." Mallory added a few drops of milk to the cup before taking a sip. "Mrs. Bauer, had there been any suggestion that Courtney testify at the killer's trial?"

"Only in the beginning, but then she got so upset, I went to the detective who'd questioned her . . . I can't think of his name, tall man, dark hair, a little extra around the middle . . ."

Mallory smiled at the description. "Detective Toricelli."

"Yes, that's the name. I spoke with him, and told him how upset she was, and since she hadn't even been there when the shooting happened, she hadn't seen anything or heard anything, I asked him if they had to call her to testify."

"And he agreed not to?"

"He was so sweet about it," Linda said. "He told me that since she couldn't testify to anything that would help them make their case, he'd recommend to the DA that they not make her come to court."

"That must have made her happy."

"Made all the difference in the world." Linda nodded. "She was better after that. I think the trauma of what had happened, and having to go into court and talk about it, had scared her half to death."

"So the police spoke with her just that one time?"

"Twice, actually. They talked to her the night of the shooting, and they came by the house the next day. And then we heard the police had picked up a suspect and they were going to try her for the killing. A young woman, twenty-five years old, can you imagine that? Shooting a kid in cold blood like that." Linda looked bewildered at the thought.

"Hard to believe, yes." Mallory paused, then asked, "Do you happen to remember the name of the suspect?"

"No. She wasn't convicted, though. The newspapers said the jury didn't have enough evidence to convict her. So whether she did it or not . . ." Linda shrugged.

"Has Courtney tried to contact you over the past few weeks?"

Linda looked at her as if she were mad.

"Are you kidding? You see these bags under my eyes? You think I've had a night's sleep since the night she went missing?" She began to weep softly. "I close my eyes at night and try to imagine where she is. Is she still alive? Would I know for certain if she wasn't? I'm her mother—aren't I supposed to know, aren't I supposed to feel it, if something terrible happened to her?"

"Mrs. Bauer . . ."

"Linda. My husband, the bastard, left me long ago. If it weren't for the kids, I'd have gone back to my maiden name. Do you know he hasn't even called one time since Courtney disappeared? Wouldn't you think he'd want to know what happened to his own daughter?"

"Is he still in the area?"

"I have no idea. I don't think he is." Linda got up from the table and took a box of tissues from the counter. "I ought to have stock in Scott Paper. I go through about five boxes of these things every week. Anyway, I haven't heard from the kids' father in years. But the story was all over the news, I'm sure even he heard about it, wherever he is. And I'm sure even he's smart enough to realize there's only one Courtney Bauer in Conroy, Pennsylvania."

"Is there a chance he's been in touch with the girls?"

"None. He didn't give either of them the time of day when he lived with us, I don't see him reaching out to them now. He never wanted either one of them, wanted me to have an abortion both times. Not that I ever told either of them that, but that's the truth."

"But could she have tracked him down somehow?"

"No." Linda shook her head. "She doesn't know him, wouldn't know how to contact him."

"But under the circumstances, would she have gone to him if she needed a place to go where no one would think to look for her?"

"She wouldn't know where to start to find him, I'm telling you."

"Give me his full name and anything you think of that could help us locate him." Mallory smiled. "Just in case."

"It's Tim. Timothy J. Bauer. Last I heard he was living somewhere out near Erie."

"Does he have family there?" Mallory took the paper and pen from her pocket and jotted down the information.

"He used to. A brother, Clark, might still live there." She shrugged. "I really don't know."

"That's okay, you've given me a starting place."

"If you find him, tell him he owes me about thirteen years in back child support."

"Will do." Mallory returned the pen and paper to her pocket. "Is there anyplace you can think of where she might go if she was going to hide out? Somewhere she used to go as a child, maybe."

"No, I can't think of anyplace." Linda appeared to think it over. "You think she's hiding someplace? You think she's alive and she and Ryan are hiding somewhere?"

"It's a possibility, yes." Mallory didn't want to give the woman false hope, but she did think it was possible since no body had been found.

Linda covered her face with her hands. "I am scared to death for my daughter. And Ryan . . . I can't bear to think about what might have happened to the two of them. Until you've had someone you love just disappear from your life like that, I guess it's hard to understand. But every minute of every day, I wonder where she is. I wake up feeling sick to my stomach, and I go to bed at night, scared to death that she's dead and scared to death that she's still alive but having something horrible happening to her and God help me, I don't know which is worse for her."

Mallory nodded. She'd handled cases where both scenarios had turned out to be true. She patted Linda's arm and said, "I'm very sorry, for you and for Courtney. I know how hard this must be for you."

Linda nodded and wiped her eyes. "Thank you." She glanced up at the clock. "Oh, crap, look at the time. I'm sorry, but I have to leave for work."

"Of course you do. I'm sorry for having kept you." Mallory stood. "Thanks for the coffee."

"I'll walk out with you." Linda pulled a small stack of tissues from the box and stuffed them into her bag. "I need a few for the road."

"Can I drop you someplace?" Mallory asked as they walked to the door.

"Thanks but no. I get the bus right there at the corner. It takes me right into town." She hesitated at the foot of the steps that led to the second floor. "I really should check on Misty before I go."

"You go ahead and do that. I'll let myself out." Mallory extended her hand to Linda. "Will you call me if you think of anything, anything at all? If you hear from her . . ."

"Yes, of course. I will." Linda squeezed Mallory's hand. "If I hear anything at all, you will be the first to know."

Mallory left the house and crossed the street to her car, where she sat for several moments until she saw Linda come out, lock the door behind her, then walk to the corner. Within minutes, a bus arrived and Linda got on board. Mallory sat behind the wheel, just watching the house for another eighteen minutes. Sure enough, as she suspected, the front door opened and a young girl emerged. Mallory got out of the car and walked across the street even before the girl had gotten to the end of the walk.

"Hello, Misty. My name is Mallory Russo. I'm looking into your sister's disappearance."

Misty Bauer was fifteen, tall and rangy, all legs and long brown hair and attitude. She stopped in her tracks at Mallory's approach and stared with suspicious eyes.

"I was here a while ago to talk with your mother about Courtney," Mallory continued casually, "and I borrowed a pen from her, and without thinking, I stuck it in my pocket." She held out the pen, and Misty stared at it. "I didn't want to forget to give it back."

The girl reached out her hand and took the pen. "Thanks. I'll give it to her when she gets home tonight."

She stood her ground, then surprised Mallory by saying, "I heard about you. You used to be a cop. Why aren't you a cop anymore?"

"Long story." Mallory shrugged off the question.

"Mrs. Mary down at the church office hired you to find Courtney and Ryan."

"She did."

"Will you? Find them?" Misty asked with what appeared to Mallory to be more curiosity than concern.

Strange reaction, Mallory thought. "If I can."

"Why did she hire you, anyway, if you're not even a cop?"

"Because I'm a good detective."

"I thought you weren't one anymore."

"Well, technically . . . ," Mallory began.

"Whatever." Misty shrugged and started to walk around her.

"Misty, while I'm here, maybe you can answer some questions for me."

"I don't know anything."

Too fast. Way too fast.

"How do you know? You don't know what questions I'm going to ask."

Misty shot Mallory the universal teen look that expressed utter exasperation, but she stopped walking.

"The night your sister and Ryan disappeared, she drove you and a few of your friends to a dance, is that right?"

"Yeah. I told the police about that." Misty appeared to relax a bit.

"I know you did. Now I'd like you to tell me."

"She drove us to the community center, that's all." Misty's shrug added the unspoken, *No big deal.*

"Was she upset about anything that night?"

"Well, yeah. Hel-lo? Penn State? Rejection?" Misty rolled her eyes. "She was really pissed off. That's why she called the guys. That's why they were all in the park. They were, like, her best buds, you know?"

"I know."

"She and Ryan didn't kill Adam and Steve." It was the first unsolicited statement Misty had uttered.

"I believe that, too."

"All that stuff in the papers and on TV? It's all wrong. They wouldn't do something like that." Misty's teary eyes looked up into Mallory's.

"I believe you. I'm on their side. But we're going to have to find Courtney and Ryan if we're going to prove that." Mallory lowered her voice. "Misty, has Courtney tried to contact you at all?"

"No." A quick shake of the head. Another answer that was faster than it should have been. "Why did you ask me that?"

"Are you sure she hasn't—"

"I said *no.*"

"How about your mom?" Mallory threw this out mostly to see Misty's reaction. She felt certain if Linda had heard from her daughter, Mallory would have sensed it, but she hadn't. "I know the three of you were close. Maybe Courtney tried to call your—"

"No. She hasn't tried to contact anyone, okay?" Misty was almost whispering.

"Do you have any idea where they might be?"

"No."

"Anyplace where Courtney would go if she wanted to hide?"

"I said no. Stop asking me. I already said no." Misty's eyes darted nervously, focused on the street behind Mallory.

"Misty, has anyone else been around asking about Courtney? Other than the police?"

"What do you mean?" Misty licked her lips as if they were suddenly very dry, her eyes still on the street. "Anyone like who?"

"Anyone at all."

"Just the police."

"You're sure?"

"I *said.*"

"Look, here's my name and number. I want you to call me if anyone—I mean anyone—asks you about Courtney. Will you do that?" Mallory handed her a card.

"Sure." Misty wrapped her fist around it.

"Anyone, Misty."

"Okay."

"Misty, do you ever hear from your father?"

Misty snorted. "My father? Are you serious?"

"I take it that's a no. How about Courtney? Do you know if he's ever been in contact with her?"

"Like he'd contact either of us." Misty rolled her eyes again. "Why would he do that? He doesn't even know we're alive."

"If he does contact you, will you let me know?"

"Right. But don't hold your breath."

Mallory nodded. It was the best she was going to get today. "You look like you're going out. Can I drop you someplace?"

"I'm just waiting for a friend."

"Was Courtney dating anyone special?"

"No."

"Mrs. Corcoran mentioned someone named Joe."

"Joe Slivinsky." Misty was back to making eye contact. "He went to Central. She went out with him a couple of times but it wasn't any big deal to either of them."

"You sure?"

Misty nodded readily. "She said he only hung with her because he liked her friend Dana. But Dana wasn't interested, either." She shrugged. "You know how those things go."

"Sure. Thanks." Mallory turned to go. "Listen, you think of any-thing . . ."

"Right. I'll be sure to call."

A little too sarcastic for a kid her age, Mallory was thinking as she walked across the street to her car. She got behind the wheel and checked her phone for messages. She listened to Charlie's and checked the clock on the dashboard. It was after one. She'd be right on time to meet him at the diner.

She started the car and pulled away from the curb, glancing at the Bauer home just in time to see Misty rip up the card Mallory'd given her into a dozen tiny pieces and toss them into the gutter.

"Son of a bitch," Mallory muttered under her breath as she drove away.

TWELVE

Mallory could see Charlie from the diner steps. She went inside and headed for his table without glancing around, then sat opposite him without waiting to be invited.

"Hi," she said.

"Hi. Guess you got my message."

She nodded. "I probably should have called, but I was only a few blocks away when I heard it." She studied his face for a moment, then said, "You look as if you've had a rough morning."

He laughed wryly. "You could say that."

"Look, if you'd rather do this some other time . . . if there's some-place you need to be . . ."

Charlie shook his head. "No time like the present."

"Well, if you're sure." She signaled to the waitress and asked for an iced tea.

"Do you want something else?" Charlie asked. "I was just going to order a sandwich."

Mallory nodded. "Good idea. I'll have a BLT."

"And for you?" The waitress eyed Charlie.

"Roast beef on rye," he told her.

"Want a refill on that coffee?"

"Water is fine, thanks." As he handed her his empty cup. To Mallory, he said, "You look like you're on to something."

"How can you tell?" She frowned. Was she that transparent?

"You have that I-know-something-you-don't-know look."

Mallory laughed. "Actually, I think I *am* on to something, but I'm not sure what it is. I'm glad you called when you did. Maybe talking it out . . ."

"Do it." He sat back against the booth. "That's what we're here for."

"There are a couple of things. First, I spent a few hours at the high school yesterday talking to several teachers who knew all four of the kids. There was nothing new there, they all said pretty much the same things, pretty much all of what we've heard before."

"Good kids, good grades, yada yada yada."

"Right. The only real news came from Sister Rosalie, the counselor. She said that after the shooting at Hazel's, Courtney had a rough time."

"I don't know about the shooting at Hazel's," he told her.

Mallory filled him in. "So after the shooting that she didn't witness and didn't know anything about, she has nightmares."

"That's not really all that uncommon, though, is it, for a teenager to react that way?" he asked. "What was she, sixteen, at the time?"

"Fifteen, sixteen," Mallory said, nodding.

"I don't think it's that unusual for a kid that age to have nightmares, coming that close to death."

"But what if she really had seen something? What if she recognized the shooter but said she hadn't seen anything because she was afraid?" She sat back while the waitress served their beverages.

"What made you think of that?" He took a sip of his drink, his eyes on her face.

"Just little things. Little things, and a feeling that I have. She told her mother that she was on the phone with a friend at the time of the shooting, so she didn't hear anything that was going on. She said she didn't even hear the gunshots."

"That wouldn't be unusual, either, a teenage girl on a cell phone. Why does that bother you?"

"I just don't remember Hazel's being so big that you wouldn't hear a gunshot. And the police never did verify the story with the girl Courtney said she'd been on the phone with."

"How do you know that?"

"Because I was with Courtney's mother this morning. That's where I was when you called."

"How does she know the police didn't talk to the girlfriend?"

"She said she would have heard if they had, she knows the girl's mother really well. She said no one ever called them."

"I'll pull the case file on Monday, see if her name shows up," he said. "You happen to get the name of the girl?"

"Callie Henderson. Father Burch can probably get her out of class for you if you want to talk to her."

"Great." He wrote the girl's name down on a small spiral-bound notebook he took from his pocket, then looked up at Mallory and said, "It's not sitting right with you, either, is it?"

"If you're referring to the fact that Courtney would have been at Hazel's the night of the shooting back then, and she's in the playground the night of the most recent shooting—then yeah," she replied, "it's not sitting right with me."

"Could mean something—or nothing." He tapped his fingers on the table. "All right, let's table that for now. See what develops."

"By the way, what did you do with the scrap of yellow fabric we found on the fence?"

"It's bagged and tagged and sitting in the glove box of my car. I'll take it in on Monday."

"And guess what else?" Mallory couldn't help but grin. In the car

on the way to the diner, she'd debated whether or not to share everything she'd learned that morning and had decided to wait to see what
her instincts told her. But she knew that if she wanted him to play
straight with her, she'd have to return the favor.

"What else?" He grinned back at her, and she felt as if they were,
if not old friends, then coconspirators at least.

"Well . . ." She paused as their sandwiches were set on the table.
When the waitress had walked away, Mallory lowered her voice and
said, "This is the big one."

"Hit me."

"Courtney's sister knows something. I feel sure of it. I think she
knows what happened that night. I think she may even know where
Courtney is."

"Whoa. That is big. She told you that?" He frowned, the sandwich halfway to his mouth.

"Not in so many words."

"What did she say?"

"It's what she didn't say." Mallory touched her napkin to the corners of her mouth. "Look, your sister is missing from a murder
scene—missing for more than two weeks—someone asks you about
her, you say, *Oh, my God, I'm so worried about her, I'm so scared that
something terrible has happened to her.*"

"Courtney's sister didn't say that?"

"She never even raised the possibility that her sister could be
dead or in any danger. She was surprisingly nonchalant about it. And
when I asked her if she'd heard from Courtney, I got a really fast *no.*
She was way too quick to deny it." Mallory picked up her sandwich.
"And when I asked her if anyone else had been around asking about
Courtney, she got really nervous. No more eye contact—eyes darting
all over the place—watching the street as if she was scared to death."

"So she was lying."

Mallory nodded. "I asked her some things I knew the answers to, things about her sister, and her reaction was different. I got straight answers, complete with eye contact."

"So you think Courtney has contacted her?"

"I do. I think she knows where she and Ryan are hiding."

"How about the mother—you think she knows, too?"

"Uh-uh." Mallory shook her head. "Linda Bauer is a total wreck over this. She looks like she's borderline breakdown."

"Maybe it's an act."

"I don't think so. I think she's genuinely sick over her daughter, not knowing if she's dead or alive. If you'd seen this woman's face, Charlie, you'd know."

"I trust your instincts. So why doesn't the younger sister tell her mother that Courtney is alive and ease her mind?"

"I think it's because someone else is looking for Courtney—someone who's approached Misty and scared the shit out of that kid. I think Misty is trying to protect her mother. Like maybe she thinks what her mother doesn't know can't hurt her."

"Because either Mom would go to Courtney and lead the scary someone to her, or Mom would go to the police. Either way, Courtney—maybe all three of them—would be exposed."

"That's what I'm thinking. Courtney gets in touch with Misty, tells her she and Ryan are okay but not to tell anyone"—Mallory talked it out—"because maybe Courtney knew this person would be coming around, trying to find out where she was . . ."

"Which would mean this person knows that Courtney is still alive . . ."

". . . because this person was at the scene and knows that Courtney and Ryan got away that night." Mallory finished the thought.

"Holy shit."

"My thoughts exactly." She took a bite of her sandwich and chewed for a moment. "For the sake of this conversation, let's assume that we're right about all this, that this person was at the park at the time of the shooting and saw Courtney and knows that Courtney saw her. Courtney's disappeared, so this person is looking for her now. Why? Because she wants to make sure that Courtney doesn't tell anyone what she saw this person do. She knows that Courtney knows who she is. Not just that she can identify her, but that Courtney knows who she is."

"You keep saying 'she,' " he noted. "I'm going to go out on a limb here and assume that that's no slip of the tongue."

"Okay, this is a stretch, right? I know that," she told him, her eyes intense, "but follow along with me for a moment, okay?"

"Go on."

"Supposing Courtney wasn't on the phone in the back room with a girlfriend the entire time the clerk was shot at Hazel's. Suppose she was in the store, and maybe ducked down behind a display. Or maybe she was outside but heard the shots and came out of the back room and saw the shooter."

"Why didn't the shooter blast her there and then and get it over with?"

"There was a customer in the store who had a cell phone and called 911. Maybe the cops were pulling up out front when Courtney came out of the back and she and the shooter saw each other. So . . . yes, I know, a lot of conjecture here, but follow me . . . the shooter has to decide whether to take the time to line up a shot on Courtney or to get out of the store before the cops get closer. She decides to run, but she knows who Courtney is."

"You're still saying 'she'—and how does she know who Courtney is?"

"The suspect who was arrested and tried in the Hazel's Market case was a woman. And she could easily have found out who Courtney was from the newspaper reports." Mallory took out her phone and used it to access the Internet. She pulled up Magellan Express and entered enough information for the search engine to locate several pages of articles on the shooting at Hazel's Market in Conroy,

Pennsylvania. She skimmed several before reading aloud, " 'Police say that Courtney Bauer, another clerk on duty at the time of the shooting, was in the back room and was not able to provide a description of the gunman.' "

"But if Courtney and the killer had seen each other, it wouldn't be too hard for the killer to find Courtney . . ."

"And give her a message she'd remember. *Keep your mouth shut or I'll kill you. Or your family.* Any threat would have worked." Mallory walked through the possibilities with him. "Courtney had already seen this woman kill. She managed to convince the detective who handled the case that she didn't know a thing so that she wouldn't even be called at trial as a witness. Her mother told me she spoke to the detective herself and asked that Courtney not be put on the stand since she really wasn't a witness to anything and the whole thing had upset her."

"The detective agreed, I take it?"

"He apparently took her name off the list and convinced the DA that she had nothing to contribute."

"Who was the detective, by the way?" he asked.

"Frank Toricelli." She pronounced the name as if it were a profanity.

Charlie raised an eyebrow.

"What?" she asked.

"Nothing." He shrugged and turned his attention to the sandwich on the plate in front of him.

"What about Toricelli?" Her eyes narrowed. She knew when someone was being evasive.

"Just that I met him the other day."

"And . . . ?"

"And he seemed friendly enough." He met her eyes across the table.

"And . . . ?" Mallory knew there was something more he wasn't saying.

"And frankly, I got the feeling he was a bit of an asshole. Which may be unfair of me, since I've only really had one conversation with him." Charlie paused for a moment, then said, "Maybe *asshole* is too strong a word since I don't really know him. Maybe just say that he didn't impress me in a favorable way."

"*Asshole* is not too strong a word, and you don't need to get to know him to figure that out."

Charlie laughed. "Some people just sort of have that aura. . . ."

"Toricelli definitely has the asshole aura." She rested an elbow on the table.

"Want to tell me about it?"

She thought about it for a minute. "Not really. At least, not now. I was on a roll, in case you hadn't noticed."

"I noticed." He smiled. "Go on. Get back on it."

"Right. Okay, so we're going to say that the shooter from Hazel's knows that Courtney knows who she is, but she's kept her mouth shut all these months."

"Why didn't the shooter just kill her after the trial so she'd never have to worry about her again?"

"I'll get to that in a minute."

"I'd think she'd have found a way to get rid of the witness at some point, but go on. Is there more?"

"You betcha. Fast-forward to the park a few weeks back. Let's put the kids in their places." She moved the salt and pepper shakers to the left side of the table. "Here are Adam and Jamey on the swings. Here's Courtney at the top of the slide, Ryan behind her on the ladder or at its base." She moved the sugar and sugar substitutes into place.

"Here's the Dumpster." The metal napkin holder was placed off to the right side.

She moved her index finger back to the swings. "Here's the shooter—she robs the two boys at gunpoint, then decides to shoot them right there where they sit. *Bang. Bang.* One bullet to the back of the head for each of them. She starts to walk away, then looks up to see Courtney at the top of the slide and recognizes her, knows she can't let her get away twice. So she chases her across the playground but can't find her in the dark. Meanwhile, Ryan has pulled Courtney off the slide and gotten her over the fence behind the Dumpster and they've disappeared into the night. The killer follows the news reports, knows that Courtney and Ryan are out there somewhere but they're in hiding. She figures that sooner or later, Courtney is going to contact someone, so she corners the little sister—maybe she's there at the house one day when Misty comes home from school while Linda is at work—and tells her to tell Courtney she'd better stay hidden because if she surfaces, she's dead."

Charlie whistled softly. "I like it. And damn, but I am impressed. It's a great theory. Whether or not it's the right one . . . I don't know. There's a lot we don't know."

"Like the name of the suspect and where she's been for the past year and a half that she hasn't taken out Courtney?

"Ahhh, but don't you just love these new phones? Internet access? The universe at your fingertips wherever you go? Damn." Mallory held up her phone. "Regina Girard, age twenty-five. Immediately after her acquittal on the Hazel's Market case—the jury said they didn't have enough evidence to convict her—she was arrested on an outstanding drug case. She was sentenced to eighteen months, which would have been up within the past month. She hadn't gone after Mallory back then, because she went from the courtroom straight to lockup on the drug charges. But maybe she's coming after her now."

"She gets out of prison, starts looking for the one person she knows can finger her for the shooting in the market." Charlie nodded thoughtfully. "If she's out, chances are she's been watching Courtney, looking for an opportunity to take her out."

"She follows her into the park, sees the guys sitting on the swings, decides to rob them, maybe, just because they're there, you know?" Mallory was talking it out. "Maybe that part was a crime of opportunity, the robbery part. But I'm thinking that wasn't what brought her into the park that night."

"Assuming it was Regina Girard."

"Right." She nodded. "Assuming it was. It is hard to believe that this young girl would *coincidentally* be a witness to two of the most brutal murders in recent Conroy history, but I suppose stranger things have happened."

"Unlikely, but yeah, stranger things have happened."

She thought for a moment. "And there's this, Charlie: If Regina Girard was the playground shooter, she knows that Courtney has seen her kill not once, but three times."

"Big-time incentive to track Courtney down and make sure she's taken out of the picture."

"When you get in on Monday, take a look at Girard's file." She sighed. "Damn, but I'd love to see the transcripts from the trial."

"You could get copies, since the case is closed," he reminded her.

"I know a lot of people in the courthouse. It might be awkward trying to explain why I'm interested in the case."

"Joe said you were writing a book on an old case. If anyone asks, you could always say you're thinking of writing something on the Hazel's Market case as well," he suggested. "Or you could let me request it and pick it up. No one knows who I am there."

"I'd be more comfortable with that, if you don't mind. Ordinarily, I wouldn't care, but I don't want to feel that I have to explain myself to anyone right now."

"I don't mind at all. I'd like to take a look at the case myself. Besides, it would give me an excuse to see you again."

"We're working the same case. Different angles, but it's the same case. So you'll see plenty of me over the next few weeks."

"I'm counting on that." He took the check from the passing waitress and said to Mallory, "So here's the game plan. I'm going to go in on Monday and check out the Hazel's Market file. If I find anything I think you should see, I'll make a copy of it. I'll also see about getting a copy of the trial transcript, and I'll follow through on the case that put Regina Girard behind bars—see if, in fact, she's already out. If so, we'll want to know who her friends are, where she went when she left prison."

"I might be able to help with that," she told him. "I have someone downtown who used to give me information. I can see if she's heard anything, see if she's still willing to talk to me. I think she will. I always played straight with her."

"What did you trade?" He turned his wrist to look at his watch.

"Mostly get-out-of-jail-free cards or reduced sentences. A couple of times, cash. She's a working girl, been at it for a long time, so she has a record."

"Let me know if she's not cooperative. We can always arrange to pick her up and bring her in, see if she's still willing to trade information for her freedom."

"If it comes to that, I'll let you know."

"So, we have our assignments. I'd say we're set."

"I'll see if I can catch up with my CI early tonight, and I'll let you know if I find out anything useful. Maybe you'll want to meet her. As I'm sure you know, there's nothing like a good CI."

"I'm tied up tonight," he told her, looking at his watch again, "and probably most of tomorrow, but starting Monday, I'll be on the job full-time."

The waitress returned to the table, and he handed her the check with a twenty he'd taken from his wallet.

"What do I owe you?" Mallory asked, reaching for her bag.

"You can get it next time."

"Okay. Thanks." She held her bag close to her side, ready to leave. It was apparent that he was anxious to go. *Back to the woman she'd heard weeping last night?* Mallory immediately wished she hadn't remembered that.

The waitress handed Charlie his change, and he dropped a few bills on the table for the tip.

"You ready?"

Mallory nodded, feeling dismissed. "Sure."

Charlie stood and pointed to the door at the end of the aisle. "I'll walk you out."

"That's okay," she told him. "I want to stop in the ladies' room before I leave."

"I'll be talking to you, then. I'll be interested in seeing if your CI has any light to shed on any of this."

"Yeah, me too."

"You know, all this sounds good, but there's always the possibility that we're way off base here."

"Of course. But you have to start somewhere."

"That's exactly what I always say." He smiled. "Great minds, I guess . . ."

"Right." She nodded. "Great minds . . ."

"Well, I'll see you."

"Right. I'll be in touch." She turned and walked to the restroom at the back of the building. She really didn't need to use the facilities as much as she'd suddenly needed to get away from him, to remove herself from his presence. There was something about the way he looked at her, something about the way she felt when he did, that drew her. The reminder that he had something going in his life had felt like a bucket of cold water dumped over her head. He was too attractive, too interesting, too much the same kind of cop she was— *had been,* she corrected herself—and apparently too much involved with someone else. The ladies' room was the only refuge she could think of, so she opened the door and went into a small room that was long overdue for an overhaul.

She washed her hands and ran the small brush she always carried with her through her hair. When she was sure he'd be gone, she walked out of the restroom area and through the door. She'd gotten as far as her car, had her hand on the driver's-side door, when she felt someone behind her.

"Well, now, this is interesting." Frank Toricelli's voice was in her ear, his hand clamped onto her shoulder. "I just stopped for a quick bite and who do I see coming out the door but our new man, Charlie Wanamaker. And here you are, just minutes behind him. Some coincidence, eh?"

"Let go of me." She landed an elbow to his gut, and he grunted.

"What are you telling the new man, bitch?" His eyes narrowed. "Or is he your new man? Does Joe know? Did you tell him you were—"

"Hey, Frank." Charlie's voice came from behind them, and Frank released his grip as he turned around. "I almost forgot, I wanted to ask you about . . ."

Charlie pretended to be seeing Mallory for the first time.

"Oh, hello," he said pleasantly, as if addressing a stranger.

Frank looked from Charlie to Mallory and back again.

"You've met Mallory Russo." It was more of a statement than a question.

"No, I haven't." Charlie extended his hand. "I know I've heard the name somewhere, but I can't place it."

"Mallory used to work for the department," Frank said with obvious suspicion.

"That must be where I heard it." Charlie smiled and went through the motions of introducing himself. "Charlie Wanamaker. I'm starting on the job on Monday."

"Oh," she said with little apparent interest. "Well, good luck with that."

"Thanks."

Frank continued to watch their faces. Mallory opened her car door and got in.

"See you around, Frank," she said as she slammed the door.

Charlie and Frank both stepped back from the car as she drove away. In the rearview mirror, she could see them standing there, Charlie talking, Frank's eyes following her car.

"Wonder all you want, Frank," she said aloud.

Nicely played, she thought as she took one more look at Charlie in the mirror. Very nicely played.

She was just parking in front of her town house when her phone rang. She checked caller ID and smiled.

"Well done, Detective Wanamaker," she said.

"What's with that asshole?" He did not sound amused.

"He saw us coming out of the diner a few minutes apart and put two and two together."

"Yeah, I figured that. I didn't want to give him the satisfaction of knowing he was right. But what's his problem?"

"I'll tell you about it sometime. In the meantime, thanks for deflecting him. I don't need any more aggravation from him or anyone else on the force than I already have. And yes, I will tell you the entire story. Suffice it to say, I don't want him to know I have any interest in Courtney's case. Sooner or later, it'll get back to him, but I'd like to keep him in the dark for as long as I can."

"He won't hear it from me, I can promise you that."

"Thanks."

"Listen, he isn't going to bother you, is he?"

"Frank has bothered me for as long as I've known him." She blew out a long breath. "But if you mean will he come here to my house, will he harass me? Only verbally, is my guess."

"If it comes to more than that, you call me, you hear?"

When she didn't respond, he said, "Hey, Mallory, you hear me?"

"I hear you."

"I've known cops like him before. Don't play with him. If it looks as if he's going to do more than jaw at you, I want to know about it."

"Okay, thanks, Charlie. I appreciate that. And thanks for backing him off at the diner. I was afraid I was going to have to hurt him."

"I believe you could," Charlie said, more relaxed now.

"So what was he saying about me after I drove away?"

"He basically warned me off you, said you were bad news and you weren't someone I'd want to know and I should stay clear."

"Did he add, *If you know what's good for you*?"

"Nah, but it was implied."

"I'm sorry."

"Why? It's not your fault he's a total a-hole."

Mallory laughed, then sobered. "He could make things . . . difficult for you."

"He can try."

"Seriously, Charlie. He's not a nice guy, and if he thinks you're a threat or if you get on his wrong side . . ."

"I'm a big boy. I can take care of myself. I don't worry about the Frank Toricellis in this world."

"Great. You haven't even worked a day yet and you've already got the department bully on your back."

"Like I said, I'm not worried about Toricelli. I have a thing about bullies."

"Well, thanks again," she said.

"Don't mention it."

"Talk to you soon." She disconnected the call and headed up the short walk to her front door. Inside, she went straight to the kitchen, where she made a cup of tea and carried it to her office. It certainly had been one hell of a day so far.

While everything was fresh in her mind, she made notes on her conversations with Linda and Misty, noting her impressions of both, the questions she had come away from the Bauer house with, the insights and theories she'd shared with Charlie. She'd forgotten to mention Courtney's father, and made a mental note to do that.

She paused, her fingers poised over the keyboard. She tried to remember the last time she'd been as attracted to anyone as she was to Charlie Wanamaker, then gave up, figuring if it was that far in her past—and it was—it wasn't worth trying to dig up.

Charlie Wanamaker drew her in like the old moth to the flame. She liked everything about him. Liked the way he looked, liked the way he thought, liked the way he laughed. Liked the way he approached an investigation. For the first time in a very long time, Mallory wished she had someone to talk to, a friend, a sister, someone she could confide in, someone she could sort out her feelings with.

Well, she reminded herself, that was the thing about being a loner. When you had something you wanted to talk about, there wasn't anyone to tell.

THIRTEEN

S arah Jo Hagan was standing beneath a weather-beaten green-and-white awning that hung over the front of a storefront church when Mallory drove up and pulled to the curb at the corner of Fifth and Chelsea avenues in one of two seedy sections of Conroy. Next to the church—aptly named the Downtown Church of the Savior—was an all-night pizza parlor; beside that, a dimly lit tavern with iron bars on the windows.

"Hey! Mustang Sally!" Mallory rolled down her window, calling the woman by her street name.

The woman turned her head and stared at the car for a moment, then walked closer, hunching over to peer inside.

"That you, Detective? My pal Mal?"

Mallory laughed. "It's me, Sally. How've you been?"

"Good, good. Fine." Sally leaned against the passenger door. "You?"

"Just fine."

"Hey, we've missed you out here. Where you been?" The pretty young woman had hair the most unnatural shade of red Mallory'd ever seen, and long thin legs that were bare twelve months of the year. On her feet were four-inch heels, and the skirt that hung low on her hips didn't measure much more. In a different life, she'd have been pretty. Only in her midtwenties, she had a shopworn aura and hard lines on her face, but she'd been the most reliable CI Mallory'd had. She'd never given bad information, and to the best of Mallory's knowledge, she'd never lied to her. The two woman, so different, had always respected—even liked—each other.

"I'm off the job," Mallory told her. "Working on a book, actually."

"Don't put me in it." Sally held her hands up in mock protest.

"Not to worry. It's about a case I worked a few years back." Mallory smiled and added, "Not one of yours."

"Good. I don't need no one back home reading about what I been up to."

"Your secret's safe with me."

"Just like always." Sally rested her forearms on the window frame. "So what's up? I know you're not cruising downtown looking for action."

"Actually, I was cruising downtown looking for you," Mallory told her.

"Me? What I do?"

"No, no, nothing like that. I just wanted to ask you a few questions."

"Like old times?"

"Just like old times."

Sally opened the door and got into the passenger seat. "Then you drive, and we talk."

Mallory waited for a car to pass, then pulled onto the roadway behind it. Driving slowly, she headed for the highway.

"So what do you need, Detective?" Sally asked.

"You know I'm not a detective anymore, right?"

"Don't matter. You'll always be Detective Russo to me." Sally turned slightly in her seat to look at Mallory.

Mallory smiled in the dark. "Sally, does the name Regina Girard mean anything to you?"

"Gina Girard? Gigi?" Sally's left eyebrow raised. "What you want with that crazy bitch?"

"You know her, then?"

"Everyone knows Gigi. She is bad news."

"Bad news in what way?"

"Every way. You pick a way." Sally almost seemed to shudder in the dark.

"Any word on the street about her?"

"Yeah. The word is she's a crazy bitch."

"I mean, lately. Anything new lately."

"Just that she's back and badder than ever."

"Back from?"

"She was at County for the past eighteen months. She got caught dealing, sold some shit to the wrong suit. I heard they wanted to keep her longer, but the amount she sold was just barely the minimum, so they had to let her go when her time was up." Sally grinned. "No time off for good behavior, though."

"Do you know where she lives or who she hangs with?"

"What do you want with her?" Sally dropped the affected street talk. Mallory knew that she had two years of college behind her. How she'd ended up in the life was her own business. Mallory had never asked, though she'd been tempted on more than one occasion. "You don't want to mess with her. She's really bad news, Detective."

"So everyone says."

"Everyone is right. She's . . ." Sally fell silent for a moment, then said, "I saw this movie once, about a person who liked to kill other people and it didn't bother him? It was like he had no conscience, not about anything? Gigi is like that. Nothing she does makes her think

twice. She never blinks. If she hurts someone, it doesn't mean anything to her. She just keeps moving, you know what I mean?"

"I do." Mallory nodded. "You sound as if you know her well."

"Not really. I mostly just know her by rep." Sally shrugged. "You
don't have to be out here long to know that much."

"So do you know where she lives?"

"I heard she had been crashing down on Hawthorne someplace,"
Sally looked away. "Don't know that she still does."

"You have an address?"

"Not if you're thinking of going there, I don't."

"That's really nice of you, Sally, but I wouldn't do that."

"Sure, you would."

"Not these days. I'm not armed, and I'm by myself. And I'm not
stupid."

"No one ever said that about you."

"I appreciate that. So where is she staying?"

Sally sat quietly, her hands in her lap. "You promise me you won't
be going after her, and you promise me, if you do, she never knows
who told you where to find her."

"I promise on both. If she's as bad as you say . . ."

"Worse."

"I would never put you in danger, Sally. I never have."

"That's God's truth." Sally nodded. "You've always played straight
with me."

"So how 'bout it?"

"I don't know. . . ."

"How 'bout a name for a name?"

"What name do you have for me?"

"The name of the detective who took my place."

"Detective Russo, no one can take your place."

Mallory smiled. "He's a real good guy, Sal. He could help you if
you needed something."

"As much help as you've been?"

"Yes."

"Okay." Sally took a deep breath. "I heard Gigi spends most nights with a guy named Jay. Like I said, he lives on Hawthorne, row house in the middle of the block, but I don't know the number."

"Does Jay have a last name?"

"I don't know it. Truth. I don't think I ever heard it."

"Okay, that's great. That's fine." Mallory nodded. *Gotcha, Regina.*

"You're serious about not going there?"

"Yes, I'm serious."

"So why did you want to know about her?"

"Just curious."

"Oh, right." Sally made no effort to hide her skepticism. "So what name do you have for me?"

"Charlie Wanamaker."

"He's the new guy?"

Mallory nodded. "He is. If you get picked up and pulled in, you ask for him when you get to the station. He'll know who you are."

"Good to know," Sally said. "I could use a friend inside. Got that nasty man on my ass all the time . . ."

"What nasty man?" Mallory had circled around and was heading back to town.

"You know what nasty man." Sally shifted uncomfortably in her seat.

"I don't."

"That asshole detective. Frank."

"Toricelli?"

"Yeah, that's his name." Sally looked out the side window. "Toricelli."

Of course it would be him. Mallory inwardly grimaced. No surprise there. "Does he bother you?"

"Does a chicken peck?"

"Bother you how?"

"Just always threatening to take me in, then says we could always barter favors. That kind of shit."

"Has he ever taken you in?"

Sally shook her head. "He doesn't work vice, and he doesn't work this end of town, and he knows I know it. Doesn't stop him from coming around, though, talking shit." Her voice dropped. "I'm pretty sure he's pulling some shit with one of the other girls."

"Do you know which one?"

"Ursula's her street name. I don't know her real name."

"Does she work this side of town?" Mallory pulled to the curb.

"Sometimes." Sally glanced over at Mallory. "You're not going to tell him I said . . ."

"I don't talk to Frank if I can avoid it. And I wouldn't put your name out there."

"He makes my skin crawl." Sally ran her hands up her arms. "He totally creeps me out."

"You're preaching to the choir on that score."

Sally reached for the door handle. "What was the name of that new cop again?"

"Charlie Wanamaker. He's a detective."

"I gotta write that down." Sally opened her bag and took out a small red notebook that had a pen inside. She leafed through until she found a clean page, then wrote for a second before dropping both pen and notebook into the bag. "Thanks. I hope I don't need it, but you never can . . ." She paused, her mouth open, looking beyond Mallory. "Oh, for Christ's sake, speak of the devil," she whispered.

Mallory turned to her side window, then jumped back. "Jesus, Toricelli, what the fuck is your problem?" she snapped.

He made a motion with his hand for her to roll down the window. She sighed heavily, then did as she was told. He was still the cop, and she was the civilian.

"Well, well, well, what have we here?" Toricelli's face hung through the open window like a full moon. "Let me guess. Mustang Sally is giving you the need-to-know, one working girl to another." He laughed harshly. "Always wondered what you'd look like in spandex, Blondie."

"In your dreams, Toricelli."

"Oh, you're in my dreams, all right." Another harsh laugh. "So what would two working girls like you be doing, sitting here together on a Saturday night? This is supposed to be your money night, isn't it, Sal?"

Sally nodded.

"So why're you wasting it with this has-been?" He poked Mallory in the upper arm. "You wouldn't be giving her info, like in the old days, because she's not a cop anymore—you knew that, right?" In the dark, Mallory could see his eyes narrow with curiosity. "What use would an ex-cop have for a CI, anyway?"

"Since you feel entitled to know," Mallory replied, "I was driving down the street and I saw Sally. Since she was, once upon a time, a trusted CI, I pulled over to say hi. She said there wasn't much action tonight, so she got into the car to chat for a few minutes."

"Ahhh, that's nice. A little girl-time. And then big bad old Frankie had to come along and spoil the party." He poked Mallory's arm again. It was all she could do to not put a fist to his face. "I suggest you drop off your pal and get your ass on home unless you want to be picked up for solicitation."

She laughed in his face. "Trust me, bucko, if I'm going to solicit, I'm going to aim a lot higher."

He smirked. "Keep it up, Russo. I'm making a note of this conversation. You get a reputation for hanging around with the wrong element, next thing you know someone's going to be thinking you're pitching the same product. What do you suppose Drabyak would say if he heard you solicited me?"

"Oh, please." She laughed out loud. "You really think anyone would believe I solicited you."

"My word against yours, Blondie. And everyone on the force knows what your word is worth." He stood up and slapped a hand on the side of her car door. "You ladies have a nice night now."

The two women watched him walk back to his car.

"I really don't like that man, Mallory," Sally said softly.

"You're not alone there."

"You think he's going to tell people you're working down here?"

"Nah, but nothing would surprise me when it comes to him." Mallory saw the worried look on Sally's face. "Don't lose any sleep over him, okay? I won't. He can jaw all he wants. He can't hurt me."

Sally bit her bottom lip, her thoughts as clear as glass: *But he could hurt me.*

"I think I'll let my former boss in on our run-in with Detective Toricelli tonight."

"Uh-uh." Sally shook her head. "I don't want him on my ass."

"He won't be," Mallory reassured her. "Joe won't say anything to him, I promise. I just want it on the record, that's all."

"You mean, in case something happens to me?" Sally opened the door.

"Nothing's going to happen to you. Frank knows I still have a hotline to the department, the one that counts. His bark is going to be worse than his bite. Trust me."

"I always have, Detective." Sally got out of the car.

"Sally, how much do you suppose you lost in business tonight, driving around with me?"

Sally shrugged. "Fifty, maybe a little more. We weren't gone all that long, and it's early yet, so it's not that busy. Him showing up might have scared a few cars away, though. Not you. Everyone knows you. And everyone knows him."

"I'll make it up to you."

"You already have." Sally slammed the door. "Charlie Wanamaker, right?"

"Right."

"See you around, Detective."

"See you, Sal."

The woman took a few steps from the car. Mallory called to her, "You'll let me know if he bothers you, right?"

"Sure."

"And you know how to get in touch with me if you hear anything you think I need to know?"

Sally turned back to the car and leaned into the window. "You still at the same number?"

Mallory nodded.

"And I can get you through this detective, right?" Sally patted her bag.

"That would work, sure."

"One thing." Sally lowered her voice. "About that other thing . . . the person you asked about? Why you asking? Why you want to know about her? You ain't even a cop no more."

Back on the street, the street slipped back into her.

"Let's just say I'm tugging on a loose thread and we'll leave it at that."

"Right. I guess I don't really want to know." She straightened up and walked in the direction of the far corner.

Mallory drove to the end of the block and sat through a red light. By the time she'd made a U-turn and driven back the way she'd come, Sally was already sauntering over to a black sedan that had pulled up to the curb. As Mallory passed by, her eyes met Sally's, but neither waved.

Mallory drove home in silence. She had a lot of information to share with Charlie, but it would have to wait until morning. It was nine thirty PM on a Saturday, and she wasn't going to make the mistake of calling him again on a weekend night. She'd go home and write up her notes, then maybe take a long hot bath and turn in early. A meeting with Sally always left her feeling tired and soul-weary.

Not that she judged Sally for the life she chose. Everyone had to find their own way, and while having sex with strangers for money was something Mallory didn't really understand, she'd never walked in Sally's shoes. Just like she'd never walked in her mother's, she reminded herself. God knew she had to fight herself from making judgments there. She supposed that was hypocritical on her part, but a twenty-four-year-old hooker and one in her midthirties with a newborn she didn't want didn't necessarily have a lot in common.

At least her mother had had the good sense to abandon her to someone she knew would take care of her, Mallory'd give her that. The fact that *that* hadn't worked out so well didn't mean that it might not have seemed like a good idea at the time.

FOURTEEN

The covered bridge was painted barn red and ran over the widest part of Coyote Creek sixty miles east of Pittsburgh. Susanna Jones was headed back to Conroy from her weekend away—one that hadn't been particularly profitable, but then again, for the most part, none of her trips had been. Disappointed that she hadn't accomplished more, she consoled herself with the thought that at least she was being proactive. That had to count for something.

She drove slowly, the bridge being narrow even for one vehicle, then picked up speed when she was back on the road. Coyote Creek Road, barely two lanes wide, wound around the mountain like a snake. How the people who lived up here managed in winter was one of life's mysteries, not that she'd seen many houses since she'd turned off first the Pennsylvania Turnpike, then the main road that ran through the small town of Ogden and onto this sidetrack. Those she did see weren't all that close together. It appeared that people in this part of the country liked their solitude.

The car picked up speed as it headed downhill, and she eased her foot onto the brake. There were many quick twists and turns, and with the bright light of the late-afternoon sun slanted at exactly the wrong angle through the windshield, it wouldn't take much to go off the side of the road. She was into another hairpin turn almost before she realized it, and she had to hit the brake solidly to avoid scraping along the guardrail on the right side. She craned her neck to look over the rail.

"Like falling off the edge of the earth," she muttered, wondering just how often cars had gone off the road in this exact spot.

She drove until she found a place where there was sufficient clearing on the shoulder to allow her to park safely, then got out of the car. She walked back to the turn, stepping around the side of the guardrail to look down.

"Some serious rocks there," she murmured as she picked her way around to the other side of the battered and scraped railing to study the vegetation. It was dense but not impenetrable. A car that went off the road here would easily be discovered if enough people were looking for it.

Convinced that this was not the right place, Susanna walked back down the road to her own car. She debated whether to head back home or to go a little farther on Coyote Creek Road.

"Oh, what the hell. I'm already here." She turned the key in the ignition and pulled back onto the road.

After all, she reasoned, you never knew what you might find around that next bend in the road. And if not the next, perhaps then the one after that or the one after that.

What she did know was that Robert Magellan would never be at peace until his wife and son were found. If it took every weekend for the rest of her life, Susanna would keep on looking for that twist in the road, that drop off the mountain that had somehow been overlooked.

Susanna had examined every conceivable explanation for their disappearance. She knew Beth Magellan all too well, enough to know that Beth was totally in love with her lifestyle—if not her husband—and never would have walked away without taking a hell of a lot with her. That her personal accounts had not been touched since the day she disappeared and none of her credit cards had been used spoke volumes as far as Susanna was concerned. The stories that had circulated for a few months had been varied, but none of them rang true to Susanna. Beth had met and fallen desperately in love with someone else and had left her husband and all his wealth behind, taking only her child with her to her new life.

Uh . . . no. Not ever. If Beth had met someone, she'd have divorced Robert and taken every penny she could get. With no prenup, she'd have drawn as much as she could from that well.

So nix the lover theory.

Another theory that had made Susanna laugh was, Beth felt stifled by her husband's enormous wealth—which would make it impossible for Ian to live a normal life—so she packed up her son and went in search of something simpler.

Too silly for words to anyone who knew Beth.

Then there was the kidnapping theory, which would have made sense except for the fact that they'd never been contacted by anyone demanding ransom. For a while, the papers had toyed with the possibility that something had gone wrong during the abduction and both Ian and Beth were killed, but Susanna couldn't imagine that the kidnappers wouldn't have tried to collect a ransom. Robert would have paid anything to have them back under any circumstances, even the worst, and he'd put that out there in the press. But there'd been no phone calls, no letters, no e-mails. So while possible, to Susanna's mind this theory wasn't probable.

Of course, she'd read the alien abduction theories, but figured even aliens would have gone after the reward money Robert had posted. For a time, Susanna and Trula had spent all their time just wading through all those calls, none of which was worth a damn.

Which left only one plausible explanation as far as Susanna was concerned: Somewhere between Gibson Springs and Conroy, Beth's car had gone off the road and down the side of a mountain. After having spent so many weekends on those narrow, twisting roads, Susanna had become convinced that if Beth and Ian were to be found, it would be at the bottom of one of those deep ravines. She'd located several such possible locations herself, and had made so many phone calls to the state police to request their follow-up that the detective in charge of the investigation knew her voice. Over the months, she'd felt his enthusiasm and interest in the case wane. After a while, she found it easier to check things out on her own. Even at this late date, wouldn't there be some telltale sign if a car had gone off the road? A scrape on a guardrail; a tree or shrub holding evidence that a car had careered off it and over the side of the road? Wouldn't there be something?

There would be, Susanna told herself as she rounded yet another tight curve in the road. She knew from the reports she'd read from the varying investigative agencies that on the morning of the disappearance, there'd been an accident on the turnpike right at the second exit past Gibson Springs. Traffic had backed up, then stopped for hours. Susanna's theory was that an ever-impatient Beth was likely to have driven on the shoulder to the exit in an attempt to circumvent the blockage. In doing so, she could easily have gotten herself on a road to nowhere and, with no cell phone aboard, kept going, figuring that sooner or later she'd find a main road, maybe even a town. Which could have worked for her as long as she stayed on one of the main roads, but here again Beth's impatience could have come into play. A series of wrong turns could have wound her around and around the mountain, and, as Susanna learned, taking one of those unexpected turns in the dark or with the sun in your eyes could be hazardous. There were miles and miles of mountains with such twisting roads between Pam's house and Beth's. It was entirely possible that Beth had become increasingly lost as the day went on, had made a bad turn, and had ended up at the bottom of one of these ravines that couldn't be seen from the road above. While the initial search had been thorough, could every gully, every rocky ledge have been discovered?

If her theory was wrong, well, no harm, no foul. But if she was correct, sooner or later Susanna would find the right mountain road, the right ravine.

Robert's life depended on it.

FIFTEEN

Charlie rubbed the back of his neck and walked to the window that overlooked the parking lot. He'd shown up early that morning, eager to start his new job, more eager still to start tracking down the files he and Mallory had discussed. He'd read straight through lunch and now, at three thirty, was certain anyone coming within a city block of his small office could hear his stomach rumbling.

He stretched, walked to the door, and opened it. He started down the hall, surprised that the department was so quiet for a Monday afternoon.

"I wondered when you'd be coming up for air," Joe said as Charlie passed by.

"I just got sucked into this case file—" Charlie paused at Joe's doorway. "—and I lost track of time. I thought I'd run out for a sandwich."

Charlie looked back at the department, which lay behind him.

The large open room was quiet and practically empty. "Where is everyone?"

"Busy day," Joe replied.

"Something you wanted . . . ?" Charlie paused.

"Nothing that can't wait. Go, eat. Stop in when you're finished."

Charlie took the steps from the second floor and exited the building through the front door. He'd noticed a deli across the street, and he headed in that direction. Fifteen minutes later, he was back at his desk, enjoying an exceptionally satisfying corned beef on rye and a large bottle of springwater.

It had been six weeks since he'd left Philly, and it felt good to be back on the job. He hadn't realized how much he'd missed it. While he ate, he glanced over his notes and made a list of things he still wanted to do. At the top of the list went a reminder to follow through on finding Courtney Bauer's father. Charlie had called Mallory on Sunday afternoon, and she'd apologized for having forgotten to tell him on Saturday that the man may be living in western Pennsylvania.

"Timothy J. Bauer," she'd said. "Courtney's mother thinks he could be living out near Erie. He had a brother, Clark, in that area, and she thinks he might be there. At the very least, there's a damned good chance that Clark would know where to find him. I'm sorry it slipped my mind yesterday. I should have referred to my notes while we were in the diner."

"If he was there yesterday, chances are he'll still be there tomorrow. I'll see what I can find on him. You think Courtney and Ryan might be hiding out with him?"

"If they're still alive, they are getting help from someone. They've been gone three weeks now. That's a long time for a couple of kids to be on the run with no money."

"There's still that missing thousand to be accounted for," he'd reminded her.

"I don't see it having happened that way."

"Frankly, neither do I, but the fact remains that the money is still out there somewhere."

"Speaking of being out there somewhere, let me tell you what I learned about Regina Girard," she'd said, then filled him in on everything she'd learned from Sally the night before.

"She's known to be a stone-cold hard-ass," she concluded. "There's no doubt in my mind that if she'd been the shooter at Hazel's and knew that Courtney saw her there, then she saw her again on the playground . . ."

"Courtney would have been scared to death."

"Scared enough to run like hell and take Ryan with her. So it's got me thinking. Maybe the meeting of the four friends in the park was about something more than poor Courtney didn't get into Penn State. Maybe she asked the guys to meet her there because she thought Regina was looking for her. Maybe Courtney saw her somewhere, thought she was following her, and got scared shitless and wanted advice from her friends."

"If Regina *was* following Courtney, she would have followed her into the park thinking she'd be able to take her out once and for all."

"Then she gets there and there are these two boys there who would be able to identify her, so Regina gets rid of them even before she goes after Courtney. If you eliminate them right off the bat, you've eliminated possible future problems." Mallory paused. "It would fit, Charlie. Sally said that Regina had no conscience, that it didn't bother her to hurt people."

"We need to share this with Joe," Charlie said. "Even though it's supposition, it's good solid supposition. It feels right."

"I already told him," Mallory said. "He's trying to figure out the best way to get to Regina. Street name, by the way, is Gigi."

"I know. I pulled her rap sheet. She's been in and out of the system since she was very young. Foster homes for a while. She spent more time in juvie than most of the guards. And she didn't slow down once she came of age. Drug possession, assault charges . . . She's been around the block."

"So what are we doing to find her?"

"Talk to Joe. He's got a couple of undercover guys trying to find her." Before he could respond, she said, "By the way, I gave Sally your name."

"Why?"

"She's a hooker," she said matter-of-factly. "She gets picked up from time to time. She needs a friend on the inside. So tag—"

"Right. I'm it."

"You won't be sorry. She's good, if she trusts you." Mallory had paused again, as if she was about to say something else. He'd waited, but she hadn't said anything more.

"So she sounded scared of Regina?"

"Totally. I just hope we find her before it's too late."

"Too late for what?" he'd asked.

"I'm not really sure . . . ," she replied.

She'd sounded worried but hadn't said why. Too bad she was off the force, he thought as he balled up the bag his sandwich had come in and tossed it into the trash can near the door. Mallory Russo would have made one hell of a partner. She was every bit as smart as the chief said, and—from what Charlie'd seen—intuitive, not afraid to think outside the box, which to his mind was just about the best thing a cop could be. He was happy for the opportunity to work with her in any capacity, he realized, officially or unofficially. Happy to get a chance to know her better, happy to have an excuse to spend more time with her.

She was certainly one hot ticket, he was thinking as he tapped on the door to Joe's office, in more ways than one. Smart and sexy.

"Come on in," Joe called from inside.

Charlie found Joe seated on a small sofa covered in a dark blue fabric. A knitted afghan was neatly folded over one of the fat arms. The chief was reading the newspaper and sipping a cup of coffee.

"Have a seat." Joe gestured to the two mismatched armchairs that stood opposite the sofa. "I was just catching up on the sports section. Haven't seen a baseball game since the season started, between the playground case and the mess this damned sniper is stirring up."

"I heard he shot at another pedestrian late on Saturday night," Charlie said as he lowered himself into one of the chairs.

"Yeah, some young father with a baby in his arms, down on Madison this time." Joe shook his head. "You gotta wonder how these people think sometimes, you know? You just wake up one day and say to yourself, *Hey, I think I'll go take potshots at some strangers?*"

"I guess you'd have to ask a profiler that."

Joe snorted. "Yeah, right. You ever talk to one of those people?"

"Actually, back in Philly . . ."

Joe waved a hand to dismiss whatever it was Charlie was about to say. "Don't want to hear it. This guy isn't out there shooting because he was potty-trained at too early an age. He's out there shooting at helpless, defenseless people because he can. And because he likes it."

"That's pretty much what a good profiler would say, I'd think."

"I don't buy in to any of that psychological crap, you need to know that right off the bat." Joe folded the paper in half. "Anyway, I understand you spoke with Mallory yesterday. I like the possible connection between the shooting at Hazel's and the playground. Could be something to it. Girard is one nasty young lady. I could see her doing both." He slapped the paper onto the coffee table that stood between the chairs and the sofa. "Then there's the sniper. Bastard's got the entire city on edge."

"Anything new there?"

"Other than the shell casings that were picked up from the various scenes, no. We sent them to the FBI lab with a request for ASAP processing, see if they can be matched, but God knows how long it will be before we have a response."

"Which reminds me, Chief, I'd like to have the shells from the

Hazel's Market and the playground shootings compared to see if they're from the same gun, but I'm not sure what lab you use."

"Give them to my secretary, Marlene, when she comes back from break. She'll get them to where they need to be."

Joe slapped the paper again on the tabletop. "So whose idea was it to connect the two shootings?"

"Mallory's," Charlie said without hesitation.

"I figured. I heard you were good—wouldn't have hired you if you weren't—so don't take offense, but that's the kind of thing she does well. Connects the dots. Not that she always connected them in the right way—too soon to say if she's right this time—but at least she was always thinking and was never afraid to be wrong." He nodded almost absently. "Be great if we could connect these two cases, though. Be brilliant if this was on the money, close two cases with the same shooter. We know she did the first one. The more I think about it, the more she feels right for the second. I'd love to put her away once and for all . . ."

"Mallory mentioned that you're trying to find her."

"She's slippery," Joe said. "We're watching the boyfriend, too. He steps over the line—any line—we'll bring him in for questioning. We get him, you can have him for a few minutes, see if you can get some information out of him that might help your case."

"Thanks. Maybe he knows what she's been up to. I'd like an opportunity to question him. In the meantime, I'm trying to track down Courtney's father. I'm guessing Mallory mentioned that possibility. I have a call into the state to see if he has a current driver's license."

"I'm one step ahead of you. I just happened to be talking to a friend this morning, and while we were on the phone, I got him to run the name. Timothy Bauer is living about eighty miles from here." Joe got up and walked to his desk. "He's in Beaver Creek. Not far from Penn State, by the way."

"I have a feeling that's supposed to be meaningful, but I'm afraid it's lost on me," Charlie admitted.

"Penn State, where Courtney suddenly decided she wanted to go to school. Some coincidence, eh?"

"So maybe Courtney got spooked and decided to run to Daddy?"

"Possibly." Joe sat in his desk chair and leaned back.

"But Courtney sent in her application back in March, before Regina got out of prison."

"Maybe Regina found a way to get a message to her: *I'll be home soon and we have some unfinished business.*"

"I'll take a drive out to speak with him. See if she's been in touch, and if so, when."

"Here's the address." Joe handed him a piece of paper. "You might want to think about asking Mallory to go with you. She knows the area."

"Did she go to school there?" Charlie frowned. Odd; she hadn't mentioned it when they were discussing Penn State last week.

"She grew up not far from there." Joe reached for his phone, which Charlie took to mean their talk was over. "Do her good to go back."

"Sure. If she wants to go."

"She'll go. She's hooked on this case." He looked at Charlie from across the expanse of his desk. "Thanks for letting her work with you."

"Like you said, she's good." Charlie shrugged then, before he thought twice, heard himself asking, "Why'd you let her go?"

"She handed in her resignation."

"Why'd you accept it?"

Joe returned the phone to its cradle, his hand still on the receiver.

"One of my detectives—off duty, that's the key here—decided to involve himself in a high-speed chase into the next town." He leaned back into his chair, his expression stony. "Unfortunately he had his six-month-old son in the backseat."

Charlie felt his jaw drop in spite of himself.

"Yeah." Joe nodded. "You get it. But my detective did not 'get it.' When he was reamed out for it, he tried to tell me that when the chase started, he was in the parking lot of a local convenience store talking to Mallory, who just happened to be there, and that he'd handed the baby off to her before he set off in pursuit."

"I take it it didn't happen that way."

The chief's expression made a reply unnecessary.

"So how did Mallory end up being the bad guy?" Charlie asked.

"She didn't lie for him." Drabyak cleared his throat. "There'd been some talk that . . ." He looked out the window as if searching for words. "Right from day one, anyone could tell that Mallory had the makings of a great cop. She made detective faster than anyone else in the department ever had. When our previous chief announced his retirement and I was moved up to fill the office, the lead detective's job was coming up for grabs. There were a couple of men who had more seniority than she, but none of them was as good. And they all knew it."

"So when an opportunity arose to push her out . . ."

"They jumped on it. Said the only reason her name was on the short list was because she and I had a thing going, if you follow."

"I follow." Charlie hesitated before asking, "Did you?"

"No. Not that it's any of your business, but no. She was just an exceptional cop, and she deserved the promotion. And for the record, the former chief was the one who put her name on the list." Drabyak looked up at Charlie. "Not that I wouldn't have recommended her. He just did it first."

"So when Mallory didn't step up as a team player to bail out this other guy's ass . . ."

"He'd been her partner."

Charlie nodded slowly. To a cop, not supporting your partner when he or she was in trouble was unforgivable. "With the lead detective spot about to open up, what better time to get rid of the opposition."

"That's pretty much what it boiled down to." Drabyak drummed his fingers on his desk and looked sad. "Anyway, suffice it to say that her coworkers were less than kind when the word was spread that she'd lied to get her partner out of the way so she'd have a better shot at the job."

"Wait a minute. Did he or didn't he have the baby in the car?"

"Oh, the kid was in the car, all right." Drabyak nodded. "But by the time the story circulated throughout the ranks, the baby had mysteriously disappeared."

"So he denied it, said she made it up, and everyone believed him?"

"Not everyone, but enough that it made her job hazardous. No one wanted to partner with her, when someone had to ride with her they ignored her . . ." The chief rolled his eyes. "It was all bullshit, but by that time the truth hardly mattered. The story was out there, and the detective was the one doing all the talking. He'd been busted back to patrol and he wasn't liking it one bit. Took it out on Mallory."

"He's still with the force? What's his name?"

"Cal Whitman. Two years away from retirement—from a nice fat pension and him with a new young wife who can't wait to move someplace warm—and he blows it to play cowboy to go after a hijacked car, then lies about it." Drabyak shook his head. "Things would have gone better for him if he hadn't made up that stupid story and brought someone else into it. The chief wanted Whitman fired on the spot, but this was three weeks before he was set to leave, and the union was up in arms, so he let it go rather than get embroiled in something that would have kept him involved in the department long after he wanted to be sitting on his patio out in Arizona with a cold beer in hand."

Drabyak reached for the phone. "Anyway, that's the story. Whitman in, Russo out."

"I still don't understand why you let her go."

"There was no one to watch her back out there. Sooner or later, she was going to get hurt," he said softly. "She wouldn't have seen it coming, and I wouldn't have been able to stop it. It was just better for her to go, with everyone lining up to pile on."

Charlie stared blankly at him. "With all due respect, sir, why couldn't you just grab the guy at the bottom of the pile and bounce his ass out of here?"

"Because it wasn't just one guy." Joe crossed his arms over his chest defensively. "It was a good portion of the force, all of the detectives lined up against her. And as for bouncing the guy responsible for creating the wall?" Joe laughed. "He's a decorated detective with over twenty years on the force and his brother-in-law is the union rep."

Charlie nodded slowly. He'd seen the union in action firsthand.

"Frankly, I was more concerned about Mallory's safety than her job. But trust me on this, Wanamaker." Joe lowered his voice. "The guy at the bottom of the pile will screw up big-time one of these days. And his brother-in-law isn't going to be able to bail him out."

"With any luck."

"When the time comes, luck won't have anything to do with it."

"Anything else you want to know?"

"Who made lead detective?"

"No one." Drabyak smiled for the first time since Charlie came into the room. "The position is still open. They're all bucking for it, but no decision's been made. And frankly, I'm not in much of a hurry to make one."

They both fell silent for a moment, then Charlie said, "Thanks for filling me in." He got up to leave. "I appreciate the history lesson."

"Everything under control at home?" Joe asked as Charlie reached the door.

"Yes. Thank you." Charlie turned around, his hand still on the doorknob. "My sister's going to go back to Riverside on Thursday. She'll be staying there. Thanks for arranging the interview for her, for getting her bumped up on the waiting list. I think being there is going to be the best thing for her. So thanks. I—we—my mother and I—appreciate your help."

"Glad there was a string I could pull. I hope everything goes well for her."

"I feel certain it will. Thanks again."

"You're welcome." Joe looked back at the phone and began to dial.

Charlie left quietly and returned to his office.

He walked through the door and found Frank Toricelli leaning over his desk.

"Something I can help you with?" Charlie stood in the doorway, blocking it.

Toricelli jumped at the sound of his voice, but when he turned, there was no trace of embarrassment or apology in his demeanor.

"Just stopped by to see how your first day on the job was going. You weren't here, so I thought I'd leave you a note. Just looking for something to write on. No need for that now, though," Frank said. "So how's it going? I see the chief has put you to work." He snapped his fingers. "That's right. He had you working before you officially started." He shook his head and chuckled drily. "Way to make points with the boss, Wanamaker. Take home work before you ever get on the clock. I see he even gave you his old office. Is this arrangement only temporary, or should we be reading something into that?"

"Was there anything in particular you wanted?"

"Nope. Just trying to be friendly." He pointed to the stack of paper on Charlie's desk. "But I see the old Hazel's Market file here. That was my case, you know? Just curious, what you'd want with that?"

"The missing girl in the playground case—Courtney Bauer—was working at Hazel's the night the kid on the cash register was killed. Some coincidence, huh?"

"How'd you know about that? About her being at Hazel's?"

"The chief mentioned it. Said he'd thought the girl's name

sounded familiar, then remembered where he'd heard it before. I thought I'd take a look at the file, read over her statement." Charlie stepped behind Frank and pulled a sheet single of paper from the file. "Doesn't look as if she had much to say, does it?"

"The statement is short because the girl wasn't in the store at the time of the shooting, so she wasn't really a witness. Didn't really know anything about what went down that night." Toricelli's eyes narrowed suspiciously. "Couldn't add a thing."

"You think she could have been lying about that?"

"What, that she wasn't there when the kid was shot?" Toricelli laughed out loud. "Nah. Why would she lie?"

Charlie wondered if the thought had ever crossed Toricelli's mind that the kid could have been scared shitless of the shooter.

"What about this suspect you had . . ." Charlie pretended to look through the file as if searching for the name.

"Gigi. Regina—Gina—Girard." Toricelli shook his head in disgust. "What a piece of shit that one is. She should have gone down for that."

"What happened? How'd she slip by?" Charlie folded his arms over his chest and leaned against his desk. "There was one witness, right? The customer who'd ducked down behind a display when he heard the shots? He said he saw her, right? Gave you a description of her and the two guys who were with her?"

"Yeah, he described her. White, tall, thin, black hair . . . like no one else in that neighborhood looks like that. And those two shitheads who were with her?" He snorted. "The wit said he only saw them from the back; he never did see their faces. But he picked out Gigi from a lineup of other tall, thin, dark-haired white women in their early twenties. He was adamant it was her in the beginning, but once trial day came around, he was nowhere to be found. Gone, no forwarding. Just vanished."

"Wasn't that convenient?" Charlie said drily.

"Yeah, no shit. We knew she had a hand in that somehow, maybe had one of her boyfriends on the outside take the guy for a ride, if you know what I mean. But we could never find a thing. The guy just disappeared one day and hasn't been heard of since. So there was no witness to testify at trial. We tried to make her think there was some-one else who saw her who was willing to testify—trying to smoke her out, you know. Even put her in a second lineup, a fake one this time—you know, made her think someone was behind the glass and all—but she just shrugged and said she wasn't there so our so-called witness must be lying."

"Who did she think the witness was? Didn't she wonder why this witness didn't testify at trial?"

"We told her that the wit was a minor and her mother wouldn't agree to have her testify."

"So, in other words, you let Regina believe that a sixteen-year-old girl witnessed her killing Christopher Jackson that night in Hazel's, and that the girl was willing to testify." It was all Charlie could do to not put his fist through Frank's face.

"We didn't tell her that, exactly."

"You think she didn't read the papers, Frank? The reports all said that no one else was in the store that night except for a sixteen-year-old high school student named Courtney Bauer who said she was in the back of the store at the time of the shooting."

"Yeah, well, Regina didn't fall for it. Besides, I never said who the witness was."

"But if Regina had seen Courtney there that night, she'd have known who it was, wouldn't she?"

"How could she have seen the girl?" Frank frowned. "The kid was in the back of the store. She never came out front. She didn't see the shooting."

"Like I said before, maybe she lied."

"Well, it don't make much difference now, because no one testified against her and she got off."

"She walked on that murder, but now she's out."

"Yeah, she walked to the back of the courtroom and we slapped cuffs on her, took her back into custody on another case. And yeah, she's out. Been out about a month. Haven't heard much about her, so I guess she's been keeping her nose clean." He laughed again. "Which would be a first."

"How about the guys who were with her at Hazel's that night? I read in the file that there were two young guys there, one on the door inside, one outside."

"Couple of yahoos from the neighborhood. Both kept their mouths shut. You know the drill, right? They weren't there. They don't know who was there. They had alibis. They didn't know a thing. So when she walked, they walked."

"They were tried together?"

"Yeah. Some genius in the DA's office thought that was a good idea." Toricelli looked disgusted. "So when he couldn't get a conviction on her, he lost all three of them."

He was leaning against the side file cabinet. "Tell me again why you're interested?"

"Just curious about the other case Courtney Bauer was involved in."

"Oh. Right." Toricelli yawned. "Well, gotta go get me some sleep. This sniper's been running me ragged, you know what I mean? Toughest case I ever handled." He stepped around Charlie on his way to the door. "You take care out there. Conroy's a dangerous place these days. You never know where that sniper will turn up next."

Charlie stood over his desk until he heard the department door close, then began to check through the papers he'd left sitting out. It was apparent that things had been moved around, though why the other detective would be interested in what was on Charlie's desk was a mystery. Charlie checked through the file, through the pages of notes he'd made during his review, and through the notes he'd made later during his conversation with Mallory. There was no indication that he'd been speaking with her, as far as he could see, though that in itself may have been of interest to Toricelli.

"Just because he's an asshole, he'd want to know about that," Charlie muttered under his breath. Talk about a dog with a bone. That was pretty much the way Toricelli seemed to be fixated on Mallory. For whatever reason, he just wasn't going to let go.

Charlie tucked the papers back into the file and closed the folder, then slipped in the pad containing his notes for safekeeping. He was annoyed as hell that Toricelli would come into his office, and annoyed with himself that he hadn't made that more clear. His first inclination had been to bodily toss the shorter man out of his office, but he'd wanted an opportunity to question him about the Hazel's Market case.

Everything's a trade-off, he reminded himself.

All in all, he'd gotten the best of the bargain anyway. There'd been nothing on his desk that Toricelli could have been interested in, but Charlie now knew that not only was Frank an asshole, he was a lazy asshole. He hadn't bothered to pin down the testimony of their key witness, and he'd taken Courtney's word that she hadn't been in the store when the shooting occurred.

And he'd probably given Regina Girard cause to paint a target on Courtney Bauer's back.

He'd just have to make it a point to remember to keep his desk clear when he was out of his office, he told himself, and to keep his files locked up.

He glanced at the clock. It was almost five in the afternoon. For some reason, if his mother was going to have a meltdown, it usually occurred around this time. He called home to see how things were going, but there was no answer. She might have turned the ringer off, he rationalized, knowing how the sound hurt Jilly's ears so. Or she could be passed out on the living room sofa.

His good mood having vanished, Charlie walked down the hall

to the department kitchen where the vending machines were located. He'd sworn off soda after having read an article spelling out the dangers of all that unnecessary sugar and had kept to his resolve to drink springwater, but between having found Toricelli hanging over his desk and not knowing what his mother was up to, Charlie was feeling peevish. He pulled an assortment of change from his pocket and plunked four quarters into the Pepsi machine. The can clattered out from its slot, and he retrieved it. He popped it open and took a long swig.

Giving in to temptation did little to improve his mood. He returned to his office and closed the door.

It was this whole thing with Toricelli, he told himself. And this thing with Mallory. She was a good investigator and she'd been totally screwed. What kind of an idiot went on a high-speed chase with a civilian—an infant civilian, for Christ's sake!—in the backseat. Was anyone really that stupid?

Apparently so.

He wondered if Cal Whitman was one of the patrol cops he'd passed on his way in to the station this morning as everyone was rolling out to their cars. He wondered, too, why any of his fellow officers would support a member of the force who'd displayed such poor judgment. Of course, he wasn't privy to just what exactly had been said and by whom. That gossip chain could be wound pretty tightly—over the years, he'd seen it ruin the career of more than one fine officer.

Charlie reached for his cell phone and dialed Mallory's number, wondering who, if anyone, had taken her part. The chief had specifically requested that he take Mallory along when he went to find Courtney's father. Today was shot, but tomorrow was wide open.

"Mallory, it's Charlie," he said when she answered her phone. "Got time to take a ride with me tomorrow?"

SIXTEEN

Waiting to leave until later in the afternoon was a good idea," Mallory noted as Charlie got back into the car after filling up the gas tank on the turnpike. "We're more likely to find Bauer at home if we arrive around dinner."

"Which could be anytime between five and seven, depending on his habits, but yeah, I think we'll have a better shot at finding him. Assuming he still lives there, assuming he works during the day and not a night shift . . ."

"Assuming he'll talk to us."

"I think he will. Unless he is a totally heartless bastard, he has to be concerned about his daughter. How could your kid be missing for three weeks and you not care?"

"He's been missing from her life for something like fourteen years now, and it hasn't bothered him too much."

"We don't know that," Charlie pointed out. "That's another assumption. You're basing your opinion on what his ex-wife said, and we both know that there are two sides to every story."

"True. And we don't know for certain that he hasn't been in touch with her. I suspect he has been."

"Your gut tell you that?"

"Yes, actually, it does."

"Good. So does mine."

They drove past farms that stretched from just off the side of the road to wooded areas far beyond the barns and farmhouses that looked to have been standing for at least a century. There were towns with tall, white-spired churches; houses that perched on the sides of the hills as if they'd been placed there by careful fingers; lakes where ducks gathered, with an occasional heron fishing apart from the others that kept careful eyes on their young lest they float too close to the predator in their midst. Mallory sighed. She'd grown up in one of those little towns, skated in winter on lakes just like the one they'd just passed. She didn't miss any of it.

"Drabyak tells me you grew up around here somewhere," Charlie said.

"Yes."

"He didn't mention the name of the town."

"We passed the exit about ten minutes ago."

"We did?" He looked surprised. "Why didn't you say something?"

"What's there to say?"

"You could have said, *Hey, there's the town where I grew up.*"

"What would be the point?" She looked out the window.

"Do you still have family there?"

"I'm not sure."

"Guess there'd be no point in asking if you want to stop on the way back and say hi."

"Guess not."

She stewed for a few minutes, debating with herself. Then, because she'd felt that door inside open just a little when he'd gotten in Toricelli's face outside the diner the other day, she said, "I had an aunt and a few cousins there. They might still be there, but I don't know for certain. We haven't been close in years."

"That's all you have, an aunt and a few cousins?"

"That's all I know about."

He looked as if he wanted to say something, but didn't, so she continued.

"When I was five days old, my mother took me to her sister's house and left me there because she didn't know what else to do with me."

He shot a glance across the front seat as if he wasn't sure he'd heard her correctly.

"She didn't want me, but she'd found out too late that she was pregnant, and couldn't get an abortion." Mallory turned to look at him. "You hear about these young girls who deliver babies before anyone even knew they were pregnant? The girls always say, *I didn't know*? I think they know. I think they're just in denial. If they admit that they know they're pregnant, they have to make some decision about what to do with the baby after it's born and they don't want to face that. So they pretend they don't know, act so shocked when they go into labor. I believe my mother was like that. From everything I've heard about her, she was in total denial about me. Once I was born, she had to do something with me, so she took me to Aunt Jess and just left me there."

"Left you on the front porch or what?"

"No. She made like she was coming to visit because she really didn't have anyplace else to go. Aunt Jess let her stay for a few days. She left in the middle of the second night. She left alone."

"And she was young, a teenager?"

"She was thirty-seven."

His eyebrows rose nearly to his hairline, but he didn't comment.

"Aunt Jess was married and respectable and was raising three sons. She didn't want another child—least of all, she didn't want me."

"But she kept you and raised you."

"To prove a point."

"Which was . . . ?"

"That she was morally superior to her sister. That she was more maternal, that she was the better person." Mallory shrugged. "And she probably was, all things considered."

"Did your mother ever contact you?"

"No."

"So your aunt and uncle adopted you?"

"No. They did have themselves declared my legal guardians, but they had no interest in claiming me as their child, didn't even give me their name. Russo is my mother's last name. My cousins did try to treat me like a little sister, I'll give them that, but mostly I was alone. My uncle was always indifferent, he was totally involved with the boys. I think he thought having another girl in the family would be good for my aunt, but it wasn't. She really didn't want me around, and never paid much attention to me unless it was to remind me that I'd have been in a foster home if she hadn't been such a good person. She had this sort of martyr attitude toward me, you know? *Well, of course I couldn't turn her away. After all, she is my flesh and blood.* But she never 'mothered' me, and for most of my childhood, I was left alone."

"I'm so sorry," Charlie said quietly. "I'm so sorry, Mallory. You deserved better than that."

"Yes, I did." She nodded.

"What about your father? Where was he?"

"I have no idea who my father was. Is." She turned her face back to the window. "My mother was a prostitute in Atlantic City. She worked the casinos until she realized she was pregnant, had me, dumped me off on her sister, and went back to work, apparently. I'm assuming that's what she did."

"There's that word again."

"Which word is that?"

"*Assume.*"

When it was apparent she wasn't going to comment, Charlie said, "Maybe something happened to her. Maybe she's no longer alive."

"That sounded nicer than, *Maybe she's dead.*"

"Either way, that could be why you never heard from her."

"Or maybe she just forgot that she ever had me. That denial thing at work again."

"Do you know her name?"

"Of course I know her name."

"Maybe you could . . ."

"No, Charlie, I could not. I do not want to look for her. I do not want to find her. Nor do I want her looking for me."

"Okay, then." He nodded and pointed to the exit sign. "Is this where we get off?"

"Yes. Stay to the left out of the tollbooth, then take a right after the stop sign. The next street is Casper on the left. Bauer's house is the fifth one on the right side."

"How do you know that?" Charlie asked as he approached the tollbooth.

"I looked it up on Magellan Express."

"I used Google but it wasn't that explicit as to which house." He paid the toll and followed her directions.

"Hey, how do you think Robert Magellan made all that money?"

"Oh, that's right. He lives outside Conroy." Charlie came to a full stop at the sign. "The guy whose wife and baby disappeared last year. Have you ever met him? Strange case, wasn't it? They never even found the car, right?"

"Yes, so I understand. It wasn't my case." She ignored his question about having met Robert. "Here's Casper. Five houses down on the right would bring us to . . . Yes, that's it. The one with the green shutters."

"I see it." He pulled to the side of the road and parked across the street from the house.

They sat and watched for a few minutes before the side door opened and a man's arm could be seen holding the screen door ajar for a large black-and-white dog that bounded down the steps and loped across the yard. When the dog was out of sight, Charlie asked, "How do you want to play it?"

"Straight up."

"I agree. Let's do it."

They got out of the car and crossed the street, walked directly to the front door, and rang the bell. Mallory stood closest to the door so that she would be the first person he'd see. She didn't say it, but they both knew that a man was more likely to open a door for a strange woman than for a strange man.

"Can I help you?" The man who opened the door was dressed in denim shorts and a T-shirt and looked to be in his midforties. He had a farmer's tan and a few extra pounds around the waist. He addressed Mallory, but Charlie answered.

"Timothy Bauer?"

"I'm Tim Bauer, yes."

"I'm Detective Charles Wanamaker from the Conroy Police Department." Charlie held up his badge. "We're investigating your daughter's disappearance, and would like a few minutes of your time."

" 'Bout time someone remembered that Courtney has a father," Bauer said. If he was surprised, he didn't show it. "How did you find me?"

"Does it matter?" Charlie replied.

"Guess not. I suppose you want to come in." Bauer held the door open for them. "You a detective, too?" he asked Mallory after they'd stepped inside.

"I was hired by Ryan Corcoran's grandmother to find Ryan and Courtney."

"So how's that going?" he asked.

"We're here, aren't we? We found you."

Bauer stared at her for a very long time, as if thinking something through very carefully. Then all the color drained from his face.

"It's Linda, right? She hired you to track me down because of the child support thing, right?"

"I think your ex-wife has more on her mind right now than child support," she told him. "And yes, I have spoken with Linda, but I don't work for her."

"So you say." He stood in the doorway that led to the living room, blocking their entrance beyond the small foyer. "You mean to tell me you're not going to run right back to her and tell her where I'm living so she can have me arrested?"

"Not if you tell me where Courtney is," Mallory said.

"I wish I knew. I swear to God, I don't know where she is or what happened to her."

"You're telling me you haven't heard from her?"

"No. I mean, yes, that's what I'm telling you."

"How long has it been?" Mallory continued to press, and Charlie let her.

He gazed out the window, his top teeth playing with his bottom lip.

"Mr. Bauer, when was the last time you spoke with your daughter?"

"The day she disappeared, I talked to her. That afternoon. She called, all upset."

"She tell you why she was upset?"

"She said she'd gotten rejected from Penn State, but it seemed like maybe there was a little more to it."

"Why do you say that?"

"She sounded more scared than upset. But I could be wrong, you know? I'm just getting to know her, so it's hard for me to read her sometimes."

"How long have you been in contact with her?" Charlie took over the questioning.

"Just since February of this year. She got my brother's phone number in Erie and called it one afternoon. I just happened to be there, and I just happened to answer the phone. I gotta say, it shocked the shit out of me. Maybe I shouldn't have let on it was me, since it had been so long, but I was just so surprised, I told her who I was as soon as she identified herself. We talked for quite a while that day."

"You hadn't been in touch with her before that?"

"No. She just sort of popped up out of the blue. Damnedest thing."

"Did you make plans to meet?"

Bauer nodded. "Just twice. I drove down to Reading to meet her there—she took the bus in. I just couldn't believe what a great kid she turned out to be. That was Linda, you know?" He paused for a moment. "You see Linda, you tell her I said that, okay? I know the credit is all hers. She must be one hell of a mom. Anyway, I bought Courtney a cell phone so that she could call me without her mother knowing about it." He hastened to add, "Not that I thought it was okay for her to keep things from her mother, don't get me wrong. It was just until I could find a way to make things right with Linda."

"Bringing her child support up-to-date would be a good start." Mallory couldn't help herself. "But even then, you did walk out on her, left her with an infant and a toddler. Disappeared, never sent her a dime, never helped out in any way. Never even bothered to let her know you were alive. How do you figure you can make that right?"

"Yeah, I know." He nodded slowly. "I thought maybe if Courtney and I were to have some type of relationship, maybe got to know each other, maybe in time, Misty would come around. And then maybe Linda and I . . . Oh, hell, I don't know what I was thinking."

"Did Courtney say why all of a sudden she decided to track you down?"

"Not really. I just figured she wanted to know her dad. She got interested in Penn State when I told her I was living near there. She said she'd decided she wanted to go away from Conroy for school. Even asked me if I thought she could stay with me if she went to summer school right after graduation."

"Does Misty know that you and Courtney have been in contact?" Charlie asked.

"Uh-uh. She does not know."

"You sound awfully sure about that," Charlie noted.

"I am. I asked Courtney to bring Misty with her when we were making plans to meet up last month, but she said no, Misty hates me. She said she'd have to warm her up a bit to the idea. She was afraid if she told Misty right away, she'd tell her mother, then the next thing I know there'd be a couple of cops at my door because of the deadbeat-dad thing." He stopped and looked from Mallory to Charlie and back again.

Charlie held up both hands and said, "Hey, that's not what I'm here for. I'm trying to find a missing kid."

"But you're going to tell her where I am."

"Probably."

Mallory watched Bauer's face. The man was trying to debate what to do. His eyes flickered in the direction of the open back door, but he made no move toward it.

"Of course, you could always step up and make some kind of arrangement to start paying what you owe," Charlie said. "You screwed up big-time when you left, but you can start making it right."

"That's what I was trying to do when Courtney disappeared. That was my plan. We talked about it. Now . . . Shit, I don't know . . ."

"Mr. Bauer, can you think of someplace that might be special to her?" Mallory asked. "Someplace she might have gone in the past where she might go now?"

He was shaking his head.

"Maybe someplace you used to take her when she was little . . ."

"I'm afraid I never took her anywhere," he said softly. "I don't even know her well enough to know what places are special to her. I wish I did."

"If you hear from her, you call me anytime. Day or night. Hear?" Charlie handed Bauer one of his business cards. His new ones hadn't come in yet, so he'd taken one of the old ones from Philly and crossed out the office number. The cell number remained the same. "She calls you, you hang up that phone and you call me. You find out where she is, but you don't tell anyone but me. Not Linda, not Misty, understand?"

Bauer nodded.

"Anyone comes around asking about Courtney, I don't care who it is, you call me ASAP."

Courtney's father's eyes were wary. "What is it that you're not saying?"

"We think she might have seen something that someone wishes she hadn't," Charlie explained. "So anyone asks about her—you haven't seen her since she was a toddler and you leave it like that. And then you call me. Anything suspicious, you think someone's watching you—whatever, something doesn't seem right, you call. Got it?"

"Yeah, man, I got it." Bauer's face had gone pale. He fingered the card Charlie had given him, then tucked it into the palm of his hand. "I got it. . . ."

Charlie glanced at his watch as they drove away. "I think we should stop someplace on the way home and grab a bite. Maybe there's a restaurant here in town, or maybe out on the highway."

"Fine with me," Mallory told him.

"Any preferences?"

"As long as it's edible, I'm happy."

They drove through the center of town—basically one intersection with a stoplight—then followed the road back toward the turn-pike.

"I think we passed a shopping center on our way to Bauer's," Mallory pointed out. "I think it was close to the exit."

"This one over here on the left? The strip mall?"

"Yes, that's it. I didn't notice if there was a restaurant or not, though." She leaned forward to get a better look. "There's a place. Looks like maybe a sandwich shop."

"Any port in a storm," he muttered as he made the turn into the parking lot, which was mostly empty. He parked right outside the storefront and turned off the engine.

"Doesn't look like there are too many people eating here. That's never a good sign," he said.

"Sometimes these little hole-in-the-wall places fool you." She unfastened her seat belt and opened her door. "Let's take a look."

Charlie followed her into the restaurant. A tinny bell rang when the door opened, and a thin woman with dyed strawberry-blond hair peered out from the kitchen.

"Be with you in a minute, hon," she called to Mallory. "Go ahead and sit anywhere you like."

There were only three empty tables out of twenty-five occupied, so Mallory walked to the table in the corner.

"This okay with you?" she asked, and Charlie nodded.

The thin woman emerged from the kitchen with a tray that she delivered to a table of three men, then handed menus to Charlie and Mallory.

"I'm a little shorthanded tonight, hons, so bear with me." The pin over her left breast spelled out CHARLENA in green sequins. "Specials are on the board right behind you. I'll be right back with water."

Mallory turned to read them. "The chicken salad looks good. I think I'll go with that."

Charlie studied the board for a moment, closed the menu, and said, "I'd like to take you out for a real dinner one of these nights."

"You don't have to take me to dinner. This is fine."

"Adequate under the circumstances, but not fine. And I meant I want to take you out. As in a date. Dinner is merely the vehicle. And I bring it up only to let you know that I know the difference between grabbing a sandwich from someplace—anyplace—and dinner with a capital *D*."

"I never date anyone I work with." Mallory looked away as she spoke. "Messy."

"Good policy. Stick with that. I agree completely. So I'm really glad we're not working together."

"What do you call this?" She leaned forward. "What we're doing on this case?"

"Oh, this?" He grinned. "This is collaborating."

Before she could respond, the waitress came over to take their menus and explain the specials.

"I think I'll go with my first choice." Mallory handed back the menu. "I'll have the chicken salad and a Diet Pepsi."

"I'll go with the burger. Medium rare. Fries. Large Coke," Charlie told her.

"Got only one cola." The waitress pointed to the sign that was neither Coke nor Pepsi. "That okay?"

Charlie and Mallory nodded.

"I'll be right back with those." The waitress hustled back to the kitchen.

Mallory sat with her right elbow on the table, her chin in her hand.

"Okay, how's this sound: Courtney gets some type of communication from Regina back in the winter, late January, maybe, or early February. She wants to find a place to hide so that Regina can't find her. What does she do? She tries to find her father, and does.

"She's thinking if she can hold on till graduation, she'll go to live with Daddy and Regina won't be able to find her."

"Why didn't she just go to the police?" Charlie wondered aloud.

"Probably because she saw the shitty way the case was investigated in the beginning, and figured her father would be a better bet."

"That reminds me, I did talk to Callie Henderson this morning. She said that she'd spoken to Courtney on the phone for about three minutes the night of the shooting, and it was an hour earlier than Courtney had told the police. She said no one ever asked her about it, so she figured it wasn't important."

"Swell." Mallory grimaced and fell into silence for a while.

"Charlie, maybe it's not a place special to Courtney. Maybe it's someplace of Ryan's," she said thoughtfully. "You know, we've been so caught up with all this business with Courtney and Regina that we've lost sight of Ryan."

Charlie looked up with interest.

"The place where they're hiding," she continued. "Maybe it's someplace special to him. And yes, we're going to *assume* they are hiding."

She took her phone from her bag and entered a number, then placed the phone to her ear.

"Mary, it's Mallory Russo . . ."

The reception inside the restaurant was poor, so she walked outside, talking as she went. She paced on the sidewalk and asked the same question in as many ways as she could think to: *Yes, I know you've been asked before, but have you been able to think of someplace that's special to Ryan, someplace that he might think of as a sort of sanctuary?*

"Please give it some more thought," Mallory said when her questions all brought the same response: no place special Mary knew of. "Maybe something will come to mind."

"Mary can't think of anyplace offhand," she told Charlie when she went back inside. "I'm thinking I should talk to Father Burch. Maybe someone at school, maybe one of his friends might have an idea. Maybe Ryan mentioned something to someone . . ." She tapped her fingers impatiently on the tabletop. "There has to be something."

"You're that sure they're alive?"

"Aren't you?" She appeared surprised by the question.

"Pretty sure, but I don't like to . . ."

"Yeah, I know, to assume." She smiled. "I feel them alive, Charlie. I feel them still part of this world."

"You got a little woo-woo thing going on there?" he asked, his eyebrows slightly raised.

"A little. Nothing weird. Just feelings I get sometimes."

"And you feel these kids are still alive." It wasn't a question.

"I do."

"Then I guess if they're going to stay that way, we're going to have to find them before Regina Girard does."

"There's a sobering thought," she said. "Everything we've heard about that woman has been scary. She sounds like your classic psychopathic personality. No conscience, no rules—and no line that she won't cross."

"Frank tells me that the customer who ducked down to hide in Hazel's when the shooting started disappeared after he ID'ed Regina from a police lineup."

"As in just . . . poof?"

"As in gone for good without leaving a forwarding address and never heard from again."

The waitress served their food, and they ate in silence for a while.

"Maybe there's a way to flush her out," Mallory said thoughtfully. "Maybe we could lure her somehow . . ."

"We can't keep her on anything right now. We could bring her in to question her, but I don't want to tip our hand yet. I'm afraid if she knows we suspect her, she'll disappear and we'll never find her. The chief wants to pull in the guy she's been staying with, see what he can get from him."

"Won't that make her suspicious?"

"Depends on what they bring him in to talk about. Chief said I'd get a chance to talk to him once they have him. We'll see if he has anything to say about his current live-in."

"You know, you might want to—"

Her thought was interrupted by his ringing cell phone.

"Excuse me," he said to her as he answered the call. "What? Where are you?"

He got out of his seat and started walking toward the door. Bad reception, Mallory thought as she watched him disappear outside. By the time he returned, she'd almost finished her meal.

"We're going to have to get on the road," he told her. He withdrew his wallet from his back pocket and took out two twenty-dollar bills.

She looked up at him, surprised. "Is something wrong?"

"Yeah. Something's wrong."

"Aren't you going to finish eating?"

"I lost my appetite," he said, his face unreadable.

"Okay. You go start the car." Mallory pushed her chair back from the table. "I'll settle up here."

"I took care of it."

"You left entirely too much. Go. Start the car. I'll be out in a minute."

She picked up the twenties and walked to the counter.

"Something wrong with your food?" Charlena asked with apparent concern.

"No. My friend just got called back to work. The chicken salad was fine," Mallory assured her. "But I'm wondering if we could wrap his burger and fries . . ."

"I got just what you need." Charlena pulled a Styrofoam container from under the counter and handed it to Mallory. "Let me get you folks some travel cups for those drinks I'll bet you barely touched."

Within minutes, Mallory was at the car. She approached the

driver's side with the brown paper bag from the restaurant in her hands.

"How about if I drive for a while so you can eat," she suggested when he rolled down the window.

"I'm okay. Get in," he said brusquely.

She walked around to the passenger side and opened the door. She had not yet fastened her seat belt when he began to back out of the parking space, then hit the gas to beat the red light at the entrance to the shopping center.

She waited until they'd gotten onto the turnpike before opening the lid of the white Styrofoam container.

"I'm assuming you can eat and drive at the same time." She passed him the burger.

"Thanks."

"I have your fries, too," she told him. "I'll leave the container on the console, if you like."

"That would be great. Thanks, Mallory."

"And your drink is in the cup holder." She placed it there.

"You're a lifesaver. Thanks for being so understanding."

"Well, I'm not, not really, since I have no idea what's going on. I didn't have much of a choice. Seems to me it came down to being left behind in Beaver Creek or packing it up and taking it with us."

"I'm sorry. I owe you an apology."

"Hey, no apology necessary. I know how work can be sometimes."

"This has nothing to do with work. This is personal."

"Oh."

She debated with herself whether or not to ask. In the end, pride won out over curiosity, and she opted out of asking about his personal life.

"So you think he was telling the truth? About not hearing from Courtney?" she asked.

"I don't think he expected anyone to come around, so he didn't have a story cooked up. At least that's how I read it. You?"

"I thought he was being straight with us—but I don't know. I'd have expected him to be a little more upset about her disappearance. Did he seem upset to you?"

"Not really. Then again, he's only seen this kid a few times since she was born," Charlie said. "Which is sad, when you think about it, but the fact that he hardly knows her could account for the lack of emotion."

"Still, he's her father. Wouldn't you expect to see a little more emotion?"

"Frankly, I think he showed more emotion over his ex finding out where he is."

"You're going to let the court know, aren't you?" she asked. "Linda and Misty have a right to know."

"I'll take care of that first thing in the morning."

He passed a tractor trailer on a curve, and Mallory held her breath. They traveled another five minutes without speaking, and it was clear to her that he was miles away. Finally, she said, "Anything you want to talk about?"

He took his time answering.

"That call . . . that was from my mother. She called to let me know she was out for the evening, so I should get home right away because my sister was alone." He accelerated and passed another truck. Traffic was light on this part of the interstate, and he was obviously taking advantage of the fact.

"How old is your sister?"

"She's twenty."

"Old enough to spend some time alone, I'd think. You're not one of those superprotective older brothers, are you?"

"I'm afraid so." He put his turn signal on and flew past a Jeep that was doing seventy-five. "I have to be. My sister is autistic. She can't be left alone."

"Oh, I'm sorry. I didn't know . . ."

"Of course you didn't. There's no reason you would have. She—

her name is Jilly—will be all right for a while. She pretty much stays in her room and does her own thing. But if she starts looking for my mother, she'll leave the house, and she'll start wandering, and God knows what could happen to her." In the dark, she could see his jaw set squarely. "On Tuesday, Jilly is going to be admitted as a resident at Riverside."

"That's the school for special-needs kids outside Conroy?"

"Yes."

"I heard there's a really long waiting list. You were lucky they could take her."

"The chief apparently knows someone there. He got the paper-work pushed through."

"His sister-in-law is one of the trustees," she told him.

"Really? I didn't ask who he knew. Anyway, she goes there on Tuesday, and she'll be living there for as long as they feel she needs to be." He slapped a palm on the steering wheel. "You'd think my mother could have waited another two days to go out partying with her girlfriends."

He cleared his throat. "My mother is an alcoholic. She's supposed to be going into rehab the Saturday after we drop off Jilly."

Mallory didn't have the heart to tell him that she knew very well who and what his mother was. "She must be very frightened" was all she said.

"Your sympathy is misplaced." When he turned to look at her, she pointed to the road ahead.

"Don't take your eyes off the road when you're doing eighty-five, please," Mallory said. "I understand you being upset and worried about your sister, but I do think your mother must be scared to death. Her daughter will be gone, and if she's in rehab, she's going to have to face whatever it is that addicts have to deal with on her own."

"It isn't that I'm not sympathetic. I know she's had a lot to deal with throughout her life. Things haven't been easy for her."

As he drove, he told Mallory about his family history and the issues his mother had dealt with over the years.

"She's had a full plate, hasn't she?" Mallory remarked when he finished. "She lost a home and a lifestyle she clearly loved, her husband died young and left her with three children, one of whom needed special care. And all those miscarriages. Your brother's death. She's really had more than her share, Charlie."

"I know," he agreed. "She's a really good person, Mal. She really is. She was a good mother. She *is* a good mother, when she isn't drinking. But she's lost control of it, and everything good that she is, is overshadowed by it. For her own sake, if not for Jilly's, she has to stop. Sooner or later, something really bad is going to happen—to her, to my sister . . ." He shook his head. "I can't let that happen."

"That's why you quit the job in Philly and came back to Conroy," she said softly. "To take care of her and your sister."

"I had to." He nodded. "There isn't anyone else."

His words hung between them in the front seat. She picked at the french fries mostly to have something to do with her hands.

"Not that I mind," he said. "I just want to clarify that. I should have come home after Danny died. I should have known how hard that was for my mother. If I had, the present situation would have been avoided."

"You don't know that," Mallory pointed out.

"I pretty much do. So now I'm playing catch-up. I need to get Jilly squared away, so that I can get Mom straightened out."

"And then what? Do you go back to Philly?"

"No. That wouldn't be fair to the chief or to the department." He shook his head. "Ideally I'd like to convince my mother to sell the house she's in. She's always hated it. Maybe if she hadn't had this drinking problem, she'd have sold it and moved on long ago, but she just hasn't had the strength to do that. I think she's been depressed, and when you're down like that, it's hard to make big decisions. So I figure if I can get her to move on, it would be really good for her to be in a new place."

"How about you?"

"I have a deposit on a town house out on Ridge Road."

"The new complex they're building? Out by the lake?"

He nodded. "I figure by the time they're completed, if all goes well, my family will be settled and I can get back to having a life again. Not that I'm complaining, but I really never saw myself living at home through my thirties," he said wryly. "I've lived alone for years now, and I can't wait to have my own place again."

"Did you have a house in Philly?"

"Yeah, a great place in a little section called Queen Village. I contacted a Realtor before I left, told her I wanted to put it on the market. Now she tells me she has a buyer and I'll make a killing on it, so I told her to go ahead and make the deal. I'm hoping the sale will be finalized around the time I'll be settling on the new one."

He slowed as he entered the Conroy city limits.

"Why don't you stop at your house and check on your sister before taking me home?" she asked.

"She might get upset," he replied. "Strangers make her nervous."

"You can just run in and check on her. I can wait in the car."

"Would you mind?"

"Not at all. I know you're really worried about her."

"Thanks. I just need to see if she's there."

"If she wasn't, where would she be?" Mallory asked as he turned onto Fourth Street.

"The few times she's wandered, it's just been through the backyards here in the neighborhood. At least, that's all I've heard about. But you never know."

He pulled in the driveway of a small ranch house and cut the engine. "I'll just be a minute."

Mallory sat alone in the dark and watched him hustle up the

front walk and unlock the front door. Inside, she could see lights go on. He was back out to the car within five minutes, notably relieved.

"She's okay?" Mallory asked.

"Jilly doesn't seem to be aware that Mom isn't there, which is a good thing. If she knew, she'd be out looking for her. So yeah, she's okay. She's in her room, drawing pictures. I ran over to our next-door neighbor's. She's agreed to stay until I get back. Today Jilly's drawing cats, so that will occupy her for a time. She really likes to draw cats."

He backed out of the drive and turned to the left. Without taking his eyes off the road, he said, "I feel a little responsible for this. Yesterday I called home and there was no answer. I jumped to the conclusion that my mother had gone out and left Jilly, but she was in the backyard, pulling weeds from her garden. I really pissed her off, and I don't blame her."

"She was pissed off because you'd lost faith in her."

"Something like that, yes."

"It's a tough situation to be in. You need to make sure that no harm comes to Jilly, but at the same time you need to support your mother. It can't be easy."

"It isn't. Thanks for understanding."

"Don't mention it. That's what friends do."

He didn't comment, and a minute later he was parking in front of her town house. He put the car in park and, without warning, reached across the console to pull her close.

"I don't think I want to be just friends," he said, right before he kissed her.

Her first thought was that his lips were softer than she would have expected, had she been thinking about it, and she wasn't sure she hadn't been. Her second thought was that he was a really good kisser, and that she wanted him to kiss her again. She had pretty much decided he might have been the best kisser she'd ever met when he moved his mouth from hers to the side of her face and kissed her there as well.

"I need to get back," he said very softly.

"You do."

"Come on." Charlie leaned forward and kissed her lightly one more time on her mouth. "I'll walk you up."

"You don't need . . ."

He was already out of the car, so she opened her door and met him on the sidewalk. He slipped an arm around her shoulder, and together they walked to her door.

"What's on your schedule for tomorrow?" he asked as if unaware that he'd just nearly turned her inside out.

"I'm going to follow up with Father Kevin and see if anyone can think of a place that might have meaning to Ryan. Maybe not necessarily somewhere you might think of as a hiding place. Maybe one of his teachers or one of the other kids might have some thoughts on that."

She took out her key and fit it into the door. "What about you?"

"I'm hoping to be able to talk to Regina's buddy, Jay, see if we can learn anything from him."

"What if we're wrong? What if it wasn't her?"

"Don't think I haven't thought about that. But in the absence of any other viable suspects, we go with what we've got."

He opened the door for her, then bent down to kiss her again. "I'll talk to you tomorrow."

"Good night. I hope things are okay at home."

"Me too."

He turned and walked back down the path to his car. She stood in the doorway and watched him pull away from the curb, one finger tracing her bottom lip where his lips had been. She closed the door slowly, and went inside. From somewhere near the back of the house, she heard Leroy squawking, "Hello, beautiful."

It was the last thing she remembered before her head exploded and the world went black.

SEVENTEEN

Mallory woke to find part of her face on the cool hardwood floor, and the rest of it on the edge of the area rug in the living room. Opening her eyes was an effort; lifting her head even more so. It felt as if a few hundred tiny little carpenters wielding heavy hammers had invaded her brain and were building themselves a residence.

"Oh, Christ."

She raised a hand to the back of her head and winced when her fingers found the source of her pain. She struggled to pull herself up. She leaned back against the front door and tried to remember what had happened.

She'd been with Charlie, she knew that, had spent the afternoon with him. They'd talked to someone . . . Bauer, that was who. She exhaled long and deep and fought the urge to touch the back of her head again.

What else? She remembered that as Charlie had driven back to

Conroy, he'd talked about his family. About how his sister was autistic and his father and brother had died, and about how his mother had dealt with all the disappointment and loss by crawling into a bottle and not coming out.

Well, she'd known the part about his mother drinking, she just hadn't known why.

Oh, and he'd brought her home and kissed her in the car, and she'd kissed him back. How could she forget that part? Then he'd walked her to the door, he'd kissed her again, and she'd stood against the wood frame to watch him walk down the path to his car. She'd closed the door and started to lock it, and . . .

And that was pretty much it. The lights went out. She raised her hand to her head and touched the place where the carpenters were doing their thing.

She grimaced when her fingers found the lump that had already risen. She went still then, having pieced it all together. Someone had been in her house, had struck her from behind. That someone might still be there.

No lights were on downstairs, which could mean that whoever had attacked her could be gone. Or they could be sitting in the dark, watching her.

Her eyes moved around the room, studying the shadows, her ears straining for the sound of breathing coming from someone other than herself. Seeing nothing, hearing no sound, she slipped off her shoes, holding one in her right hand, heel-first. Her bag was right where it had fallen, and she looped it over one arm and rose clumsily. She made her way through the living room, pausing at the entry to the dining room, which was smaller and offered few hiding places. But why hide when whoever had struck her was armed with something—whatever had hit her—and she was armed with . . . one black leather flat with floral cutouts and a madras Dooney & Bourke shoulder bag.

She made a cursory check under the dining room table, but there was no one there, so she ventured into the kitchen. Someone could still be upstairs.

Here there was light creeping in through the open door from Jacky's second-floor deck. She slipped outside and pulled her phone from her bag.

Her first impulse was to call Charlie, but she hesitated. If she called him, she suspected he'd turn the car around and come back. He'd be caught between helping her and taking care of Jilly. She thought maybe Jilly needed him more.

Mallory called 911 first, then put a call in to Joe. She knew there was a damned good chance that the patrol officers who showed up would be some of those who had a beef with her, and she wasn't in the mood to be messed with. They could talk all they wanted, but her house had been broken into, damnit, and she was going to have someone there who cared enough to make sure that her attacker was gone and that any prints that might have been left behind were properly lifted. She wrapped a towel around a handful of ice, held it to the back of her head, and sat on one of the patio chairs until she heard commotion at the front of the house. She went back in through the kitchen, careful not to touch anything, and opened the front door, steeling herself from whoever might be on the other side.

"Miss Russo." A deliberately indifferent Officer Michelle Crandall addressed her formally. "We had a report of a break-in at this address."

"Please come in." Mallory stepped aside to let in Crandall and her partner—a male officer Mallory did not recognize. She could tell by his demeanor that he'd been apprised of all her past sins.

Mallory turned on the overhead light in the living room.

"I'd been out since about four this afternoon," she told the officers, "and arrived home about . . ."

She looked at her watch and tried to calculate.

"About thirty minutes ago. I unlocked the front door and came inside, and when I turned to close the door, I was struck from behind."

"Are you injured?"

Crandall asked without any real interest. Mallory met her cold stare with one of her own.

"I was hit with sufficient force to knock me out cold, so I'd say yes. Yes, I was injured."

"Where were you injured?"

"The back of my head where I was struck."

"Would you like us to call an ambulance?"

"No, I would like you to check upstairs to make sure that the person who broke into my home has left. And then I'd like you to see if you can lift prints from the back door where my assailant apparently gained entry to my house." Mallory stood with her hands on her hips, trying to ignore the pounding in the back of her head. She fought back the sarcasm that was welling inside her. *Perhaps I could assist you in dusting for prints, Officer Crandall? May I borrow your gun and your flashlight so that I might check upstairs myself?*

"We'll take a look upstairs." Michelle Crandall motioned for her young partner to accompany her.

Mallory turned on the light switch to illuminate the stairwell, then listened to their footsteps on the floor overhead before they stopped in her office.

A moment later the young officer called down to her, "Miss, have you been up here since you arrived home?"

"No. As soon as I came to, I called 911," she replied. "Why?"

She started up the steps, but her head began to throb, and she had to force herself to slow down. She reached the office door and gasped. The room was a mess, with papers strewn all over the floor and her files emptied on the desk where her laptop had stood.

"Can you tell if anything's missing?" Crandall asked.

"Yes, my laptop is gone." Mallory walked to the desk and started to go through her papers.

"Anything else?"

"I don't know." Mallory shook her head.

"Word is you're writing a book," Crandall noted sarcastically. "Maybe someone wants to beat you to the punch, steal your notes."

"Maybe." Mallory refused to bite.

"Mallory?" Joe called from the first floor.

"Up here," she called back.

He came up the steps and appeared in the doorway. Crandall's attitude vanished the second the chief of police walked into the room.

"Officer Crandall. Officer Stuart." He nodded as he entered. "You all right, Mallory?"

"Except for this lump on the back of my head, I'm fine." She held up the towel that held the dripping remains of the ice. "This has helped a little."

He looked around the room. "Would it be too much to hope that this was a routine burglary?"

"My laptop's gone, maybe some of my notes. I haven't looked in my bedroom yet. I don't have any jewelry of any value, though, so I can't imagine what might have been taken from there."

Without being asked, Crandall walked into the other second-floor room and turned on the lights. "Miss Russo, would you come in here and take a look around?"

Mallory nodded and followed her. Before she left the room, she turned back and said, "Thanks, Chief. I appreciate you coming over. I'm sorry, I just wasn't sure . . ."

"Don't apologize." He shook his head.

She went into the bedroom and looked around, but it didn't appear that anything there had been touched, and she so advised the police officer.

"Looks like the only thing that was taken was the laptop," Mallory told the chief when she came back into her office. "And maybe some of my notes."

"Notes from . . ."

"My current project," she said meaningfully.

"I see." He stood with his hands on his hips. From his expression, Mallory took it that he was struggling not to ask questions specific enough that Crandall might realize Mallory was working hand in hand—albeit unofficially—with the department on an open case.

"I see," he repeated. "Any idea who . . . ?"

"None." She shook her head.

She could have said, *Maybe one of my former colleagues,* but she didn't. Would any of them have actually broken into her home? And if they had would they have actually struck her with enough force to have knocked her out?

Duh.

By the time prints were lifted and the house was hers again, it was three in the morning and Mallory was sitting at her desk, sipping a soothing cup of tea. She'd knocked back more than the recommended dosage of Advil, then picked up the papers that had littered the floor and reorganized them. Next she went through them to see what, if anything, was missing, but she couldn't really tell. Most of what had been tossed on the floor pertained to the book she was working on. Almost all of her notes regarding her efforts to find the missing kids were on her computer. The thought of someone hacking into the machine and accessing the pages of information made her nervous. What would someone—anyone—else want with those notes?

Maybe it was just the computer, she rationalized. There was always the chance that it had been a random burglary. The fact that neither the downstairs nor the bedroom had been ransacked didn't mean a whole lot. She didn't really have anything worth stealing.

Besides, access to her computer was protected. To get into her files, a series of passwords was needed. So unless the thief was a really good hacker, he'd be unable to read her files, wouldn't he?

Wouldn't he?

The pain reliever began to kick in, and while it really hadn't reduced the pain, it had slowed down the pounding. She'd declined a trip to the hospital, but since she did suspect she might have a concussion, she promised Joe she'd stay awake for the rest of the night—not that she'd be able to sleep anyway. The thought that someone, somewhere, right at that moment, might be booting up her computer and reading her files made her crazy.

But what would be the point, she wondered. Who would be so curious about what she was doing that they'd break into her home to find out?

Toricelli, maybe? Or maybe one of the other officers who'd lined the drive the other day? Maybe someone started asking questions around the building and found out where she'd been and why she was there. She'd been tempted to voice her suspicion to Joe, but she had nothing to back them up. Besides, any accusations she might make would only serve to add fuel to the fire. And if she was wrong, she'd be even more reviled than she already was.

If one of her former fellow officers was behind the break-in, she'd need proof if she intended on taking it to the chief of police. How she'd get such proof, she had no idea.

Then there was this case of hers. She pondered that possibility for a while.

And cop or not, the questions still remained: who and why.

EIGHTEEN

The phone rang in her ear with all the clarity of a church bell.

"Oh, dear God." She fumbled under her pillow for the cell phone she'd tucked under there before she finally went to bed around seven AM.

"Mallory, it's Charlie," the voice on the other end said. "What the hell is going on?"

"What?" She frowned and struggled to sit up, then groaned. Those hateful little carpenters were at it again.

"I just heard there was a break-in at your house last night." He sounded angry, and she wasn't sure why.

"Yeah. Yeah, there was." She leaned back against the pillow and turned the clock around so she could see the time. Nine thirty. Good. She woke up. She would probably live.

"Are you all right? I heard you were attacked."

"I was smacked on the back of the head with something hard, not sure what," she told him. "I guess I walked in on someone after you dropped me off and—"

"Wait a minute, you mean this happened while I was still outside?"

"No, you'd driven away by then. I closed the door after you left, and that's all I remember."

"Why didn't you call me?"

"My first thought when I came to was to call 911. That's what you're supposed to do when you need the police ASAP."

"I am the police," he reminded her. "You found time to call the chief."

"I called Joe because . . . well, because he's Joe, and I didn't want someone showing up here and giving me a hard time because I'm Mallory Russo, former cop." She sighed. "And I didn't call you because you needed to be home. You had your own thing to take care of. If I'd called you, you would have been torn between turning around and coming back or going home to take care of your sister. I didn't want to put you in that position, Charlie. It wouldn't have been fair."

When he didn't respond, she said, "How is everything? How was your sister when you got home?"

"She was okay." He paused. "I just wanted to make sure you were all right."

"I have one bitch of an egg on the back of my head, and one nasty headache, but other than that I'm okay. Thanks for asking."

"Chief says your laptop was stolen."

"Yeah. That's the bad news. All of my notes on this investigation are on there. The computer has several layers of security, but still, someone with more knowledge of computers than I have could probably get into the files if they really wanted to. I just don't know why anyone would want to. Which makes me wonder if it wasn't a random burglary."

"That seem probable to you?"

"I guess anything is possible, but probable? Not so much."

"Any thoughts on who might be behind it?"

She hesitated just a little too long.

"You don't really think that someone here . . ." He lowered his voice.

"I honestly don't know what to think, Charlie. But I imagine if one of Conroy's finest had a hand in it, sooner or later you'll hear about it."

"I'll keep my ears to the ground. You mention this to Joe?"

"No, and I'd appreciate it if you didn't raise that concern to him. That's all I need, for it to get around that I ran to the chief and told him the other kids were picking on me."

"Good point. But you'll let me know if anything else happens, okay." He paused. "And then there's always the possibility that the lady we're looking for is on to you. How she could be, I have no idea, but it's a possibility."

"More of a possibility than a random burglary, I'd say. But I still think it's more likely that someone there was involved. I've been a little too visible lately, and I think that's stirred the pot a little."

"Look, Mal, would you want to stay with us tonight? I can sleep on the sofa and you can—"

"No, no. I'm fine. It's probably done. I think whoever it was won't be back. But I really appreciate the offer. And I can arm myself."

"It stands, if you change your mind. If you start feeling uneasy tonight . . ."

"Thanks, Charlie. I'll call. I will."

"So you're going to take it easy today, right?"

"I need to check in with Father Burch to see if I can talk to a few people at school. Maybe someone will recall a place Ryan may have mentioned that might be meaningful to him."

"Are you sure you're okay?"

"I'll be fine. That wasn't the first shot I've taken to the head. It probably won't be the last. Besides, I'm so pissed off that someone broke into my home, took my stuff . . ." She blew out a long breath. "I'll feel better working than I would not."

"Just be careful."

"I will."

"And you'll call me if you need anything."

"I promise."

Mallory closed the phone and swung her legs over the side of the bed. Her head was slightly woozy, and her stomach unsettled, but not enough to keep her from standing and gathering her robe around her. First, a shower, then coffee. She needed to do whatever it would take to clear her head. She had an agenda planned for the day, and she was going to stick to it.

"Wanamaker." The chief's voice came through Charlie's intercom.

"Yes, Chief?" Charlie set down the file he'd just lifted from the floor.

"Come in here."

Charlie was at Drabyak's door in an instant.

"I just got a call from downstairs. Guy named Arlo Pickett was brought in last night for driving without a license. All manner of assorted goodies were found in the trunk of his car . . . guns for which he had no permits, a small amount of drugs. A little of this, a little of that. Nothing major, but enough that we could pull him in."

"Arlo Pickett." Charlie frowned. "Why is that name familiar?"

"Because he's one of the two men who went on trial with Regina Girard for the shooting at Hazel's Market." Joe sat back in his chair and smiled.

"Where can I find him?"

"Room two seventeen. One floor down, to the right of the elevator. My guess is that he'll be arraigned this afternoon and out on bail before the day is over, so you might want to spend some quality time with him while we've got him."

"Thanks, Chief. I'm on my way."

"You talk to Mallory today?" The words stopped Charlie in the doorway.

"Just a little while ago."

"How's she feeling?" Drabyak asked.

"She says she's okay."

"Any ideas on who might want to target her?"

"Not off the top of my head," Charlie told him. He hated covering for anyone who might have been involved, but it was Mallory's call to make, and she'd asked him not to let the chief know her suspicions.

"You hear any scuttlebutt out there"—Drabyak pointed in the general direction of the squad room—"I want to know about it."

"If I hear, you'll hear." Charlie turned to leave again.

"You don't think it had anything to do with this case, do you?" The chief rubbed the back of his neck as if in pain. "Someone connected with it, maybe. Someone who's getting antsy about her asking questions."

Charlie thought about that for a moment.

"I think if someone wanted to stop her from asking questions, they'd have done more than knock her out," he said, believing it.

"Good point," Drabyak said.

Charlie took the stairs and within minutes was standing at the door to room 217, looking through the glass at the young man seated at the wooden table. In his midtwenties, close-cropped hair, skin the color of mahogany, dressed for the street in a T-shirt and baggy jeans. When he looked up at the glass, his eyes narrowed uneasily as he studied the detective. Charlie tapped on the door, then opened it.

"Detective Wanamaker," he identified himself to the officer who appeared to be wrapping up his interview. "I can come back if you're . . ."

"No, no. I was just about finished." The officer stood. "The chief called down, told me to give you as much time as you want. I'll be outside if you need me."

"Thanks." Charlie took the seat the departing officer had just vacated. He folded his arms over his chest and stared across the table just long enough to make the younger man squirm just a little.

"Arlo Pickett," he said evenly. "Whatcha in for today, Arlo?"

"Some petty shit." Pickett leaned back in his chair and tried to look defiant.

"Some petty shit." Charlie nodded. "Petty as in, jaywalking? Petty as in running a red light? Or petty as in being identified as having been present when a store clerk was shot and killed?"

Pickett looked genuinely confused. "Don't be bringing that up. I wasn't convicted of none of that. Uh-uh. Besides, there's that double-jeopardy thing."

"You still see your buddies from back in the day, Arlo? Demetrious Brand? And how 'bout . . . what was her name now? Ginger? No, no, Gina. Regina Girard. You ever see your old friends, Arlo?"

"Last I heard, Demetrious moved to Baltimore."

"And Regina? What's the last you heard about her?"

Arlo shrugged. "Don't hear nothing."

"Really? That's funny, you know, because I know she's back in town, and you'd think she'd have been in touch. I mean, after all the two of you went through together a year or two back, and all."

Arlo shifted uneasily.

"So if she's not hanging with you, who's she pals with these days?"

"Gigi has no pals," he snorted. "She ain't friends with no one."

"You haven't seen her with anyone?"

"Nope."

"Well, I doubt she's been all alone this past month or so since she's been in Conroy." Charlie rubbed his chin thoughtfully. "So I'm thinking maybe you're not being straight with me. Maybe you're still her BFF."

"Her what?"

"Her best friend forever. Maybe the one she was hanging out with the night of the playground shooting."

Arlo's eyes widened and he shoved back from the table. "Uh-uh. No way, man. That was not me."

"Then who was it, Arlo?"

"I don't know nothing about that. Uhh-uhh." He shook his head adamantly.

"Oh, come on. You must have some ideas. . . ."

"I got no ideas about that. I swear. I don't know nothing about that." Arlo looked genuinely frightened.

"Any thoughts on who might?"

Arlo shook his head again.

"Maybe you could think of someone, someone you might have seen hanging out with Gigi." Charlie stared at him. "It's a small city, Arlo. She's been in town for at least a month. You cannot tell me you haven't seen her even once. Come on. Between you and me."

"Between you and me." Arlo repeated sarcastically. "I see what's in it for you, what's in it for me?"

"I can talk to the arresting officer. See what we can do about those charges that are currently pending for your 'petty shit.' " Actually, he'd be talking directly with the chief, but Arlo didn't need to know the details.

"But no one knows we talked, right?" Arlo leaned forward.

"No one but you and me." And the chief. And Mallory . . .

"I might have seen her with this guy, Malcolm. Back when she was first in town."

"Malcolm have a last name?"

"Wilson, I think. But I haven't seen him in a while."

"How long's a while?"

"Couple of weeks, maybe. Like I said, when she first got back to town."

"Anyone else?"

"I don't know, man. Maybe Malcolm's cousin."

"Where would I find him?"

"Don't know his name, but he sometimes hangs with a guy named Gracy down at the car wash, Ninth and Mill."

"How about Jay? I thought she hung out with him most nights."

"She stays with him when she feels like it. Least, that's what I hear."

"Where does she stay when she doesn't feel like staying with Jay?"

"I don't know, man. That's the truth. I just seen her maybe the one time. I try to keep my distance, you know what I mean?"

Charlie pushed back the chair and walked to the door.

"You think of anything else you think I might want to know about . . ."

"Yeah. I'll call. Right. Hey, you're gonna talk to that jackass who arrested me, right? Just like you said?"

"I'm going to take care of it right now."

Charlie left Arlo Pickett in the small room. From the look on his face, Arlo was having second thoughts about having spoken with the detective. There'd be no way he'd be calling in anything else.

At least I have a name I didn't have before, Charlie thought as he took the stairs up to the third floor. He stopped in the chief's office and filled him in.

"I'll see what I can do about getting Pickett back on the street," Drabyak told him.

"Think we could have a man follow him? See where he goes?"

"You're thinking he might run right to Girard, let her know the cops are asking about her."

"Yeah. I think that's exactly what he's going to do. In the meantime, I'm going to run the name he gave me, see what pops up in the computer. I'll bet this kid Wilson has an interesting past."

"Let me know if you find anything interesting. In the meantime, I'll see if we can find him, bring him in and see what he has to say." Drabyak said just as his secretary, Marlene, buzzed him.

"Chief, Tom from the mayor's office is on line seven. They want an update on the sniper . . ."

"If it isn't one thing, it's another around here these days," he muttered. To Marlene, he said, "Tell Tom I'll be with him in a minute."

"No leads at all on this guy, Chief?" Charlie said as he made his way to the door.

"None. I never saw anything like it. I got everyone I can spare and then some working on this case, and there's nothing. You'd think someone would come up with something." He shook his head. "Jesus, you've got to wonder what the hell is going on in this city. . . ."

NINETEEN

ather Burch, thanks for making time to talk with me." Mallory met the priest in the lobby of the high school. "Especially on short notice."

"I told you, anytime." He patted her on the arm. "Let's take a walk outside, shall we? It's a beautiful morning, and we can sit in the garden and talk privately. I'm assuming you're here to talk about your job."

He opened one of the double doors on the side of the building and held it for her.

"My . . . oh, my job." She laughed self-consciously. She been so engrossed in the case that she'd all but forgotten she'd taken it on as employment. "Yes, I had an idea."

"How about here?" He gestured toward a wooden bench. "This is one of my favorite places in Conroy. The botany students designed and planted the garden, the wood shop kids made the benches, and the kids in Mrs. Winters's art classes made the sculptures. Wonderful, isn't it?"

"It is beautiful." She ran a hand along the arm of the bench and admired its smoothness. "Very nice."

"So, tell me where you are in your investigation."

Before she could reply, he added, "Susanna was just asking me this morning if I'd heard from you, and I had to admit I hadn't heard since Friday."

"I wasn't aware I was expected to check in with anyone." She realized how defensive she sounded, and tried to soften her response. "Is that a problem?"

Father Burch smiled but remained standing. "When you worked for the police department, how often did you fill in Chief Drabyak on your open cases."

"Depends. Active cases, I kept him pretty much in the loop . . ." She paused, then nodded. "Okay, I get it."

"Yeah. Susanna likes to be kept in the loop. That way, when Robert asks, *Anything happening with that case that Kevin has gotten me involved in?* Susanna can say something besides, *I don't know.*" He joined Mallory on the bench. "She hates not knowing. She's supposed to be in charge, and when she isn't, she starts feeling cranky."

"I understand. I'll give her a call."

"Better still, stop in and see her."

"All right."

"So, what is this idea that you had?"

"You know that I still believe that Courtney and Ryan are alive. . . ."

"Good," he said, nodding. "So do I."

"Well, they have to be hiding someplace." She felt silly stating the obvious. "Someplace where they know they will be safe."

"Safe from the police?" He shook his head. "That just never has rung true to me. I can't see them running from the police."

"I agree. I think they're running from the killer." She told him the theory she and Charlie had been working on.

"That makes much more sense to me, yes. I could see Courtney being afraid of someone she'd seen kill in cold blood. Of course she would be terrified, and of course they'd run," he said thoughtfully. "So the question is, where would they go where no one could find them."

"Exactly. I've spoken to Courtney's family, but there doesn't seem to be anyplace in particular where she'd go. I called Mary and asked her if she could think of someplace that was special to Ryan, but she didn't know of any. I was hoping perhaps one of his teachers might know something—maybe in conversation sometime he mentioned something . . ." She blew out a long breath. "I know it's a long shot, Father, but I can't think of anything else right now."

"So you want to talk to some of Ryan's friends, and to all the teachers you missed the last time around?"

"I'm thinking maybe the people he was closest to, the people he might have confided in. I might have spoken with some of them last week, but maybe I didn't ask the right questions."

"Well, you might want to talk to Dirk Petersen. He teaches the class on film. Ryan was his star pupil. He often spoke about the work Ryan did on his projects."

"What kind of projects?"

"Some films they made over the past two years. Dirk's told me many times how gifted he thinks Ryan is."

"Why didn't I speak with him the last time I was here?"

"He might have been out that day. He's only in three days each week, teaches two classes. Let me see if today is one of his days . . ."

As they walked back into the building, Father Burch asked, "Is there anyone else I can line up for you while you're here?"

"Let's wait to see what Mr. Petersen has to say," she told him. "Oh, I would like to speak with Misty Bauer. I understand she's a freshman."

"Yes, I'll check on her as well." They were back in the lobby where they'd met earlier. "I'll be right back."

He disappeared into the main office, and the door closed quietly behind him while Mallory paced in the hall. She was feeling a bit nervous, hopeful that today she'd find the key, fearful that she would not. Her headache had returned with a vengeance, so she shook two tablets from the plastic container of Advil she carried with her and looked for a water fountain. She was just walking back to the office when the door opened and Father Burch stepped out.

"Dirk Petersen's in his classroom." Father Burch was smiling when he rejoined Mallory. "The third-period class is over in about seven minutes. I'll walk down with you, introduce you, and you can take it from there."

"Great."

Mallory followed the priest down one hall and around a corner to a second, longer hallway. He stopped close to the end and pointed to a door.

"Room one thirty-three. The film lab."

She began pacing again. Father Burch watched her with some apparent amusement.

"You take your work very seriously, don't you?" he said when she'd paced herself back to where he stood leaning against the wall.

"Yes, I do."

"Good. This is serious business, this disappearance of children." His face went suddenly sad and his voice dropped. "This shooting of children in a playground. Taking innocent lives for no reason." He looked at her with apologetic eyes. "I know that Jesus says to hate the sin but love the sinner, but it's damned hard sometimes, Mallory."

She started to remind him that the Bible also said something about an eye for an eye, and that she wasn't sure which—revenge or forgiveness—was more appropriate under the circumstances, but they were both spared the debate when the bell rang and all twenty-some of the third-period film class spilled out into the hall.

Father Burch escorted her into the classroom, where Dirk Petersen was removing a video tape from a VCR.

"Dirk," Father Burch greeted.

The man looked up. "Father Burch." His face lit with surprise. "Good to see you."

The priest introduced Mallory and explained that she was working with Ryan Corcoran's family to determine what had happened in the playground and, hopefully, to find Ryan.

"That would be wonderful, Ms. Russo, if those two kids were found alive." He shook her hand. "I don't know Courtney very well—actually, I only know her because Ryan had filmed her several times, and . . ."

"Ryan filmed Courtney?"

"Yes, as I said, she was in several of his films."

"What sort of films has he made?"

"He's done several documentaries, all very good. Excellent, in fact." Petersen's head bobbed up and down. "He's done one on comparative religions, one on the problems of housing wild animals in zoos. Oh, and the one he did on the Underground Railroad was really quite remarkable. The boy really has a lot of promise."

"Would it be possible for me to view his work?"

"Sure thing. We entered two of his films in a contest for student filmmakers, and I asked him to make several copies at the time, in case we had to submit to the next level of judges. I think he has a very good chance to win, or at the very least to place high nationally."

"He's that good?"

"The best I've ever had." Petersen turned his back and went to a file cabinet. A moment later he turned back, two flat DVD cases in his hand. "Here are the two I mentioned. Take them home, take a look. Bring them back whenever you're finished."

"Mr. Petersen, to the best of your knowledge, was there any one place that Ryan liked especially to film? Someplace that was really special to him for some reason?"

The teacher thought the question over, then shook his head. "Not that I know of. He's never mentioned anything like that. Of course, if there was, he may have filmed it, but I can't think of anyplace he's gone back to more than once to shoot, say, in different lightings or different times of the year."

She handed him a card. "If you think of anything, would you give me a call?"

"Sure thing."

"I'll get these back to you as soon as I can," she told him.

"No rush. At least, until Ryan comes back, there's no rush, so take your time."

"Thanks."

She deposited the DVDs into her bag while she and Father Burch walked back to the front of the building.

"You wanted to speak with Misty Bauer," he reminded her when they rounded the corner near the office. "Let me get her for you."

"Could I maybe meet with her outside, in that little courtyard where you and I sat?" Mallory asked. "Maybe she'll be more relaxed outside the school building."

"Sure thing. I'll send her out." Father Burch went into the office, and Mallory returned to the bench in the garden. Something had her blood humming—she didn't know how else to describe the feeling she had when something felt right. Somehow, before the day was over, she'd learn something important that she didn't already know. She could sense it.

She was wondering what that something could be when she looked up to see Misty walking toward her.

"Did you find out something about my sister?" Misty asked. "Do you know where she is?"

"No, but I think you do."

"That's crazy. If I knew where she's hiding, why wouldn't I tell you?"

"Because Courtney has made you promise not to tell anyone. And you haven't. Not even your mother," Mallory said softly. "You and Courtney both know that someone very, very bad is looking for her. And we both know who that very bad person is, don't we, Misty?"

"I don't know what you're talking about." The blood drained from Misty's face. She turned back toward the school.

"Misty, this isn't a game. I know you promised your sister, but she's in terrible danger. The person who is looking for her wants to kill her, you know that, right?"

"I don't know what you're talking about," Misty repeated, and kept walking.

"Misty, I have to find Courtney before someone else does. I can help her. You can help me do that."

The girl slowed for a moment before resuming her pace.

Mallory caught up with her and held out her hand.

"Misty. Put this in your wallet or wherever you keep important things."

Misty looked down at the paper in Mallory's hand.

"It's my business card," Mallory said. "Don't throw this one away. Trust me. You're going to need it."

Misty folded the card in half and closed her fingers around it. She went back into the school, and the door closed behind her.

"Well, that went well," Mallory muttered.

She found Father Burch waiting just outside the office and thanked him.

"Let me know if there's anyone else you want to speak with or if there's anything else I can do to help," he said as he walked her to the front steps. "And don't forget, you need to—"

"—call Susanna, yes, I'll do that." Mallory smiled. And she would. Later. Right now, she was on her way home to watch the DVDs Ryan had made. Hopefully, one or both would tell her something that she needed to know.

Mallory watched the DVD on religions twice before deciding there was nothing there. While interesting and well done, there was no scene where the camera lingered over any particular place, no one building or setting that recurred. She removed the disk from the DVD player and slipped the second one in. As soon as the film began, she got goose bumps, and her ears began to hum again.

The opening shot was of a neatly tended farm, the camera panning across the field and over the pastures where goats and sheep grazed together. The scene was filmed from someplace high—the second floor of a barn, maybe. The credits were written across the screen, but she barely saw them.

The narrative began, the voice-over telling the story of how people who'd lived in and around Conroy in the nineteenth century had helped runaway slaves escape north to Canada and remote parts of New England. There were a remarkable number of Underground Railroad stops in the area. She'd never have guessed there'd been so many.

She watched the DVD in its entirety, then replayed it several times over. The answer was there in her hands; she knew it. By late afternoon, she had a list of places that had appeared on the screen. She rewrote the list in order of the number of times each had appeared.

When she finished compiling her list, she reached for the phone, excited to share her news with Charlie. Disappointed when she had to leave voice mail, she disconnected—then true to her word—dialed Susanna's number.

"Susanna, hi, it's Mallory Russo," she said when the call was answered.

"Oh, Mallory. How are you?" Susanna seemed pleased to hear from her. "What's going on? Any leads yet?"

"I have a few ideas. I'll stop in the office tomorrow or the next day and go over it with you, if you're going to be in."

"I'll be here all week. Just give me a call when you're on your way. I'm sure I'll be here. I have no plans to travel until Friday."

"Oh? You're taking a trip?"

"What?"

"You said you wouldn't be traveling until Friday, so I assumed you meant that you were going somewhere then."

"Oh. No real trip. Just weekend stuff. You know."

"Sure."

"So, will you be bringing me a bill for your time?"

"Not until I get my license," Mallory told her. Remembering she hadn't checked the mail when she'd arrived home earlier, she went to the front of the house and walked outside.

"Are you sure that's necessary?" Susanna was asking.

"It's the law." Mallory peeked inside the mailbox, spotting several envelopes and a magazine or two.

"Well, you are keeping track of your hours, your mileage, that sort of thing, aren't you?"

"Pretty much." She lifted the lid and brought the stack inside.

"How much longer do you think before you have your license?"

"Maybe another week or so. There shouldn't be a problem with it. I had some excellent references."

"I'm sure you did. Well, give me a call and let me know when you'll be coming in. Even if I can't pay you yet, I'd like to see your preliminary reports."

"That might be a problem." Mallory placed the mail on the coffee table. "My house was broken into last night and my laptop was stolen. All my notes were on the laptop."

"Good Lord, are you all right? You weren't home at the time, were you?" Susanna sounded genuinely alarmed.

"No. Actually, I came in right as the person or persons were leaving, I guess. I took a good crack to the back of my head, but I don't think there's any permanent damage."

"Was this a random attack? I mean, you don't suppose this has anything to do with this investigation, do you?"

"No, no, I'm sure." She wasn't, but she didn't want to discuss that with Robert Magellan's right hand. If she couldn't even defend herself or her home, what the hell kind of private investigator was she?

She began to flip through the mail, then stopped at the white envelope bearing an official-looking seal as the return address. She slit the back of the envelope open with a fingernail and slid out the contents.

Her permit to carry a concealed weapon.

She concluded her conversation with Susanna, then hung up. Gleefully, she went upstairs and into her bedroom closet. From inside a box on the shelf, hidden behind her sweaters, she retrieved a small handgun and its holster.

"Come to Mama," she crooned.

She fastened the holster around her waist and tucked the gun into the small of her back, then patted it.

"Welcome back." She grinned as she stood before the mirror and turned so she could see the reflection of the small bulge beneath her waistband. "Mama's missed you."

She hadn't realized just how much she'd missed that weight, that slight pressure at the back of her waist. Wearing it felt like fitting in that last piece of a puzzle, and she was unexpectedly grateful to have it there. She couldn't help but wonder: If she'd had the gun strapped on last night, would she still have been attacked? Would her home have been robbed?

Probably, she admitted. For one thing, she'd never seen it coming, and so wouldn't have had time to reach for it before she was knocked out. For another, as much as she genuinely loved guns, as much as she liked target shooting, she knew that once you pulled the gun, you had to be prepared to use it. As a cop, she'd fired warning shots at suspects before, but she'd never shot another human being. Way different from shooting at an inanimate target, she knew.

Maybe just as well. If she'd had the gun last night, she might have shot someone. While she didn't like the fact that she'd been a victim, that someone had come into her house and helped himself to her things and made her feel vulnerable for the first time in a very long time, she didn't relish the thought of possibly ruining someone's life for the sake of saving a laptop.

Leaving the gun in its holster, she went back downstairs and replayed Ryan's DVD one more time.

TWENTY

"Y ou look happy." Robert came into Susanna's office and dropped a few envelopes on her desk. "Today's bills," he told her.

She stacked the bills into a neat pile and placed them on the right side of her desk.

"I am happy," she replied, giving him a huge bright smile as proof.

"Want to share the joy?" He sat on the edge of her desk.

"Actually, you will be sharing."

"I'm not following you."

"Remember the bet we made about Mallory Russo?"

"Mallory Rus . . . the PI?"

"Yes. I'm impressed. You remembered her name."

"What was the bet?"

"The bet was that she'd add her hours on from last week to this week's, and in essence, pad the bill."

"What makes you think she won't?"

"Because she isn't billing this week."

"She take the week off?"

"No. She isn't billing until she gets her license. Which is the concept that started that conversation about her billing or not billing."

"So you're saying you think you're going to win the bet."

"I'm definitely winning this one. All I have to do is decide what to pack."

"Pack for what?" He frowned.

"Ah, so you not only don't recall making the bet, you've forgotten the wager."

"What was the wager?"

"Loser buys dinner."

"That's not so big a deal. We've bought each other dinner before."

"In Paris."

"Ah. Transportation provided, I'm assuming."

"You volunteered your plane, win or lose."

"Did I now?"

"You did. And I will hold you to that. I hate commercial flying these days. It's a big pain in the ass."

"I agree. Which is why I don't do it." He got off the desk. "And how clever of you to have stipulated that use of my plane was included, regardless of who was buying dinner."

"You don't recall that conversation at all, do you?"

"Not really. But I believe you when you tell me we had it."

He went to the window and gazed out.

"It looks like there are eggs in the mockingbird nest again," he told her.

"I know. I'm not sure what laid them, though. I think I read somewhere that sometimes some birds will take over an existing nest once the previous tenants have moved on. Maybe that's what happened there."

"What happens if the first bird comes back and decides she wants her nest back?"

"I don't know." Because it was a question she'd asked herself many times in one form or another, Susanna moved on. "Her house was broken into and she was knocked out cold."

"Who?"

"Mallory Russo."

"Great choice of a detective."

"I think she was. She's really caught up in this investigation."

"She should be. She's being paid to be." Robert stood halfway to the door, his hands in his pant pockets. "Was she hurt?"

"I suspect she has a good-sized lump on her head, and she was probably seeing stars there for a time, but she seemed to be okay on the phone."

"I think I need to see what her bills look like before I admit defeat."

Susanna laughed. "Fine with me. I still think I'm going to win this one."

He glanced at his watch. "I think I'll go see what Trula has cooked up for dinner. Want to join us?"

"I'll be down in a minute. I have one more call to make."

"I'll tell Trula to set an extra plate."

He was almost through the door when she called to him, "Robert, I think this is a very good thing you're doing."

"What thing is that?" He turned in the doorway.

"Hiring Mallory to look for Ryan Corcoran and the Bauer girl. I was speaking with Kevin earlier. He believes in her. He thinks she's going to find them."

"What do you think?"

"I think if anyone finds them, it will be Mallory."

"Is anyone else even looking for them?"

"Not the police, apparently. They're all tied up with this sniper. Oh, there is one detective who's been sort of working with Mallory—someone new—but other than that, she's pretty much alone in this, I think."

"Then you're right. If anyone finds the kids, it's probably going to be her."

"Cynic."

He shrugged.

"Anyway, I think it's a wonderful thing you're doing for Mary Corcoran."

"I'm doing it for Kevin."

"Still, it's a great idea, you know, using your resources to help people who don't have any. Helping people who are running out of hope."

"Did Kevin tell you to say that?"

"No, why?"

"It just sounds like something he'd say. Actually, it was something he said."

"Just think how good you'll feel when those two kids are found alive and returned to their families."

He stared at her for a moment, then left the room, saying, "I'll see you at dinner."

"Oh, shit," she muttered, her face flushing red as she realized what she'd said. "Of all the thoughtless, stupid things to say . . ."

Her phone rang and she took the call, still slightly flustered. She finished the arrangements for the meeting she was setting up between Robert and his Realtor to discuss the offer they'd received on the beach house, made some notes for him, and hung up. She had no doubt that he was going to accept the offer, even though it was lower by far than the asking price, and she wondered how he was going to feel once the house was sold. She saw it as a first step for him to accept the inevitable, and hoped in time he'd be relieved to be rid of it. As well as she knew him, she sometimes wondered these days if she knew him at all. He was becoming more withdrawn, more sarcastic, more cynical, than he'd ever been.

Sooner or later, she knew, something would have to give.

TWENTY-ONE

I'm seeing a pattern in Ryan's film—there are a couple of places he's shot from several angles and obviously on different days, judging from the weather and the season," Mallory told Charlie when he returned her call early that evening. "But I don't recognize any of them. Well, one I might recognize. The barn at one property reminds me of an old barn that is out on Josephine Road, but in the film, you only see it from the back." The teakettle shrieked from the stove, and she walked into the kitchen to turn off the burner. "Then again, so much of the architecture around here is similar, it's tough to know for certain."

"But you think there's enough repetition that maybe one of these spots could be their hiding place?"

"Right now, it's the only possibility we have, so I think we have to take it as far as we can."

"I agree."

"I'd like you to take a look at the film as soon as possible. Think you can fit in a quick trip to my place?"

"Not until tomorrow at the earliest, I'm afraid. We take Jilly to Riverside first thing in the morning, and we need to pack for her tonight. My mother was afraid if she packed too early, Jilly would get upset."

"I thought Jilly liked it there."

"She did, but I don't know if she remembers liking it. She might when she gets there." He paused, and in the pause, she could feel the tension deepening. "Getting her there will be a battle. I hope this was the right thing to do."

"Are you having second thoughts?"

He hesitated, and she sensed he was debating with himself. Finally, he said, "Not really. I know it's the best thing for her. I think my mom feels she's bailing on her daughter, but Jilly really needs to be in a residential setting. Regardless of how it affects us, this is what Jilly needs."

"Then I guess you need to remember that. You're doing this for her."

"You're right, and I know that. I should remind my mom of that when she starts feeling weepy."

"How is she doing?"

"She's hanging in there. We'll see how things go on Saturday."

"What happens on Saturday?"

"She goes into rehab."

"Good for her. I wish her all the best."

"Thanks, Mal." He cleared his throat. "Anyway, I guess I'll catch up with you tomorrow. I'll give you a call when I get back from Riverside."

"Hey, if you feel you need to talk . . ."

"Yeah. Thanks. I appreciate that."

They ended the call, and she set the phone on the counter while she poured hot water over the tea bags she'd placed in a pitcher to make iced tea. She'd envisioned him dropping everything to come over on his way home to watch Ryan's film—it was that important.

But she totally understood that his obligations had to take precedence. It was apparent that he was conflicted about both his sister and his mother, and she respected that. Not ever having had either, however, she didn't really understand the emotion. She knew it was the right way to feel; she just hadn't ever experienced it herself. She couldn't help but wonder what it was like, to have a mother who loved you. To have a sibling you cared for so much, you'd put everything on hold—your job, your life—for their sake.

Then again, Mallory didn't know for certain that she didn't have a sister or a brother somewhere. Maybe someday she'd try to find out. Maybe.

It was, she told herself, something she might want to think about some other day. Today she had a job to do, and it was easier to focus her thoughts on someone else than to turn them inward. She knew this was avoidance in its purest form—something she'd practiced most of her life—but so far it had worked for her. Focus on doing good—on saving a life, on solving a crime, on comforting a victim—and she wouldn't have to focus on herself.

She sliced a lemon and filled a tall, thick plastic glass with ice, then poured herself some tea. The ice crackled under the hot liquid, and a spire of steam rose. She locked the back door, took her tea into the living room, and prepared to watch Ryan's film one more time.

"Hey, Wanamaker, the chief's looking for you." Frank Toricelli appeared in Charlie's office at almost the same time Charlie did.

"Thanks." Charlie was in no mood for conversation. He'd just dropped off his sobbing mother at home after taking a frightened Jilly back to Riverside, this time to stay. The last person he felt like dealing with was Toricelli. He had no patience left; his last nerve had been worn down to the quick.

Toricelli opened his mouth and began to say something, but Charlie walked around him and into the hall. At the chief's doorway,

Charlie paused and looked in. Drabyak looked up and motioned for him to enter.

"How'd it go this morning?" the chief asked.

"It went, sir. Thank you."

The chief nodded as if he understood. Rather than belabor the issue, he said, "There's a present waiting for you downstairs in one of the holding cells."

Charlie looked at him quizzically.

Drabyak smiled. "Malcolm Wilson was brought in last night around eleven after blowing a red light and then deciding he'd rather outrun the patrol car that was following him than pull over. A number of stolen items were found in the car. Including a laptop with a smashed screen. Malcolm had an interesting story explaining where it came from and how it got smashed." Drabyak smiled. "You might want to hear the story directly from him. It's a doozy."

"I'm on my way."

"Malcolm Wilson still inside?" Charlie asked at the desk outside the holding cells.

"He's the only one we have right now." The woman looked up to inspect Charlie's badge, then buzzed him through.

"Hello, Malcolm." Charlie stopped in front of the occupied cell.

The man inside barely looked at him.

"I'm Detective Wanamaker. I hear you had a bad night."

There was a folding chair next to the door, and Charlie brought it to the front of the cell and opened it.

"I hear they found some interesting items in your car, Malcolm. I'm guessing you were on your way to unloading some of it when you ran that red light. Not a good idea to do that when a cop's sitting right there at the intersection."

"I never saw that cop car," Malcolm muttered, shaking his head. "Fucker came out of nowhere."

"Yeah, well, cops have a way of doing that sometimes." Charlie nodded, turned the chair around, and straddled it. He rested both arms on the back. "There's one thing I'm real curious about."

"What's that?" Malcolm remained slumped on the mattress.

"The laptop. How the hell were you going to fence a laptop with a broken screen?"

"Wasn't going to fence that. A friend asked me to get rid of it for her."

"Oh? I suppose it belonged to her and she dropped it accidentally."

"Something like that."

"I guess Gigi must have picked up some computer skills when she was away, huh?"

Malcolm's head shot up. "Don't know no Gigi."

"Oh, give me a break." Charlie laughed. "Three sets of prints were lifted from that laptop, Malcolm. Yours, Regina Girard's, and the ex-cop's who owned the laptop." It wasn't true, but Charlie bet it would turn out to be.

"Ex-cop?"

"Yep. I guess Gigi didn't tell you that the house she had you break into belonged to an ex-cop?"

"I didn't break into the house, she just asked me to come with her to this house over on Essex in case . . ." He realized what he'd said and shut up fast.

"The house over on Essex is owned by a former Conroy detective. Now, how do you think the police department feels about one of their former fellow cops being burglarized and brutally attacked?" Charlie left out the fact that there would probably be applause in the squad room once it got around.

"There wasn't no brutal attack, man. I just . . ." Malcolm got up and began to pace. "Shit. She didn't say nothing about no ex-cop."

"This your first arrest for burglary, Malcolm?"

The young man shook his head. "No."

"Guess it isn't going to go so well for you, is it?"

"I do not want to go back inside, man." He spoke more to himself than Charlie.

"Why don't you tell me what your involvement was? We know you weren't behind the break-in, Malcolm."

Malcolm continued to pace.

"I'm guessing that Gigi asked you to come with her to serve as a lookout while she went through the house." Charlie offered him an opening.

"That was all it was supposed to be. Gigi said she needed something in this house, all I had to do was stand at the front door and keep an eye out in case someone came home while she searched the place. That's all."

"She tell you what she was looking for?"

"No. She looked around the first floor for a while, then she went upstairs. She was up there when the woman came home. I called up to her, told her someone was coming, she told me to take care of her. Gigi was going out the back door when the woman was unlocking the door."

"By 'take care of her' she meant . . . ?"

"I don't know what she meant. This woman unlocked the door and came inside, she was closing the door and I clocked her from behind. She went down. Gigi hollered from the back of the house for me to do her, I didn't see no need for that, she was already out cold, she hadn't seen me, so I left her there."

"What did you take from the house?"

"I didn't take nothing, I swear. Gigi had the laptop and a bunch of papers in her hand, that's all I seen her take."

"What happened next?"

"We went back to this place Gigi's staying over on Hawthorne. She turned on the computer, but she got real pissed when she couldn't get any information out of it. She didn't have the password and she couldn't get into it no how. She smashed the screen with the heel of her shoe and told me to get rid of it."

"What about the papers she took. You see them? Any idea what was on them?"

"Nah, didn't see 'em. She sat at the table reading them for a while. Must have been something, though, 'cause she got real mad and started cursing. Then she asked me to drive her to Academy Street. Said she wanted to check out an address."

"She say whose?"

"Some hooker, she said."

It didn't take a genius to figure out who the hooker was and what had set Gigi off.

"Did she find the house?"

"Yeah, but no one was home, so we left. I took Gigi back to Hawthorne and dropped her off. I haven't seen her since."

"Thanks, Malcolm." Charlie folded the chair and leaned it against the wall where he'd found it. "I'll tell the chief you were very cooperative. Maybe we can do something about reducing the charges, maybe get you out a little early."

"You goin' after Gigi?"

"Yeah. We're going after Gigi."

"You going to let her know I talked about her?" Malcolm sat back on the mattress. "Because if you do, I may be better off right here, where I am. At least, until you bring her in. She's one crazy bitch, man."

"So I've heard." Charlie buzzed to get out.

On his way back upstairs, Charlie called Mallory and left a message.

"It's important that you call me as soon as you get this message, Mal." He briefly related what he'd learned from Malcolm Wilson. "Depending on which notes Regina Girard lifted from your house and how much you'd written down, she may know everything that you know right now. And if that's true, she knows you've connected the dots between the shooting at Hazel's and the shooting in the playground. And to my mind, that makes you a real big target. This is one irrational woman, Mal. If you're on her list, we've got a big problem." He'd taken the steps two at a time, and he stopped at the top of the stairs to catch his breath. "And that's not the only problem we have. Malcolm mentioned that after Gigi read your notes, she got really pissed off—something about a hooker, he said—and she had him drive her to a house on Academy Street. I'm hoping that your CI doesn't live on Academy, because if she does, Gigi's going after her. I'm on my way in to talk to the chief right now, see if we can get a car over there. In the meantime, if you can get in touch with her, you need to warn her that she could be in danger. Please call me so that I know you got the message. I have a really bad feeling that this is about to blow up, and you and your friend Sally are going to be right in the middle of it when it does."

TWENTY-TWO

Mallory stopped at the drive-through ATM and frowned when she read the OUT OF ORDER sign. She parked in the first space she came to; taking her wallet and her keys, she locked the car and went to the walk-up inside the bank lobby. She took out the fifty dollars she felt she owed Sally and returned to her car. She tucked the bills into the top of her bag, which was sitting on the seat where she'd left it. As she drove away, she turned on the radio, smiling when she realized that the song playing was one of her all-time favorites, one that brought back one of her best childhood memories.

She'd danced to the song—Journey's "Lights"—in her ballet recital when she was thirteen years old. She'd loved that dance, loved the costume—pink tulle with a fluffy skirt, the girliest thing she'd ever worn. To this day, she could remember every step. Every time she heard the words, she was thirteen again and feeling pretty for the first time in her life. Her dance instructor had wanted all the girls who had long hair to wear it in a French braid, but having had short hair all her life and having given birth to only boys, Mallory's aunt hadn't a clue how to construct such a thing.

Fortunately, Mallory's friend Kelly's mother was a hairdresser, and had offered to fix up both girls before the performance. Mrs. Allen had looped Mallory's hair into a perfect braid and had touched her cheeks with pale pink blush. When she'd looked into the mirror, she'd barely recognized herself. That image—the reflection she'd seen that day—had never really left her. It had been one of the happiest days in an otherwise forgettable childhood.

Mallory turned onto Academy Street, wondering what had happened to her old friend, and thinking that if there was one person from her past she'd want to see again, it would be Kelly Allen.

She parked across the street from the house Sally shared with three other girls, the fourth one in from the corner in a straight line of identical row houses. She figured if she were to find Sally at home, it would be in early afternoon, before she set out for working the streets. Morning might have been too early; later in the day she'd have missed her. Mallory got out of her car and walked across the street. From a block away, she could hear children at recess playing in the East Conroy Elementary school yard. She rang the doorbell and waited. When no one answered, it occurred to her that she probably should have called first, so she took her phone from her bag. The screen alerted her to having missed two calls, and she'd just started to check those numbers when the door opened.

"Hey, it's my pal Mal." Sally smiled and stepped outside in bare feet and cutoff jeans. "What are you doing here?"

"I felt bad about costing you the other night," Mallory said, thinking how young and pretty Sally looked, with her red hair toned down just a bit and pulled back in a ponytail, her face clean of makeup. She reached into her bag and took out the bills she'd gotten from the ATM. "I wanted to make it up to you."

"You don't have to do that. It was early, there wasn't much going on anyway," Sally told her. "Besides, I didn't give you much."

"You still lost some work time." Mallory folded the bills into Sally's hand.

"Really, Detective, I . . ." Sally looked past Mallory, a curious expression on her face.

Mallory turned toward the street just as a brown sedan with dark-tinted windows pulled up. Later, Mallory would recall that at that second, everything seemed to move in slow motion: the car window rolling down, the burst of fire, the explosion of red that rose into the air in liquid streams and solid splinters as Sally shattered into a million pieces before her eyes.

She'd recall reaching behind her into her waistband at the same time she'd heard the sound of return gunfire, and she'd remember being surprised, because she'd tried but hadn't been able to draw her handgun, her fingers unexpectedly slippery with what she would later realize was Sally's blood. She'd know that she'd slumped to the ground, cradling Sally, and that when the shooting stopped, she'd looked up to find Charlie leaning over her, his phone in one hand as he called for backup, his other hand wiping something wet and sticky from her face.

At some point, Joe had shown up, and she'd heard him tell Charlie to take her out of there, to get her home, and Charlie's quiet words: "I'll take care of her. . . ."

TWENTY-THREE

Charlie opened Mallory's bag and sorted through its contents, searching for her keys. Pocketing them, he got out of the car and walked around to the passenger side. He opened the door and reached over Mallory's still form to unfasten her seat belt.

"Come on, Mal," he said softly. "We need to get you inside, get you cleaned up."

It didn't take an EMT to tell she was in shock, and he wasn't sure he shouldn't take her directly to the nearest emergency room. He was debating that possibility when she moved toward the door. He helped her out and supported her as she walked with a staggered gait. Charlie fumbled momentarily with the key, then pushed the front door open and slammed it closed behind them with his foot. Once inside, he dropped her bag to the floor.

"We need to get you cleaned up," he repeated, wondering just how they were going to do that. "Guess your shower's upstairs, right?"

He took her hand and helped her up the steps. At the top of the stairs, he rightly guessed that the middle door of three on the left was the bathroom, and he steered her in. Mallory stood like a mannequin, her face pasty under the smears of blood where he'd tried to wipe away the worst of it. Her shirt was covered in bits and pieces of Sally's bone and blood and tissue, and he realized there was no way she was capable of removing anything.

He turned on the shower and adjusted the temperature to moderately warm. Then, because she began to shake, he increased the hot water a little.

"Under other circumstances, I'd be enjoying this," he told her as he began to strip off her clothing. "As a matter of fact, I've been thinking a lot about doing exactly this, these past few days."

He dropped the bloodied clothing on the floor and turned her body in the direction of the shower. "But right now . . . not so much . . ."

He redirected the showerhead so that the water would rain down on her head. He unbuttoned his own shirt and took it off, then pulled his T-shirt over his head.

"Nope, not the way I planned it, Mal." He helped her into the shower and stood just beyond the plastic curtain. "I know this isn't the time, but I gotta tell you, you're one beautiful woman."

He wet a washcloth and wiped the blood from her face and neck, moved on to her chest.

"I promise I'll tell you again, when the time's better." He rinsed the cloth and muttered to himself between clenched teeth, "Take one for the team, Wanamaker. Sometimes you have to take one for the team. . . ."

When she'd been washed clean, he turned off the water and wrapped her in a towel, then sat her on the toilet seat and dried her hair as best he could. There was a white terry-cloth robe on the back of the bathroom door, and he wrapped her in it and tied it at the waist, then led her down the hall to her bedroom. He pulled back the light blue coverlet and helped her to lie down.

"I'm going to make you some . . . I don't know, tea or something." He debated. Did she drink hot tea? He tried to recall if he'd seen her drink hot anything. He had heard a kettle whistling in the background last night on the phone. "So, tea, yeah. We'll go with tea. You stay right here, Mal. I'll be right back."

He was back in five minutes, steaming-hot tea in a white mug. Placing it atop a magazine on the bedside table, he sat down on the bed next to her still body and took her hands.

"Mallory." He waited, hoping her eyes would follow the sound of his voice. He'd been just about ready to give up, just about to decide that both he and the chief had been wrong, that she should have gone to the ER, just about to call 911 for an ambulance, when she turned her head.

"I did this to her," she whispered, her eyes brimming.

"No, Mallory. Regina Girard did this to Sally. Not you."

"Somehow she knew. That Sally talked to me. Told me where she was. Or else she was following me." She covered her face with her hands. "She was afraid that Regina would find out she talked to me, and I promised her she'd never know. I promised her I'd never put her in danger, and she believed me. She trusted me and now she's dead."

"It isn't your fault."

"Yes, it is. I should have . . ." She started to sit upright.

"Listen to me." Charlie placed his hands on her shoulders and gently pushed her back down. "Regina Girard is a psychopath. Sally didn't give you any information about Regina that we wouldn't have gotten sooner or later anyway."

"Then why did she kill her?"

"Because she wanted to. Because she felt like it. Because she could."

Her hands still covering her face, Mallory began to weep, long racking sobs that seemed to come from someplace deep within her. Charlie rested her against his chest and let her ride out the storm.

When it finally subsided, she said, "I never really knew her. I don't know where she came from or how she came to do what she did. I used her to get information when I needed it, and every once in a while I'd toss her a few bucks for her time. But I never bothered to get to know her. All I knew about her could fit on one side of an index card."

"Could be she wanted it that way," he told her. "Some people are like that, you know? They don't want anyone getting too close."

Take you, for instance, he could have said, but didn't. It wasn't the time. They would have a conversation about her, one of these days, but it wasn't going to be today.

"Did you get her?" she asked.

"No," he told her. "Whoever was driving for her moved too damned fast for me to get a good shot. Which is probably why she missed hitting you. The car took off while she was still shooting."

"So how do we get her?" She was resting against him, her breath warm on his bare chest.

"I don't know." His hand moved the length of her back from her neck to her waist and back again, hoping to soothe. "We will get her, I promise you."

"I want to be there," she told him. "I want to be the one to pull the trigger."

"No, you don't. You're a civilian. You'll be charged with murder."

"I don't care."

He understood her frustration and her anger, her need to retaliate, to seek revenge. He'd felt it a hundred times, when he'd brought in someone who'd left a sad trail of victims behind, someone he knew could get around the system and be back on the streets in too short a time.

"You worry about finding Ryan and Courtney, okay? Let me take care of Regina Girard."

"How did she know?"

He hesitated, then told her, "She and some street punk were the ones who broke into your house the other night. She grabbed a handful of your notes. I'm guessing you'd jotted down something after you spoke with Sally last Saturday night, and she found it."

"Sally didn't really tell me anything except where Regina was staying sometimes, you know that."

"Yes, but Regina didn't."

"Why would she have broken into my house? How would she have even known that Sally and I spoke the other night?"

"Someone obviously saw you with Sally, maybe someone who might have known you've been asking questions about the playground shooting."

"There has to be a connection I'm not seeing."

Mallory sat quietly for a while, then pushed against him.

"Misty Bauer," she said. "When I spoke with her the first time, she kept watching the street—remember I told you how nervous she seemed? She even ripped up the card I'd given her and made a thing about dropping the pieces in the street."

"Ah," Charlie replied. "Yes, if Regina was convinced that Courtney had contacted her sister—or that she would contact her—she would have kept an eye on her. Watched where she went, who she spoke with."

"And if she knew I'd spoken with Misty, she might have thought I'd be worth watching, too . . ." Mallory frowned. "Maybe word was out that I was looking for Courtney."

"She'd have known who you were, all those years she was on the street, while you were on the force. No big secret there," he pointed out. "Conroy isn't that big, and there aren't that many women detectives."

"We need to talk to Linda Bauer," Mallory said. "She needs to keep a real close eye on Misty until this thing is over."

She started to get up.

"Where do you think you're going?" he asked.

"To get my phone."

"Use mine. And stay put for a minute, will you? Shit, Mal, you were so white there for a while . . ." He stopped and shook his head. It didn't matter now. She was okay, seemed like herself again. The anger and frustration had brought her back. He knew what that was like, too.

He took his phone from his pocket and handed it to her.

"I don't know the number. It's in my phone."

"In the bag you had this morning?"

"Yes."

"I'll get it. Just sit here and wait a minute." He ran downstairs and found the bag on the floor where he'd dropped it. He opened it up and shifted things around, searching for the phone, wondering why women felt it necessary to carry around so much stuff: a brush, several tubes of lip balm, a small notebook, a couple of pens, a tiny tin of mints.

He found the phone in a side compartment, went back upstairs, and handed it to her.

"Call Linda Bauer, check up on Misty, then drink your tea."

"What tea?" She began to look up the number.

"The tea I made you." He pointed to the bedside table.

"You made me tea?" Her smile started slowly. She looked up. "What else did you do for me?"

"Cleaned you up." He shifted on the edge of the bed at the reminder.

"I guess I was a mess, wasn't I?"

"I've seen worse." Actually, he hadn't, but he didn't think that would be the best thing to say, under the circumstances.

"Where are my clothes?" she asked. "The ones I was wearing when—"

"In the bathroom," he cut in. "I can put them in the washer for you, if you tell me where it is."

"No," she told him. "I want to do that. I need to see it."

Her jaw set firmly, and she began to dial.

"Crap," she said and made a face. "Voice mail. I guess Linda's not home from work yet. . . ."

She waited a second, then said, "Linda, hello, it's Mallory Russo. If you could give me a call when you get in . . . or Misty, if you hear this message before your mom gets home, please give me a call. It's very important. Here's my number again. . . ."

She repeated the number, then ended the call.

"I wonder if I should have been more explicit." She frowned.

"What could you have said on a message that wouldn't have sent that woman into a panic?"

"Good point." She nodded. "Then again, a little panic might be a good thing."

She lay back against the pillows and seemed to be studying his face. When she reached for him and pulled him to her, he offered no resistance.

"Where's your shirt, Detective Wanamaker?" she asked.

"With yours, on the bathroom floor."

"Did you get into the shower with me?"

"Don't you remember?"

"No."

"Then if I said yes, we showered together, would you think we'd already passed that hurdle?"

"Which hurdle is that?"

"Seeing each other naked."

"Ha. Nice try." She tried unsuccessfully to smile. "I think I'd re-member that."

"I'm crushed that you don't remember." He tucked the quilt up around her. Despite the warmth of the late-afternoon sun coming in through the window, her skin was still cool to the touch.

"You want a window open?" he asked.

"Just the back one, maybe." Her eyes were at half-mast, but they followed him across the room.

He pulled up the shade and opened the window. A refreshing breeze blew in.

"You've had a really bad couple of days here." He returned to her bedside, leaned over her, and kissed the side of her mouth. "Try to get a little sleep, and . . ."

"We need to look at the film that Ryan made," she protested and started to sit up.

"Uh-uh. I can look at them while you rest."

"I feel fine, honest." She pushed his arms away. "We need to go out and look . . ."

"It's too late in the day, it'll be dark soon. I'll watch Ryan's films and later we'll compare notes, okay? And first thing in the morning, we'll see if we can locate any of the places that look promising."

"Don't you need to get home with your mom?"

He glanced at the clock on her bedside table. "She won't be home for a while yet."

"Is she . . . out?" Mallory hesitated to say it.

"She's at AA." He nodded when he saw Mallory's eyes widen slightly. "Yeah. She figured she needed to go a few times before she leaves for rehab this weekend."

"At least she's trying."

"I think that her knowing that Jilly is being taken care of has removed a huge weight from her shoulders. I think she was really overwhelmed. Maybe now she feels more free to take care of her own issues."

"Good for her," she said, her voice starting to drop, her eyelids fluttering.

"I'll be downstairs," he told her.

"Charlie?"

"Yeah?"

"How long are you going to stay?"

"As long as you want," he told her. "As long as you need me . . ."

It was just after six the next morning when Mallory's phone began to ring. She struggled to sit up, then fumbled with first her quilt, then her bag, as she searched in the semi-darkness for her phone. By the time she found it, the ringing had stopped. She stretched and yawned, then sat back down on the side of the bed, engulfed by a great sadness as she recalled the events of the previous afternoon.

In her mind's eye she saw Sally standing in her doorway, saw the look of curiosity in her eyes when she first spied the car that had pulled up. Then there'd been that loud and unexpected blast that had stunned her and had blown Sally away, leaving her to slump onto Mallory. She could remember feeling for her gun, but her hands had been too slippery to hold on to it. Then that sense of helplessness had swept over her as she'd tried to keep Sally on her feet, even while she'd known the woman was dead. Remembering was worse than the worst dream she'd ever had.

Mallory shuddered, sick inside.

"*I would never put you in danger, Sally. I never have,*" she'd said. "*That's God's truth . . .*"

Shaken by the memory, she stood and walked to the bathroom. She paused in the doorway, expecting to see her bloody clothes, but they were gone. She looked in the hamper, but they weren't in there, either. When she was finished in the bathroom, she stood at the top of the steps. The house was very quiet, and she assumed Charlie had left.

He'd been wonderful to her yesterday, she remembered that. Kind and sweet and thoughtful and strong. The knowledge that he'd stripped her of her clothes and showered her should have caused her to blush, but didn't. That he'd cared enough to do that for her so that she wouldn't have to do it herself—now, that made her heart beat a little faster.

She was almost to the stairwell when she heard sounds from the first floor.

Please God, not again. She froze, one hand on the railing.

"Mal?" Charlie's voice called up to her.

"Yes." She cleared her throat and tried to ignore the fact that, for a moment, her knees had gone weak.

"Was that Linda Bauer on the phone?" He'd come to the bottom of the steps and was looking up at her.

"I missed the call," she told him, and turned back to the bedroom for her bag and phone.

She looked up the last incoming call. It was a local number, and it took a minute for her to recognize it.

"Oh," she called down to him. "It's the Bauers' number. I guess Linda finally got my message."

She hit the button to return the last call and waited for someone to pick up. When she heard Linda's voice, she said, "Linda, hi. It's Mallory Russo. I just missed a call from this number a minute ago."

"That was me," Linda told her. "I meant to call you last night, but I had to work late. By the time I got your message, it was too late to call. You said it was important, but I'm guessing you haven't found Courtney or you'd be much more excited than you are."

"No, we haven't found them yet, but I do have a lead that might work out. I'll definitely let you know about that. In the meantime, we need to talk about Misty."

"What about her?"

"I'm almost positive that she knows where Courtney and Ryan are."

"Impossible." Linda brushed off the possibility. "If she knew, she'd have told me, and we'd have gone there and brought her home."

"That's exactly why she didn't tell you, Linda. Courtney doesn't want to be found. She's afraid you'll come after her. I think Courtney made her sister promise not to let anyone know where they are."

"That's crazy. Why would she do that? Of course I'd come for her. She's my daughter." Linda's voice rose in anger. "Why would she put me through this, put Mary Corcoran and everyone else through this?"

"Because Courtney knows that the police weren't the only ones looking for them." She explained her theory to Linda.

"Oh, dear God," Linda gasped. "You think this woman . . . this killer . . . is looking for Courtney?"

"I do. And I think she suspects that Courtney's been in touch with Misty, and I think she's been keeping an eye on her."

"Misty? She's been watching Misty?" The panic in Linda's voice was unmistakable.

"I think so. I suspect she's been in contact with Misty, but I have no proof of that. I asked Misty but she denied it."

"Why didn't you tell me this sooner?"

"Because all I had were suspicions, Linda. I don't know that it would have helped your situation to know what I suspected since I had no proof."

"And now you do?"

Mallory debated on whether or not to tell Linda about Sally.

"Let's just say that now my suspicions are stronger."

"Dear God." Linda began to cry. "I couldn't take it if something were to happen to Misty."

"We're going to do our best to make sure that nothing does, Linda." Even as she spoke the words, Mallory knew there was little she could do to protect the younger Bauer daughter short of asking Joe to put a guard on her. Which might not be a bad idea, she reasoned. "Linda, has Misty left for school yet?"

"About fifteen minutes ago. She had to be in early for some project she's working on."

"What time does school let out?"

"Two forty-five."

"With your permission, I'd like to ask Father Burch to keep Misty there when school is over until we can have someone pick her up and bring her home," Mallory offered.

"Could you do that?"

"Sure. If I have to, I'll drive over and pick her up myself."

"Maybe I should bring her home. Maybe I should take the day off and—"

Mallory interrupted. "I think the best thing everyone can do right now is to maintain their normal routine. She might be better off in school, where there are a lot of people around her."

"You're probably right." Linda sighed deeply. "And you don't even know for sure that your theory is the right one, do you?"

"No. It's the only one we have right now, but no. We aren't certain of anything. Which is why we haven't had this discussion sooner. I didn't want to upset you unnecessarily. You already have enough to worry about."

"I appreciate that, please don't think I don't." Linda paused, then said, "I got a call from my ex yesterday. He's agreed to work on bringing us up-to-date with child support." She paused again.

"That's terrific, Linda. I'm glad to hear it."

"Yes, well, all that back support isn't going to be of any use if something horrible happens to both my kids."

"We're doing our best to prevent that, Linda," Mallory told her. She ended the call praying that their best was going to be good enough.

TWENTY-FOUR

Mallory handed Charlie a cup of coffee.

"I can't believe you slept on my sofa all night. You were so sweet to do that." She took a sip from her mug. "But what about your mother? Was she all right by herself?"

"She wasn't by herself. She and one of her friends—her oldest friend who is her most loyal drinking buddy, by the way—had a girls' night last night after the AA meeting."

"Was that a good idea? With your mom going into rehab in a few days?"

"Gail went to AA with her. She and my mom apparently spent most of the night talking things out. Upshot is that Gail's thinking now might be a good time for her to stop drinking, too."

"Wow. That would be great for both of them."

"Yeah, it would. We'll see if either or both of them make it. I hope they do. Might be easier for them if they have each other to do things with—things besides meet at the corner bar. On the other hand, it might be more difficult in the long run. If one of them leaves rehab before completing the program, or later falls off the wagon, it could hurt the other's chances of succeeding. But at least they're both making an effort right now. We'll see what happens."

"Well, I appreciate you staying here with me."

"I couldn't very well leave you alone."

"You could have. I slept like the dead." She made a face. "Poor choice of words."

She took a sip of coffee before asking, "Charlie, what happened to my clothes?"

"Joe sent someone over to pick them up last night. I put them in a bag and handed them over. You were out cold, so I didn't bother to wake you."

"They wanted my clothes for evidence?"

He nodded.

"Thanks." She took another sip. "I want to fill you in on my conversation with Linda Bauer."

When she finished, she added, "Before I came downstairs, I called Father Burch. He's going to track down Misty's schedule, and they'll be keeping an eye on her. And he's having the school on a very quiet lockdown."

"Why doesn't he just tell Misty what's going on and lock her in the office for the day? What the hell is a 'quiet' lockdown?"

"He doesn't want to scare her, so he's not going to isolate her. And quiet lockdown, according to Father Burch, means that all the doors except the front door will be locked, and he'll be hanging around the front for the day."

"Oh, right. A man in a white collar and a black suit should have no trouble turning back a gun-toting psychopath. Good idea." Charlie frowned. "Then again, maybe he'll be able to stop her dead with one of those big crosses."

"Very funny. Let's just hope that we're wrong about Regina using Misty to get to Courtney. Maybe we're giving her too much credit. Maybe she isn't as smart as we think she is."

"I think she's smarter."

Mallory turned on the power to her DVD player. "This is it. If the answer is here, we have to find it now. Today. We're out of time, Charlie."

"Are you sure you feel up to this?"

"I really don't have a choice."

Charlie took a seat on the sofa opposite the television screen. There'd been no reason to reply. She was right and he knew it. They were down to the wire. They could not take the chance that Regina Girard—or anyone else—was looking for the two teenagers.

Mallory sat next to Charlie and pushed START on the remote. Blue sky filled the screen as the title—*Hidden Paths to Freedom: A Film by Ryan Corcoran*—appeared.

"He starts this so well, don't you think?" Mallory pointed to the TV. "His film teacher was justifiably proud. Watch the screen off to the right; see that small dot against the sky?"

"I'm watching. I hadn't noticed that before."

They both leaned forward as the dot grew larger and took the shape of a hawk that rode a shaft of air ever higher.

"He captures that feeling of freedom, you see? Now watch as the camera comes back down to earth. Watch that grove of trees there, the ones next to that barn."

Shadows shifted and moved along the tree line toward the barn.

They watched three figures emerge from amid the trees and slip along the side of the barn, where a door opened and closed so quickly they'd have missed it if it hadn't swallowed up the three moving shapes.

"And just that quickly, three more runaway slaves moved closer to safety. Closer to freedom," Charlie said quietly.

The camera closed in on the barn, then swept the farm quickly.

"Does that place look familiar to you?" she asked.

"It's hard to tell, he panned the landscape so fast. I reran this section several times already this morning, but I don't know. Maybe in slow motion."

"We can come back to that. Keep watching. There are about eight different places on this film. Did you recognize any of them?"

"Maybe. I'm not sure. I might know a few of them."

They watched mostly in silence, with only an occasional comment from Charlie. Finally, when they'd come to the end, he said, "There are images from that first farm in several other places throughout the film, though it's not really apparent if you don't know the place. The tractor in the wheat field, the well with the red scarves tied to the crosspiece, and the second-floor hayloft in that last frame. I'm almost positive it's the old Mansfield place out near Druid's Hill. There are three or four other places there that I recognized as well."

"Is that old church—the one with the boarded-up windows—is that the one out on Malvern Road?"

"I think so, yes."

"Let's put them all in order of closest to farthest, and we'll start checking them out." Mallory rose and grabbed her bag. "I'll even let you drive."

"Not so fast." He grabbed her arm. "We need to call Joe and let him know what's going on."

"I'll do that from the car. Come on."

"And I'm not so sure we shouldn't call for backup," he said thoughtfully.

She laughed. "Backup from who? There's no one on the Conroy police force I'd trust with my back, except for you. I think my chances for survival are better with Regina Girard than with any of my former fellows on the force."

Charlie looked unconvinced.

"Besides," she continued, "Joe isn't likely to take anyone off the sniper case to follow us around the countryside on little more than a feeling that maybe the kids are hiding in one of these places. If he thinks we need backup, he'll say so."

It was a tough point to argue.

She was right about Joe not taking anyone off the sniper case, but not for the reason she assumed. When she called his office, she was told by a very excited Marlene that the chief was in city hall getting ready for a press conference.

"Haven't you heard?" Marlene said excitedly. "They caught the sniper this morning!"

"No, I hadn't heard. That's wonderful. I'm sure the chief is relieved."

"Oh, he's beside himself," Marlene went on. "It's a shame they couldn't have brought him in alive, but I doubt anyone's going to be mourning this guy. He's kept this city tied up like a pretzel for the last few weeks, scared the bejesus out of everyone, not to mention those folks he shot at."

"Who was it?"

"Some homeless guy."

"I'm glad that's over with. I know it was a nightmare for everyone down there. I'll try to get in touch with the chief myself, but just in case he's not answering his cell, please let him know it's important that we talk today. Tell him that Detective Wanamaker and I are checking out a few locations. He'll know what it's about."

"Will do." Marlene lowered her voice. "Mallory, are you all right? The chief told me what happened yesterday. Shame that girl had to get shot like that, and you being right there in the middle of it. And you not even being on duty anymore."

"I'm okay, thanks for asking."

"I was worried about you, Mal. You know that despite—"

"I do know, Marlene. And I appreciate it."

"I have another call coming in, honey. I'll let the chief know you called."

"Thanks. Oh, and Marlene . . . who brought down the sniper?"

Marlene's voice dropped even lower.

"That's the crazy part, if you ask me. It was your old partner, Cal Whitman. Brought him down with one shot to the head."

Mallory was quiet for a very long moment after closing the phone.

"What?" Charlie asked.

She told him the news.

"So what's your problem with that?"

"Cal Whitman barely qualifies on the range every year."

"Maybe he got lucky."

"He'd have to have gotten real lucky." She rolled down the window, and the light scent of wild roses wafted in. She leaned on the armrest and thought about Cal Whitman, and wondered if it was bitterness on her part that made her so skeptical. Maybe it had been a lucky shot.

And what did it matter, really, if the threat to the city was over and justice had been served?

It didn't matter, she told herself. The important thing was that the sniper was off the streets and was no longer terrorizing Conroy.

Still, if she'd had to make a list of the cops least likely to bag the sniper, Whitman's name would have been at the very top.

"I think we can eliminate the Townsends' farm," Charlie was saying as he drove farther into the countryside.

"Why?"

"Because people are living there, see?" He slowed the car and pulled to the side of the road. "There are several cars in the drive, and you can see the fields are being worked. I think it would be damned hard to be hiding out in a place like that. If you want to stop, I don't have a problem with it, but I think it's probably a waste of time."

"I agree. We can always stop back there if we turn up empty at all the others. What's the next closest?"

"Let me see the list."

She handed it to him, and he studied it for a minute.

"The Sumner place is about sixteen, seventeen miles from here." He gave back the list and started driving. "It's out near Boone. Do you know that area?"

"I don't."

"I only remember it because we used to play against the high school out there in football."

"That's one advantage of having grown up in the area. You know how to find places and things."

"If that doesn't work out, we'll move on to Lisfield and that barn Ryan spent so much time photographing. From there, I guess we'll try the Hoffmans' farm—that place was abandoned when I was a kid. I can't imagine it's been vacant all these years."

"Well, they say the housing market's tough."

He smiled. "This is the place on the film that had all the little out-buildings."

"All good places to hide, if you're hiding out," she noted, "though all those farms seemed to have a lot of little outbuildings."

She rested her head back against the seat. "Where would you go, if you were hiding?"

"Me? I'd probably go to a city. The bigger the crowd, the easier it is to disappear into it. How about you? Where would you go?"

"I'd hide in plain sight."

"That pretty much eliminates just about every place on our list," he reminded her. "They're all pretty much out of the way."

A mile later, he made a right turn onto a dirt-and-gravel road. Mallory sat up, taking in the scenery. There was dense hedgerow on both sides of the road.

"This would be a good place to hide," she said, and realized she was thinking out loud. "Who the hell would think to come looking for you here?"

"We did."

There was a lane off to the left, and Charlie followed it all the way through woods to a clearing where a dilapidated farmhouse stood. As in the film, the paint was worn off the clapboard and the chimney tilted at an odd angle.

"Doesn't look too safe, does it?" she noted.

"To Ryan and Courtney, just about anyplace probably looked safer than Conroy."

"Good point."

They got out of the car and began to look around. Charlie tested the steps leading up to the front of the house and found them soft, as were the deck boards on the porch. The front door pushed open with a good shove, and they stepped inside.

"If they're staying here, they haven't been in the front of the house." Charlie pointed to the floor. "There's an inch of dust, and it hasn't been disturbed."

"Maybe around the back."

"We'll walk around and look, but I doubt it. I can't imagine being in a place like this for three or more weeks and not going through the entire house at least once."

"Let's check the back, then."

They walked around to the rear of the house and found the back door open. There was evidence that some small animals—raccoons, most likely, or squirrels—had made themselves at home, but no sign of recent human habitation.

"We'll take a look in the barn, but I don't think this is the place," Charlie told her.

One look inside proved he was most likely right. The roof had fallen in a long time ago.

"I don't remember seeing that in the film," Mallory remarked as they walked back to the car.

Charlie turned and stared at the barn.

"Because it wasn't this farm," he said. "The barn in the film definitely had a roof. This isn't the place."

"Charlie, do you think we're just spinning our wheels?"

"Probably. If you have any better ideas, I'm all ears."

"I don't."

"Well, then, doing something is better than nothing. Just my opinion, of course."

When they were back on the road, Mallory asked, "How can people leave places like that to just rot? Especially places that could have some historical significance."

"Maybe that was one of the reasons behind Ryan making the film he made. Maybe he was trying to bring these places to light, make sure they got some attention so that they could be preserved."

"If they weren't well known, where did he get his information? How did he even know about these old farms?"

"Good question."

"Charlie, did you notice, in his credits, Ryan thanked someone for the stories," she said. "Corina something."

"Corina Rayburn?"

"That sounds right."

"He thanked Corina Rayburn?"

"You know her?"

"Sort of. She's Conroy's unofficial historian. Every town has one. You know, one person who knows everyone who ever lived in every house, going back a couple of hundred years. In Miz Rayburn's case, she probably did know everyone personally. She must be about nine hundred years old by now." He stopped at a stop sign, then made a right turn onto the paved road that eventually would take them back to the four-lane they'd driven in on. "She used to come to the schools each year and talk to the kids at assembly, tell them about the people who settled the town. She said she was the great-granddaughter of runaway slaves, that's how she knew so much about the subject, I guess."

Charlie paused, then turned to meet Mallory's eyes. They stared at each other thoughtfully for a long moment before he turned back to the road.

"Where does she live?" Mallory asked.

"She used to live on the farm she grew up on. The farm her father bought. The one where supposedly her great-grandparents hid out right before the end of the Civil War." He made a U-turn and headed back toward Conroy. "It's outside the city on Rayburn Road. She's preserved the farm, opens it several days a week as a sort of living history project."

"And she's how old?"

"Actually, my best guess, she'd be in her mideighties now. Last I heard, she had volunteers—including a few of her grandkids—working the farm."

"You think she'd hide Courtney and Ryan?"

"Who better to understand that sometimes, in order to stay alive, you have to stay out of sight?"

They had just pulled into the drive on Rayburn Road when Mallory's phone rang.

"Mallory, Kevin Burch here."

"Hi, Father. What's—"

He cut her off without apology. "Misty Bauer never showed up here at school this morning."

"What? Her mother said she left the house early, that she got a ride—"

"She never got here." The priest was obviously rattled.

"Did you call the police?"

"Yes."

"Does her mother know?"

"I just called her. I'm on my way over to her workplace right now."

"Maybe Misty decided to skip school today, maybe she and a friend—"

"I've spoken with all her friends. I thought the same thing at first. They're all here. She's the only one missing."

"The friend whose mother drove them in this morning . . ."

"She said Misty got up to the front door and said there was something she needed to do, that she'd be right in."

"Thanks for the heads-up, Father. Let me know if she turns up." Mallory turned to Charlie with worried eyes.

"Misty's not at school," she told him.

"I figured that. So the question is, where is she?"

"My guess is that she's either looking for Courtney or she's hiding from Regina or . . ."

"Or Regina has her and they're looking for Courtney together."

"Shit." Mallory slapped the dashboard with an open palm.

There were two vehicles parked in the yard between the neatly kept old farmhouse and the barn. Charlie pulled up next to a beat-up red pickup and cut the engine.

"Miz Rayburn used to have this set up just the way it would have been in the mid–eighteen hundreds," Charlie told Mallory. "Farm animals—cows, sheep, pigs, goats, chickens, that sort of thing—that kids could come and see close up. For a lot of city kids, that was as close as they'd ever get, you know? The local schools would come here for class trips. Maybe they still do. Miz Rayburn would give a talk about farm life and about slavery, and she'd explain the Underground Railroad and how many runaways passed through this area. I remember her telling us how proud we could be that people right here around Conroy were brave enough to take a stand and risk their lives so that other people could live free."

He unfastened his seat belt. "It was very moving, actually."

"It must have been. You still remember it so vividly."

"She made a big impression on me. I can't believe I didn't think of her sooner." He looked at the house. "Let's go let her know we're here, see what we can find out."

Mallory followed Charlie around the house to the front door.

"It's so quiet out here," she said.

Charlie frowned. "Maybe too quiet."

He rang the doorbell, and they heard it echo through the house. When no one answered, he knocked several times, but there was no response.

"Maybe she doesn't live here anymore," Mallory suggested.

She stood on tiptoes to peer through the front windows.

"There's still furniture in there. Someone's living here."

Charlie stood on the top step and surveyed the property. "Late morning on a working farm, you'd expect people to be out and about."

She pointed beyond the barn where several black-and-white cows shared the pasture with as many goats and three horses. "Someone's been here to let the animals out. Maybe they went somewhere. Or maybe they're in the big barn there."

"Let's take a look."

The barn door was partially open, but rather than swing it wide, Charlie paused as if listening. Mallory leaned her head toward the opening but couldn't hear a sound from within. He motioned for her to get behind him as he drew his gun from inside his jacket; she pulled hers from the small of her back. He opened the door slightly and slid in, and she followed. They crouched low in the dim light and looked around. There were stalls on both sides of the barn, and they all appeared empty.

"I don't hear anything," she whispered.

"Neither do I."

"Let's check the outbuildings," she suggested. "You take the small barn, I'll take the icehouse."

"All right," he said. "Do you have your phone with you?"

"It's in my bag, in the car."

"Stop and get it, then dial my number. Leave the line open, keep in touch. It'll act sort of like a walkie-talkie."

She did just that, tucking the phone into the pocket of her light linen jacket.

"Hey, Mallory," he called to her as she turned toward the icehouse. "Don't be a hero. If you think something isn't right, it probably isn't. Let me know."

"You, too."

There were leaves piled around the bottom of the icehouse door. Mallory figured if someone was hiding in there, the leaves would have been swept to one side, but she checked inside anyway. There were moss-covered stone steps leading down to a running stream between two large rocks. It was obvious no one had been there for a while. She backed out and reached for her phone.

"Charlie, I don't think anyone's been in the icehouse in a long time. I'm moving on to the chicken house." She paused, waiting for a response. "Charlie?"

She frowned, the phone held close to her face. The call had dropped. She dialed again and listened in vain. No service.

She dropped the phone into her pocket and headed toward the back of the chicken house. She hesitated outside the door, then opened it just enough to slip through. Inside it was dark and warm and humid and smelled of straw and feathers. The windows were cloudy with dust and cobwebs and let in precious little light. Mallory took three steps along the wall, her gun in her right hand. Wooden bins sat waist-high off the floor on both sides of the narrow room; in several, hens sat on straw nests as if on thrones. She lowered her gun hand and stepped into the aisle between the roosts. By the time she heard the *whoosh* sound, it was too late to react. Mallory fell face-forward as something struck the back of her knees and her legs were cut out from under her.

"Drop the gun!" someone demanded, then, "Get it. Pick it up."

Mallory turned her face and looked up as Misty Bauer grabbed the handgun from the floor and backed away in a flash. She pointed the gun at Mallory with violently shaking hands.

"Misty, for God's sake, put it down before you shoot someone," Mallory told her. "It's Mallory Russo . . ."

She heard the floorboards squeak as Misty drew near.

"Pick your head up so I can see your face." Misty leaned over slightly, looked down at Mallory, and then raised her head.

"It's her. The detective I told you about. She's okay, Court."

"Stand up." The voice from behind Mallory ordered. "Get up slowly. Misty, give me the gun."

"Courtney, I—"

"I said, give me the gun."

"It's okay," Mallory turned to Misty. "Give it to her. Carefully, though. That's not a toy."

Misty passed the pistol to her sister.

"Courtney, I'm so glad you're safe. You, too, Misty. Everyone is worried about you."

The gun shook in Courtney's unsteady hands.

"I'm here to help you. You and Ryan." Mallory looked around the small space. "Where is Ryan?"

"She shot him." Courtney's eyes welled with tears. "She *shot* him."

No need to ask who *she* was.

"Where is he?"

"In the little barn," Courtney told her.

"Where is she?" Mallory asked.

"I don't know." Courtney shook her head.

"Is Ryan still alive?"

"I don't know," Courtney said.

Misty's words came in a rush. "She had me and Courtney in the barn and Ryan came in and she turned around and she shot him and Courtney hit her with a rake and she fell and she started to get up and we ran . . ."

"Okay, okay." Mallory reached for the gun. "I'm going to need to have that back now."

Courtney handed it over without protest.

"There's a detective here with me, he's going . . ." She stopped in midsentence. "Shit."

She remembered where Charlie had been headed.

"Stay here. Don't—"

Two shots rang out.

"You stay here until I come back for you. Do not leave, hear?"

Both girls nodded silently. Mallory pushed open the door. She stepped outside into the bright sunlight, momentarily blinded. She heard another shot and ducked behind a rusted-out tractor that stood between the chicken house and the small barn.

She sat as still as possible and listened.

The shots were all contained inside the small barn, but who had fired them? Had any of those shots hit its mark? Which way in would be the safest?

She studied the building. There was a door on the second floor that most likely led to a hayloft, but there was no way to get to it. Crouching close to the ground, she ran to the back of the barn and tried the door she found there. It opened quietly. She held it in place for a moment, listening. When there was no sound from within, she opened it another inch or two and peered through. The door opened into a tack room. Saddles were slung over sawhorses, and several bridles hung from hooks on the wall. She slipped through the opening and crouched down, then crawled on her hands and knees to the opening that she suspected led into the rest of the barn.

Her back to the wall, she sat and listened for movement. She could hear the sound of deliberate footfalls on the straw floor, but they weren't close. She crept around the corner, and fell over Ryan Corcoran's body.

She sought a pulse and found one, stronger than she'd expected. At her touch, he opened his eyes, and she put a hand over his mouth.

"Shhh," she told him, and pointed to the room beyond.

Ryan nodded slowly and reached for her hand.

"Where were you hit?" she asked.

He moved her hand to his abdomen, and her fingers touched the warm stickiness of his blood on his shirt. Her fingers felt the skin beneath the shirt, found the entry wound. While still bleeding, it wasn't a steady flow, which she hoped was a good sign.

"Hang on, Ryan," she whispered. "We'll get you out as soon as we can."

She opened her phone, hoping to find there was service, but the line was dead.

"Courtney . . ."

"She's fine. She and Misty are fine. Now you hold on, okay?" She gave his hand a squeeze, then let go and began to inch along the floor behind a stack of hay bales.

"Oh, come on out and play," Mallory heard a woman's voice cooing. "Come on, big fella. Come on out."

She peeked between a stack of bales and saw a thin woman with short spiky black hair standing in the center of the room, her legs spread wide, one hand on her hip. Mallory couldn't see her other hand, but from the way it was extended, she knew it held a firearm, and she knew it was pointed at Charlie.

And since Charlie wasn't shooting, she reasoned, he must have taken a hit.

Mallory had never imagined a time when she'd raise a gun to shoot someone in the back. She didn't relish the thought, even if that someone was Regina Girard.

"Come on, I know you're back there," Regina taunted. "You can't hide forever. You know I'm gonna find you."

The woman fired at some farm equipment parked on the opposite side of the room, then laughed.

"I'm real good with this little baby, don't think I'm not. I been practicing," she said. "You're a fun guy, you know, but I got other business to attend to here, so I'm just going to have to finish this now. Wish we had a little more time, I could show you just how much fun I can be.

"So we're going on three here." She walked slowly in Charlie's direction, and the countdown began. "One ... two ..."

Mallory stood and took aim. Hearing her, Regina turned, the gun pointed directly at Mallory, who managed to fire off the first shot. She hit her target square in the chest, and the gun fell from Regina's hand as she dropped to her knees on the dirt floor. Mallory came forward from the shadows and kicked Regina's gun across the room, then knelt and felt for a pulse. The woman was still alive, but bloody foam was bubbling up at her lips.

"Charlie!" Mallory called.

Charlie was already walking toward her from at least twenty feet away from where Regina had aimed.

"What are you doing over there?" Mallory frowned. "I thought she was shooting at you over *here*. I thought you were wounded and she was getting ready to finish you off."

"Guess I'm a better actor than I thought I was." He looked down at Regina. Her eyes were open, but she wasn't moving.

Mallory stared at Charlie. "I thought she was going to kill you."

"If she could have, she would have." He nodded. "No question."

"She shot Ryan, left him for dead," Mallory told him. "He's still alive." She searched her pocket for her phone, but her pockets were empty. "I must have dropped it. Didn't get any reception anyway. See if you have better luck."

He dialed and the call went right through.

"Ambulance is on its way." He put an arm around her and drew her close, kissed her mouth. "I'm so glad you shot before she did. I don't know what I'd have done if she'd shot first."

"Neither do I." She kissed him back, drinking in the feel of his lips. She pulled away long before she was satisfied. "We need to let

Ryan know that the ambulance will be here soon. He's scared out of his mind."

"Where is he?"

"Back there, right outside the tack room."

"Did you find Courtney?"

Mallory nodded. "She and Misty are in the henhouse. I'll get them, you take care of Ryan."

She started toward the door, but he grabbed her by the arm and held her for just a second.

"Mal, I'm really grateful that you're a better shot than she was."

"So am I." Mallory nodded. "So am I . . ."

TWENTY-FIVE

The ambulances arrived only minutes before the car that brought Linda Bauer and Chief Drabyak. Notified by the chief that her grandson had been found alive, Mary Corcoran had run to the high school and begged Father Burch to drive her to the Rayburn farm. They were followed up the lane to the farmhouse by a very confused Corina Rayburn and her equally befuddled niece.

Charlie watched as the gurney carrying Ryan was lifted into the back of the ambulance. After much discussion, Mary still was not permitted to accompany him, so Father Burch steered her back into his car and followed closely behind as the EMTs rushed the boy to the hospital.

"The medics said his vital signs were pretty strong, considering." Chief Drabyak walked toward Charlie. "You did a hell of a job, Wanamaker. Nice debut."

"I can't take all the credit, you know that," Charlie told him.

"Yeah, I do know that."

Their eyes followed Mallory, who was joining Linda Bauer and her daughters on the back steps of the house where Corina Rayburn stood.

"You make a good team," Drabyak observed.

Charlie nodded. "Yeah."

"Wish I could bring her back," the chief said.

"Ever think of that? Offering her job back?"

Drabyak shook his head. "It wouldn't be good for her. Those bastards would eat her alive."

It was on Charlie's tongue to suggest that maybe the chief could do with a few less bastards, but he held it. It wasn't his place to tell Drabyak how to run his department. Besides, he knew how it was when cops closed ranks. He'd been part of that himself, once upon a time. He understood.

"Much as I'd like to, for her own sake, I can't bring her back."

The chief turned to Charlie and said, "Be careful with her. She's not as tough as she'd like you to think. And she isn't as much of a loner as she'd like to be."

Charlie had already figured that out for himself, but didn't say so. He just let the chief talk.

"You seem to know her pretty well."

"Probably better than anyone." Drabyak glanced over at Charlie. "Not the way you're thinking."

"I wasn't thinking that."

"She was top in her class, she tell you that?" Charlie shook his head, and the chief smiled. "I didn't think so. She had all the makings of a great cop. She was a great cop. She moved up quickly through the ranks, faster than anyone I had here. Not because of what they said about her and me. That was just ludicrous. I did have a personal relationship with her—still do—but it was more like father–daughter, you understand?"

Charlie thought he did.

"My wife and I never had kids. Wanted them, but never had them. Then this kid came out from the academy, so smart, so insightful—I told my wife she reminded me of myself when I was that young." Drabyak smiled again, this time, Charlie thought, maybe from the memory. "June—that's my wife—met her a few times, we had her over for dinner now and then, this before I was chief, by the way. Over the years, we grew close. June and I really care about her. She doesn't really have anyone, understand?"

"Why are you telling me this?" Charlie asked.

"Because I don't want you to believe what you've heard about her and me. I don't want you even to wonder about it."

"I really hadn't, sir."

"She never had a father, did you know that?"

"She told me, yes."

"Did she?" Drabyak looked surprised at first, then smiled again. "Good. That's good. She told you that. She tell you everything?"

"I don't know about everything, but she told me about her mother . . . her aunt not really wanting her . . ."

"Makes you wonder what some people are thinking, you know? June and I, well, we would have done just about anything you could think of to have had a daughter like Mallory." Drabyak blew out a long breath. "Well, that's a conversation for another day. In the meantime, we didn't have this one, you and I. Capisce?"

Charlie nodded. He understood perfectly.

"Hey, Chief. You've had a big day today." Mallory was walking toward them. "You bag the sniper, your new man brings home the missing kids, and a killer is down for the count."

"Doesn't get much bigger than that around here," the chief replied. "Congratulations on your part in finding the kids and helping to take down Girard."

"She did that on her own, Chief," Charlie said.

Drabyak looked at Mallory. "Is that right? You shot her?"

Mallory nodded.

"I'm going to have to get statements from both of you. This is going to require an investigation, you know that." He looked annoyed. "It's a technicality, but it's going to be a pain in the ass."

"It was justifiable, Chief, she—," Charlie began, and Drabyak cut him off.

"There's no question in my mind that it was, but there's still going to be questions about why she was there, why she was armed, and why she was the one who was doing the shooting." He held out his hand to Mallory. "I'm going to need that SIG I know you have tucked in your waistband."

"Like you said, it's a technicality," Mallory said as she handed over the pistol. "I've weathered a lot worse than that from the department, Joe. Just assign someone to the investigation and get on with it."

"Right." The chief stood with hands in his pockets and watched the ambulance carrying Regina Girard speed away.

"I'll assign someone . . . maybe Hendricks. He never got caught up in all the bullshit, and he's an honest cop."

"There you go," Mallory said cheerfully—mostly, Charlie suspected, for the chief's benefit. "I'm available anytime he wants to talk to me."

"Did you get a shot off?" Drabyak turned to Charlie, who nodded and turned over his gun without waiting to be asked. He knew the drill. You fire the weapon, you forfeit it until the investigation has been completed.

"The press is going to be all over this," the chief said as if it had just occurred to him that this was newsworthy. "We were having a press conference at six PM to talk about the sniper case, but we'll do this at the same time." He turned to Charlie and said, "Go home and get cleaned up. Tonight you make your debut on local TV."

"What about Mallory?" Charlie asked.

"I'm not going to be part of this." She shook her head. "You're the cop, you tell the tale, you take the glory."

"Doesn't seem fair," he protested.

"Doesn't matter," she said firmly. "I don't want any part of the publicity. The department has had one hell of a big day. Take the credit, look good for the hometown crew. Leave me out of it."

She turned to the chief and said, "I hear Cal brought the sniper down."

"That's the story I got."

"Interesting."

"I thought so, too." The chief nodded without conviction.

"So who was this guy, this sniper? What's his name? Where's he from?" she asked.

"He's been identified as Hector Gomez. He's originally from Florida, been up here for about a dozen or so years. Lived with the other street people down in that shelter they made under the Melrose Bridge."

Mallory and the chief stared at each other. Charlie had the sense they were almost reading each other's minds.

"The newspapers have been saying the sniper was using an assault weapon."

Drabyak nodded. "He was."

"So where did a guy who's been living on the streets for over a decade get an assault weapon with enough firepower to have kept this city under siege for weeks? And how was it that he never actually shot anyone? What kind of a sniper ties up a town like that, but never hits a target?"

"Been asking myself the same question," the chief replied.

"I'm guessing he had military training, though, right?"

"None that I've heard about." Drabyak shook his head slowly. "We found a brother in Miami who tells us as far as he knows, Hector's never even owned a handgun."

"Curious." Mallory nodded. "But how lucky for the city of Conroy that Patrolman Whitman was there to disarm him and take him out."

"Lucky, yes." The chief raised both eyebrows. "Lucky, too, that Detective Toricelli just happened to be closing in on Gomez at the same time his good buddy Whitman was taking the shot."

"Well, now, wasn't that a coincidence?" Mallory said flatly.

"Wasn't it, though?"

"How do you suppose that coincidence came about?"

"I'm still waiting for a plausible explanation." The chief turned and pointed to the news van that was just pulling up the drive. "I'm going to try to head them off for now. Why don't you take off while you can? Charlie, I'll see you a little before six in the mayor's press room. Second floor, city hall. Mal, we'll be in touch."

"I saw you speaking with the Bauers," Charlie said after Drabyak walked away. "How are they holding up?"

"Great. Terrific." Mallory smiled. "When you think about what could have happened out here . . . when you consider how this could have ended . . ."

"It ended just right." He took her hand. "It ended the way it's supposed to."

He tugged on her hand. "Come on, I'll drive you home."

On the way, they listened to the news station on the radio, where the afternoon talk show was all abuzz about the capture of the sniper. The story of the missing teens being found hadn't yet hit, though Charlie knew it was only a matter of time. He wasn't happy that the part Mallory played was going to be shoved under the table as much as possible. It bothered him a lot more than it seemed to bother her.

"Go get handsome for the cameras," Mallory told him when he pulled up in front of her house. "And call your mother. Let her know you're a hero."

"You're the hero."

"Bullshit. Take the credit for the department, if not for yourself. Make Joe look good, make yourself look good. Maybe the mayor will free up some funds so that Joe can finally buy another squad car or two." She smiled. "It's all politics, you know that. So take the commendation for your file and move on to the next case."

Charlie nodded. He understood what she was saying even if he didn't totally agree with it. She gave him a quick kiss on the chin and got out of the car. He watched her walk away thinking he'd rather be following her inside than going to city hall.

Mallory lifted the mail from the box and glanced through it briefly, noting that the second piece in the pile bore the county's seal.

Hopefully, my license. About time.

She ripped open the envelope and studied the license with satisfaction. Not that she'd need the license again, but at least now she could bill Robert Magellan for her hours.

She tucked the mail under her arm while she unlocked the front door and closed it behind her. She went directly to the kitchen, opened the refrigerator, and studied the contents. She hadn't eaten all day and was starving, but she hadn't been food shopping in a while so there wasn't much there. She opened a can of Diet Pepsi and drank from it, leaning back against the counter. She was hot and tired and hungry and just a little annoyed that she wasn't still with the department to take part in that press conference. As much as she'd denied it, it rankled just a little to step into the background. She knew it was strictly her ego at work, but she'd have loved a commendation in her personnel file for bringing in someone like Regina Girard.

Of course, she no longer had an active personnel file, and after today she wouldn't have a job, either.

She looked in the pantry for something she could fix, but all she had was soup and some Shredded Wheat. It was too hot out for the soup, and the cereal was past its prime. She drank a little more of the soda and thought about calling for a pizza. She thought she'd seen a flyer advertising a new place downtown, and she sorted through the stack of mail in search of it.

A plain white envelope slipped from the pile and fell to the floor as if pushed by an unseen finger. It was addressed to her in neat handwriting and had no return address. The postmark was some-place in New Jersey called Elm Hill. Curious, she slit open the back with a fingernail, and took out the single sheet of paper. She read with increasing confusion:

Dear Mallory,

I don't really know how to start this letter—I've already thrown away about thirty tries—so I decided I should just say what I have to say right up front. I know you've never heard of me, but I think we might be sisters. Well, half sisters anyway. Guess that got your attention, huh?

You are probably wondering how I found you—it's a story I'd like to share with you. But you're going to have to contact me if you want to know. I'm afraid you won't get in touch without that incentive, so I'm going to leave it at that, and hope you follow through. I pray you do. If you're at all curious, well, it's in your hands.

Sincerely,
Callen MacKenzie
1305 Campbell Road
Elm Hill, NJ
609-555-1793

Mallory read the letter over and over, as if she thought perhaps the contents might change with enough readings. But the message remained the same.

But was it true?

It couldn't be true. Maybe it was some of her former coworkers, harassing her again.

She'd find that easy enough to believe, except for one thing. Callen was her maternal grandmother's maiden name, and no one—

no one outside of her aunt Jess's immediate family—would know that.

So who was Callen MacKenzie, and how had she found out about Mallory?

Mallory was still sitting on the sofa in the living room asking herself that question when the doorbell rang.

She looked through the front window and was surprised to see that not only was it almost dark, but Charlie was on her top step holding a large white bag. She unlocked the door and opened it.

"Nice showing at the press conference," she said with a smile. "Good job, Detective Wanamaker. I'll bet your mama was proud."

He grunted noncommitedly, then held up the bag. "I'm guessing you didn't eat."

He walked past her and straight into the kitchen.

"And even if you did, you can watch me eat. I'm starving, how 'bout you?"

"Starving," she said, following him. Whatever was in the bag smelled incredible.

"I wasn't sure what you liked, so I picked up . . . Could you get a couple of plates? I wasn't kidding when I said I was starving. Forks would be nice, too, though I don't have a problem using my hands if I have to. Don't know if you have any thoughts on that one way or the other." He lifted several plastic containers from the bag. "Anyway, we have one meat loaf with a baked potato and green beans, and one roast chicken with mashed and . . . I think carrots in that one." He dipped into the bag again. "Salads . . . got a selection of dressings here because, like I said, I don't know what you like. Three different desserts—we have a chocolate cake, a lemon meringue pie, and some sort of fruit tart, because—"

"—because you don't know what I like," she finished offhandedly.

"I want to know, Mal." He put the containers on the table and turned to her, his eyes solemn. "I want to know whether you like your potatoes baked or mashed. And whether you prefer lemon to chocolate. Cake or pie. Ranch, Italian, or vinaigrette. I want to know those things about you. I want to take it day by day, and learn as we go."

Despite her best efforts not to, she began to cry, the tears rolling down her face in fat drops. He gathered her into his arms and held her as if he understood, even if she wasn't sure she did, where the tears came from.

When she'd cried it out, she wiped her face with her hands and said, "Wow. Sorry. You come here to bring me dinner and you get flooded out for your efforts. Sorry. It's just that . . ."

She struggled with her words.

"Take your time," he said softly. "We have all night."

"Don't you have to get home . . . ?"

"My mother took herself to rehab a day early. Well, her friend took her, they went together. She left me a note."

"She didn't get to see you on TV. She'd have been so proud."

"I'm more proud of her. Hers is the bigger accomplishment. I had help. She didn't."

He reached up and pulled something from her hair.

"Straw." He held it up for her inspection. "I think I see a little more there."

"I'm not surprised, crawling around barns, falling face-first in the henhouse, who knows what's in my hair. I haven't had a shower yet."

"Hmmmm. Neither have I." He nuzzled the side of her face. "And the way I see it, you owe me one."

Mallory laughed and took him by the hand. "You're right. And it's the least I can do."

She led him through the living room and up the steps to the second floor. Later, she would try, but could not remember who took off whose clothes, or how warm the water was, or who soaped who first.

He'd murmured something in her ear, but she couldn't remember the words. All she recalled was that moment when he'd lifted her and leaned her back against the cool tile wall. She'd stared into his eyes, watched them go from dark blue to smoky, and she was lost. His mouth had been hot on hers, on the skin of her neck, her breasts, and an urgency swept through her that had left her weak. She'd wrapped her legs around his hips, seeking completion, aching desperately to take him inside, then reached up and wound her arms around his neck, and held on for the ride.

TWENTY-SIX

A phone was ringing somewhere, but Mallory couldn't place the sound.

"That's mine," Charlie mumbled from the other side of the bed.

His hand reached out from under the sheet and groped clumsily on the bedside table.

"Hello," he said. "Yeah. Sure. Be there in twenty minutes."

Mallory rolled onto her side and raised herself on one elbow. "You can't get anywhere from here in twenty minutes. Unless you're planning to go as you are."

"It's still my first week on the job," he told her as he turned to her. "I think I need to behave myself for the first month or so."

He leaned down and kissed her mouth. "That was Drabyak. He wants to see me before the shift begins." He glanced at the clock. "Which is in less than thirty minutes."

"You better get moving, then. Traffic into the city is tough this time of the morning."

He disappeared into the hall, and several minutes later returned wearing his slacks and buttoning up the front of his shirt. He finished dressing, then leaned over to kiss her again.

"Did Joe give you any idea of what he wanted to talk to you about?"

"None. Just said it was important."

"I'm sure it is for him to call you in on a Saturday morning."

He took his watch from the table next to the bed and strapped it on, then leaned over and kissed her good-bye. "I'll call you later."

She sat up and listened to his footfalls on the stairs, heard the front door open and close quietly. Then she lay back against the pillows and stared at the ceiling, and remembered that she hadn't told him about the letter from Callen MacKenzie.

She got out of bed and went downstairs for coffee, picking the letter up as she passed through the living room. She read it again while she measured coffee into a paper filter and poured water into the top of the coffeemaker, and wondered if Callen MacKenzie had grown up feeling as lost as she herself had. There had never been a day in her childhood when she'd felt as if she belonged anywhere, to anyone. Had Callen felt that way, too? Who had their mother passed Callen off to? Or had she kept her?

"Connie Theresa Russo." Mallory spoke her mother's name aloud for the first time in a very long time.

The coffeemaker beeped to let her know it had done its job. She poured herself a cup, then poked in the open bags that were left on the kitchen table and found the fruit tart untouched. She got a fork from the drawer and was just about to dig in when the phone rang again.

"Hello?"

"When I get back there, I expect that tart to be right where we left it," Charlie said.

She laughed. "Are you looking through the window?" She walked to the back door and peered out, expecting to see him through the glass.

"No, I just figured you for a dessert-in-the-morning kind of gal."

"You figured right." She gazed at it longingly. "I'm standing here with fork in hand."

"I'll bring you another one tonight." He paused. "Pecan or apple?"

"Another apple," she told him. "It's my favorite."

"Apple it is," he said, then added, "It's my favorite, too."

She hung up and polished off the tart, standing with her back against the counter and staring out the window, pushed Connie Russo back into that dark corner where she kept the name, and turned her attention to the now. How she would spend her day? There was the book she was working on, she reminded herself, but working on it wasn't the same as working a case. She envied Charlie, having someplace to go, a new case to dive into. She hadn't permitted herself the luxury of missing the job these past few months. Getting back into it, even for a few weeks and on a limited basis, had reminded her of all the reasons why she'd wanted to be a cop in the first place.

She was just about to open the back door for a breath of fresh air when the phone rang again.

"Mallory, it's Susanna Jones. Congratulations. We saw the news this morning. Well done."

"Thank you. I'm just glad things turned out the way they did."

"We'd like to settle up with you. Is there a time that's convenient for you to drive out to the house to pick up a check?"

"My license finally arrived, so yes, I can drive out today. I'll need some time to get my hours together. When my house was broken into, my laptop was stolen along with some of my notes."

"I'm sure you'll be able to re-create a reasonable time line. Is two o'clock all right?"

"I should be able to make it by two."

"We'll see you then."

Mallory took her coffee out back and sat on one of the plastic chairs. It wobbled slightly when she sat, and she thought maybe this year might be the year to buy a few real chairs. Maybe a small table with a glass top where she and Charlie could have dinner sometime.

Assuming Charlie was still around.

She pondered that possibility for a while before admitting to herself that there was a good chance he might stick. The realization that she wanted him to didn't surprise her as much as she once thought such feelings might. She couldn't remember the last time she felt that connected to anyone.

"Like the man said, day by day," she said aloud, and went back into the house to prepare her time sheets.

TWENTY-SEVEN

Robert Magellan stood in his kitchen and eyed the fresh-from-the-oven scones.

"Strawberries and pecans, I think," he murmured as he reached for one.

"Don't even think about it," Trula warned. "Those are for Father Kevin and Mrs. Corcoran. You can have an English muffin."

"How does Kevin rate fresh scones and I get a dried-up English muffin?" Robert protested. "It's the priest thing, isn't it? You figure, the better you feed him, the harder he'll be praying for you."

"I don't have to bribe Kevin to pray for me," she sniffed. "And I made scones for you last week."

"That was then, this is now." He stared longingly at the baking rack.

"You'll have one later, when our company arrives."

"Only one?" He frowned. "And since when is Kevin company?"

"He isn't. Mary Corcoran is." She shooed him away from the counter.

"Remind me again why she's coming."

"She wants to thank you for saving her grandson's life."

"I didn't save him. I was playing golf when he was saved."

"You hired the woman who found him. Same thing."

"It's not the same thing. And she could just as easily thank Kevin for both of us. It was his idea to hire the detective, not mine. And she already thanked me on the phone. Three times, last night."

"She wants to thank you in person. It's the polite thing to do." She turned and scowled. "Honestly, Robert, I don't know what's wrong with you. You've turned into a curmudgeony old recluse and I don't like it. Not one bit."

"I'm not a recluse. I talk to you, to Kevin, to Suse—"

"You avoid people like the plague." Her voice softened. "That's no way to live, son. And you have a lot to live for."

"Had," he corrected her. "I had a lot to live for."

"If Beth could hear you, she'd . . . well, I don't know what she'd do, but I know she wouldn't like it one bit. And tell me this: If you had been the one to have gone missing, would you want Beth to throw away the rest of her life, the way you're doing? Or would you want her to live, to find some good to do, to find someone else to—?"

Before she could finish, a horn blew outside the kitchen window. They both turned toward the sound. Kevin had pulled up behind the house and was helping Mary Corcoran out of the car.

"Swell," he grumbled.

"And don't even think about slipping off to your office," Trula said as she opened the back door. "Father Kevin, Mrs. Corcoran. Please come in . . ."

Mary Corcoran's eyes were rimmed with red, but her smile lit her face.

"Mr. Magellan." She crossed the room to Robert, both hands out reaching for his.

He'd started to flinch, to pull back, but behind Mary, Trula stood like a sentinel. Mary squeezed his hands before letting go, her eyes welling with tears, and she touched his face.

"There are no words to thank you for what you've done," she whispered, her mouth quivering, her voice charged with quiet emotion. "Because of you—your kindness, your generosity—my grandson is alive. Courtney—her sister—home with their mother, where they belong. There are no words, Mr. Magellan . . ."

He patted her awkwardly.

"Robert," he said. "I'd rather you called me Robert."

"I'd all but given up hope," Mary went on. "Before you sent Mallory . . ."

"Actually, it was Kevin and Susanna who . . ."

"I was so afraid I'd never see him again. I know you know that pain, Mr. Magellan. I know your heartache. The not knowing is the worst, isn't it?" She dabbed at her face with a tissue. "Fear the last thing you feel at night, the first thing you feel in the morning? There were days these past few weeks when the pain was so great, I felt I couldn't contain it. How you have been able to hang on for so long . . . over a year now, I think."

"Fifteen months," he told her. "Since February 11, 2007."

"My heart breaks for you. It's so hard to carry that pain alone. Sometimes that hole inside feels so big, you know if you fall into it, you'll never stop. Never reach the bottom." She nodded in Kevin's direction. "Through Father Burch, I found a support group. Parents of missing children. They helped me so much. Despite their own terrible losses, they reached out to me. Maybe they could help you, too, with your pain."

"I'm afraid I'm not much of a joiner, Mrs. Corcoran, but thank you."

"They're a wonderful group. They're all still waiting for their miracles, you know. I pray for them every day. Just as I pray for you, Mr. Magellan."

"Thank you. I appreciate that." He wasn't sure prayers would help at this late date, but her sincerity all but broke his heart.

"You know, I was going to take out a second mortgage on my house—a bank loan—whatever it would have taken to have put together enough money to hire someone to find Ryan. I knew the police were not going to find him, Mr. Magellan. Not alive, anyway. Because of you, I still have my grandson. May God show you the same mercy you've shown me, Mr. Magellan. May he bless you with a miracle of your own."

Mary turned and nodded to Kevin, who took her arm and wordlessly led her back to the car. Trula and Robert watched in silence as the car made a circle around the drive and continued on toward the front gate. After it had disappeared from sight, Robert put his mug down on the counter and left the kitchen, seeking the solace of the den at the end of the hall.

He sat by the window and stared out at the garden Trula had designed over the winter and worked on all spring. She'd been out there every day since the end of March, directing the gardeners where to plant what, where to lay the path she had in mind. She hadn't asked his permission, but neither had she required it. She wanted a garden, she planted one. His house was her house, pretty much. It was a promise he'd made to an old woman he'd loved deeply, one he'd never go back on, and never regretted.

Well, most of the time, anyway.

He heard her footsteps coming down the hall and braced himself for an interrogation, thinking wryly that this might be one of those times.

She knocked once—a quick knuckle rap—before opening the door and coming in. She balanced a tray, which she placed on the table in front of him.

"Can't let the scones go to waste," she told him. "Might as well have them with our morning tea."

"Trula, you're the only one who regularly has morning tea," he reminded her.

"Well, everyone should. It's civilized. Gives you a few minutes to sit back, take stock. It's a more relaxing drink than coffee. Tea is a dreamer's drink, I suppose."

"What's coffee?"

"A doer's drink." She leaned over to pour the tea. "These were your grandmother's cups. She had a lovely collection. Picked them up wherever she went. Most are antiques, you know."

"I know. And then there are all those mugs with those pithy sayings."

"Mine, as you well know." Trula laughed. "My favorite is that one with the *X-Files* saying on it."

"About the truth being out there somewhere."

"It certainly is." Trula handed him one of the cups. "She'd have been proud of you, of what you did."

"All I did was write a check." He hesitated, then added, "And I haven't even done that yet. All I did was agree to pay the bill."

"But that's the point, don't you see?" She sat down in the chair opposite him. "Most people—everyday people—can't afford to hire private detectives when something like this happens. Most people just have to sit and wait for the police to find their missing person— or not. How many of those people—the ones Mary spoke of, the ones in her support group—how many of them do you think can afford to hire people to track down their loved ones, especially those who have been gone for a long time? Most people simply do not have the resources."

"I have the resources, Trula. Fat lot of good it did me. In real life, every story doesn't have a happy ending."

"Sometimes money isn't enough, of course it isn't. But sometimes, it turns out to be the difference between finding and not finding. Between a happy ending, and none."

"Maybe Mallory just got lucky."

"Maybe. I certainly don't discount luck."

"Was there a point to this conversation?"

Trula smiled at his impatience. "Just that it was a good thing that you did. Your grandmother would have been pleased—proud—that you used your wealth in such a way."

"I give money to a lot of charities," he reminded her.

"Ah, but it isn't the same as doing good for one person, face-to-face, is it?" She smiled in triumph.

He was still trying to think of a response when they heard Kevin calling his name in the hall.

"We're in here, Father," Trula called back. "Come join us. I'll get you some tea."

Kevin came into the room carrying a bottle of springwater.

"No need, Trula. I brought along my beverage of choice. I've been thinking I should drink more water. I hear it's healthier."

"Healthier than what?" Robert asked.

"Healthier than drinking other stuff all the time."

"Sit and have a scone." She rose and patted him on the shoulder. "I have some things to tend to."

"Thanks. I think I will." Kevin slid into the seat she vacated. He inspected the tray of scones. "Are those strawberry?" He picked one up and sniffed. "And pecans, if I'm not mistaken."

"I think I'll go see if there are any more of those late tulips blooming that I can cut for the breakfast room. I feel like a little color in there this morning." Trula took her cup and drifted from the room.

"Mary's right, you know," Kevin said as he reached for a napkin. "Those kids would most likely be dead if not for you."

"I'm getting a little tired of saying this, but all I did was agree to pay the bill."

"That's what it took, Rob. Someone who cared enough to pay the bill."

"Mallory did a good job putting the pieces together. She and that new detective the city hired—I saw him on the news last night and again this morning. No mention of Mallory's part in it, though."

"Isn't that the way you wanted it? No publicity?"

"I guess. Just seems a shame, she isn't getting any credit."

"She'll get paid, that's what she agreed to. And she has the satisfaction of knowing what she did mattered. I think that would be important to someone like her." Kevin took a bite of scone. "Chief Drabyak was right about her, though. She has good instincts. Have you thought about hiring her to look for Beth and Ian?"

"What do you think she could do that no one else has done?"

Kevin shrugged. "I don't know. I think it's worth a try, though."

"I'll think about it."

"Think about it before someone else decides to hire her. Mary was right about there being a lot of missing persons out there." He finished the scone and took a long drink of water. "There are a lot of folks, still waiting for their miracles."

Robert made a face.

"You could make it happen, you know," Kevin said quietly.

"Make what happen?"

"The miracles."

"I haven't done much in the way of miracles for myself. Mallory just got lucky." He repeated his earlier statement.

"Do you ever think about your purpose in life, Rob?"

"Not recently."

"Maybe you should."

"Maybe you should shut up."

"Show some respect for a man of the cloth, will you? Lightning could come down from the sky and strike you for that."

"If lightning was going to strike me, it would have a long time ago. Maybe it already has." Robert studied his cousin's face. "I know this is all leading up to something. I'm just not sure what it is."

"After I dropped Mary off at the hospital—Ryan is going to be fine, by the way—I started thinking about what she said."

"I guess it's too much to hope for that you'd keep it to yourself."

Kevin smiled. "I was thinking about all the others, the people who don't have the connections that Mary had. Who don't have the resources that you have."

"And . . . ?" Robert gestured for Kevin to continue.

"And I was thinking that it shouldn't come down to money. It all too often does, but it shouldn't. Whether or not you get your miracle shouldn't depend on whether or not you can afford it."

"All the money in the world can't guarantee a miracle, Kevin."

"No, but sometimes, like I said, it can make the difference." Kevin drained the water bottle and sat it on the table. "Your money could make a difference for some of those people, Rob. Just like it made a difference for Ryan and Courtney."

"Are you asking me to keep a PI on call?" Robert mimicked a late-night TV pitch man. "Loved one missing? Call Rob's Miracles to Go . . ."

Robert stood, his hands on his hips.

"Is that what you're asking me to do? Start a missing persons bureau? Because last I heard, the FBI has one of those already."

"I'm thinking more along the lines of a facilitator," Kevin replied.

"A facilitator," Robert repeated flatly. "And what might we be facilitating?"

"Hope. Mercy . . ."

Robert cut him off.

"Hope is an empty word, Kev, and mercy comes from God."

"Think about it before you write it off. What else do you have to do with your money? Sit and watch it grow? Isn't that a nice life."

"I did have a nice life. . . ."

"And now it's gone, and you're going to spend the rest of your life mourning your loss, just staring out that window, your heart growing smaller and smaller and you getting more and more lonely and depressed until you can't take it anymore." Kevin grabbed him by the arm. "Don't think I don't know what's been going through your mind, Rob. And don't think I'm going to stand for it. I will do anything—say anything—to make you understand that there's still a life worth living. That maybe God has other plans for you. I will not sit by and let you take your life."

Robert looked away.

"Robert, do something that would make Beth proud."

"I don't think she's coming back," Robert whispered. "I don't feel her anymore."

"If she's moved on from this world, do something worthy of her memory. Give her something to smile about when she looks back."

Kevin tucked the empty water bottle under his arm and patted his cousin on the back.

"You have a very rare opportunity to change people's lives the way you've changed the lives of Ryan and Courtney. There are others who could use your help. Think it over, Rob. Maybe there's something better to do with all that money besides watching it grow . . ."

TWENTY-EIGHT

I t was midafternoon when Trula came into the den and pulled the window shades halfway down.

"The sun is going to fade out those nice brown leather chairs," she told him. "It comes in at such an angle back here this time of the day."

She fussed with some dead leaves on a massive philodendron that sat on the sill and spilled over the sides of its pot. "Mallory Russo is here," she added. "I sent her to Susanna's office."

"Thanks, Trula."

"Are you all right, Robert?" Her voice held gentle concern. "Son?"

"I'm good, Trula. Thanks." He got up and kissed her cheek. "I'm good."

He walked across the hall and knocked on the open door.

"May I join you?" he asked from the doorway.

"Sure. I was just going to come looking for you." Susanna smiled.

"Nice job, Mallory," Robert said as he entered the room.

"I had a lot of help." Mallory turned to look over her shoulder at him.

"The new Conroy detective, yes, I heard. What was his name?"

"Charlie Wanamaker," Mallory told him.

"Wanamaker, right. There used to be a department store in Philadelphia, Wanamaker's."

Neither Mallory nor Susanna commented, but Robert could feel Suse's eyes on him. He sat next to Mallory and asked, "So, what's next for you?"

Mallory shrugged. "I guess I'll go back to working on the book I was writing when I took this job."

"Iffy business, I would think." He stretched his legs out in front. "Writing books. Unless it's sold already." He turned to her. "Have you sold your book yet?"

"No."

Robert looked across the desk at Susanna and asked, "Have you settled up with her?"

Susanna shook her head. "We were just discussing that."

He reached for the checkbook lying open in front of Susanna and took the pen from her hand.

"Two *l*'s?" he asked.

"What?" Susanna frowned.

"Two *l*'s in *Mallory*?"

"Yes," Susanna told him.

He wrote on the check, tore it from the book, and handed it to Mallory.

"That should cover it, I would think," he said.

Mallory looked at the check, her eyebrows rising almost to her hairline.

"Mr. Magellan . . ."

"Robert."

"This is way too much. Susanna and I were just discussing my hours, which expenses were reimbursable . . ."

He waved her away. "You found the kids alive, you got them home. You're entitled to the reward."

"What reward?" Susanna frowned.

"Didn't I mention I was putting up a reward for the safe return of the kids?"

"No. This is the first I've heard about it."

"Well, there was a reward, and I just paid it."

"Really, Robert, I'm not entitled to all this." Mallory appeared to be still in shock. "I didn't work this alone, I didn't—"

"Wanamaker." Robert nodded. "Is he very good? Your opinion?"

"Yes, he's very good, he's—"

"Does he like being a detective?"

"I suppose he does," Mallory replied.

"Did you like being a detective?" Robert asked.

"Yes," she said. "I did. Very much."

"I'm not going to ask you why you quit—that's your business. What I'd like to know is, would you be interested in doing more of this type of work?"

"Looking for missing kids?"

"Missing kids, missing adults." He glanced over at Susanna, who appeared totally baffled. The thought made him smile. He realized he liked throwing her a curve once in a while. He hadn't done enough of that lately. He wondered why she'd stuck with him all this time, boring and moody as he was. "I suppose we shouldn't restrict our efforts to just children. What do you think, Suse?"

"I have no idea what you're talking about, Robert," she said flatly.

"What if I were to offer you a job, Mallory? Would you be interested?"

"You mean, looking for your wife and son?"

"My wife, my son . . . and others."

"What others?" Susanna and Mallory both asked at the same time.

"Others who are missing."

"Robert, may I speak with you in private?" Susanna pushed her chair back from her desk.

"It's like Mary Corcoran said this morning," he continued, ignoring Susanna. "That she was lucky because someone was willing to help her—that most people don't have the means necessary to pick up where law enforcement leaves off. It started me thinking. The police did the best they could to find Beth and Ian—I really believe they worked tirelessly to find them. And if no one else had been killed or gone missing after my family did, I believe the police would still be looking for them. Maybe they still are. But something Chief Drabyak told me last year keeps coming back to me. There are only so many man-hours, only so much time that can be devoted to any one case before the next one comes in."

"He's right, of course. The newer case has a greater chance to be solved because it's—well—newer. Witnesses are easier to locate, the evidence is fresher. A lot of cases—not just missing persons, but murders, other suspicious deaths—get put aside because there's always another case. A lot of cases just go cold because there's not enough time to follow every lead, to check and recheck things over and over. A lot of families stay in that state of limbo, never knowing what happened to their daughter or son, their parent or sibling. If missing, are they dead or alive? If dead, how did they get that way?"

"With the right people, the right resources, how many of those missing people might be found? How many murders solved?"

Mallory shook her head. "There's no way to know for certain."

"But some probably could."

She nodded. "Some, probably, yes."

"Robert, are you thinking about starting your own little private police force?" Susanna asked, one eyebrow raised.

"Not exactly, but that's good, Suse. I'm thinking of something more along the lines of a private firm that acts like a . . ." He searched for the right word. "A catalyst. That's what I think we should be. A catalyst for solving cases that everyone else has pretty much given up on."

He turned back to Mallory. "What would it take to start up such an undertaking?"

"God, I don't know." She shook her head. "You'd need personnel . . ."

"Such as?"

"Such as more than one investigator. If you're going to be looking at old crimes, you're going to want someone who can reconstruct the scene and analyze it. A forensics specialist, maybe. Maybe a criminologist." Mallory grinned wryly. "And if you're really going for it, why not go all the way and throw in your own lab?"

Robert nodded thoughtfully. "Which would require at least one or two lab techs. Yes, I can see where we could need a lab."

Seeing he was serious, Mallory said, "How many investigators, how many experts, it's going to depend on the caseload."

"Right."

"How would you decide which cases to take on?" Mallory asked, intrigued. "As you say, there are so many people who have gone missing and never have been found. So many unsolved deaths. Where would the cases come from?"

"From people who contact us and ask us for help. We'd look into the cases and decide which one to take on."

"Which *one*?"

"One at a time."

"How would you make that decision?" Susanna asked. "How do you decide which case is most worthy of your attention, who's most worthy to be found?"

"I guess we'd talk about it. You, me, Mallory—and whoever else we hire." He turned to Mallory. "Would you think it over? And if you're interested, make a list of what you think would be required for something like this. And maybe jot down your thoughts on the criteria we should consider when choosing a case."

"Robert, this is overwhelming, but yes. I'll think about it." She laughed self-consciously. "I probably won't be able to stop thinking about it. It's the most intriguing idea I've ever heard." She tucked the check he'd given her into her wallet. "How would you know what to charge people?"

"We're not charging. See, that's the whole point. I'll set up a foundation and people who need our help will apply, sort of like the way they'd apply for a grant or a scholarship."

"Like I said, intriguing."

"But you're interested."

"Definitely." Mallory nodded.

"How 'bout Detective Wanamaker, you think he'd be interested in talking to me?"

"I have no way of knowing. I can mention it to him." Mallory stood and gathered her bag.

"Please do that. Tell him to give me a call if he thinks it sounds like something he'd like to do."

"I will. Thank you for the offer. I feel a little dazed by the whole idea."

"You're not the only one," Susanna said.

After he'd walked Mallory to the front door, Robert returned to Susanna's office.

"I messed up your weekend," Robert said. "But I appreciate you coming in on Saturday. You can always take Monday off, you know, if you want both days."

"I just might do that."

"So what do you think of my idea, Suse?"

"I think it's a very novel idea." She seemed to choose her words carefully. "What are you planning on naming this new venture of yours?"

He thought it over for a moment. "I don't know. I haven't had time to think about it."

"Think about what?" Kevin appeared in the doorway.

Robert explained his brainchild.

When he finished, he said, "We were just discussing what to call this organization. Any thoughts?"

"Something with *mercy* in the name," the priest replied, "because like Mary said, mercy is what all of those lost souls are praying for. And this new venture of yours, isn't this supposed to be for those who really have no other place to go to seek help?"

"So our foundation should be the vehicle . . . the road . . . to finding a miracle." Robert toyed with the words. "Mercy Road. Miracle Road. Mercy Way . . ."

"Mercy Street," Kevin said. "Like the old Peter Gabriel song. Mercy Street."

"I like that." Susanna smiled. "I like that a lot."

"You're a Peter Gabriel fan?" Robert frowned. "I didn't know you went in for all that world-music stuff."

"Like I said, it's an old song, but a good one," Kevin said. "And a good name, I think, for what you have in mind."

"So Mercy Street it is?" Robert looked around the room at the others.

"I think it should be The Mercy Street Foundation," Susanna pointed out.

"Even better," Robert readily agreed. "The Mercy Street Foundation it is . . ."

TWENTY-NINE

S o how was your day?" Charlie asked after he and Mallory had been seated and their waiter had handed them menus.

"You first," she told him. She wanted his take on Robert Magellan's offer—but was more interested in finding out why Joe had called Charlie in early on a Saturday morning, and just what were the "startling rumors" that "swirled around the sniper case" a TV reporter had hinted at. She decided there was no point in beating around the bush. "What did Joe want so early this morning?"

"He's a really smart guy, you know?" Charlie looked up from his menu. "I'll bet he was one hell of a cop."

"He's a really smart guy, and he was—still is—a hell of a cop."

"Right. He . . . ahhh, he . . ." Charlie paused while their water glasses were served. The requisite lemon slices bobbed atop the crushed ice. When the busboy walked away, Charlie lowered his voice. "The chief has this theory about this whole sniper thing."

"Which theory is that?" She was trying to read the menu and

listen at the same time. She finally made a quick decision on dinner then folded the menu and placed it next to her plate.

"He's never bought into that whole homeless-guy-gets-his-hands-on-an-assault-rifle-and-starts-shooting-at-the-residents thing. So he started picking at the seams of it. You know, how did Whitman just happen to be in the park at the same time the supposed sniper was there? And how did Gomez—the homeless guy—acquire his marksman skills?"

"So how did Whitman end up in the park?"

"He says—Whitman says—he saw the guy enter the park from Ninth Street, looked like he was carrying something suspicious, so he followed him. Says the guy turned on him and started shooting, so Whitman fired back. Says he chased him through the park as far as the fountain, where he—Whitman—was able to bring him down."

"I'm assuming the spent shells were all there to back up his story."

"Sure enough. But here's where the story gets really interesting: There was a woman sleeping behind the fountain who swears that Gomez was in the park when she got there, a good hour or so before she heard the shots. Says she knows he didn't leave because he told her he'd stepped on some glass and cut his left foot and he couldn't walk, so he was going to sleep on one of the benches. Says he showed her the gash."

"How credible is she?"

"Under other circumstances, maybe not very. But I checked with the morgue. Gomez had a damned good slice on the bottom of his left foot. No way would he have been running through the park."

"Who found the woman?"

"The chief asked me to ask around, see if there were any witnesses that might have been overlooked."

"And you found her?"

"She'd never left the park. She's waiting for some stargate or something to come for her. So when you say 'credible,' I guess it's all relative. She's a little shaky. But the gash on Gomez's foot is just where she said, just as she described it."

"She would have had to have seen the rifle, though, right?"

"She says he didn't have one. Says he didn't have anything with him."

"But the news reports all say that after the shooting, he called for backup . . ."

"And that your best friend, Detective Toricelli, was first on the scene."

"Frank backed up whatever Cal told him," she said, thinking aloud.

"Right. Says he found Gomez with the rifle still in his hand, blah, blah, blah. You know the drill."

"So no matter what anyone suspects, without any evidence to the contrary, Cal Whitman is the hero who brought down the Conroy Sniper." She bit the inside of her bottom lip. "Would it be cynical if I said something like, *Way to get your old job back* or *Way to hang on to the pension?*"

"Apparently that's exactly what the chief was thinking when he started talking to a few of his old CIs on the sly."

"And . . ."

"And someone put him on to a hooker downtown who's been harassed a bit by Frank over the past year. Threatens to bring her in for soliciting, but will look the other way in exchange for a little 'consideration.' According to her, he's been shaking her down for sex for the past year."

"Ursula," Mallory said.

"How did you know?" Charlie frowned.

"Sally mentioned it."

"You told the chief?"

Mallory nodded.

"So that's where that tip came from." Charlie grinned. "Just one more reason for Frank to love you, babe."

"I'm going to go out on a limb here and assume you've spoken to Ursula."

"Got an earful. Frank likes to talk, you know?"

She rolled her eyes.

"Yeah, I know," Charlie said. "I was shocked, too. Anyway, apparently he came around one night last week, tries to get her into his squad car. She's balking, and he tells her to get the fuck in the car or he'll do her like they did the others, and the sniper would get blamed."

"Whoa!"

"Yeah. But it gets better. Last night, he has her in his squad car doing her thing when he gets a call. He practically pushes her out of the car and takes off like a bat out of hell."

"And this blows a hole in the case how?"

"Because Ursula said he got pissed off and yelled at the caller, 'Cal, you dumb shit, you were supposed to wait for me. What if someone comes along before I get there?' Then he tells the caller to put the piece where it's supposed to be, then wait until he gets there before he does anything else."

"Holy shit. They set Gomez up?" Mallory went wide-eyed at the thought.

"The chief thinks—this is the worst part—they set it all up. That there was no sniper."

"But all those shootings . . . those people who were shot at, scared shitless . . ."

"All by the same rifle that allegedly was fired by Gomez at Whitman."

"But that would mean that Cal . . ." She sputtered. "Cal was the shooter all along?"

"The chief thinks probably he and Toricelli were splitting the duties, so that they would each have something on the other."

"You can't rat me out because I'll rat on you."

"Insurance." Charlie nodded.

"So what next?" Mallory asked.

"The chief is bumping it over to IA. He doesn't want anyone in his department involved in the investigation from here on out."

"I'm just stunned."

"Yeah, so's the chief. He said he knew Frank was a jerk and that Cal was still pissed about being busted back to patrol, but he never suspected either one of them would do something like this."

"Why would they have done something so terrible?"

"Cal wanted his detective job back, Frank wanted the lead detective job. They figured if they manufactured a sniper, shot at a few folks, got the town into a frenzy, then they could go together on the collar and look like superstars. The chief looked up the time line—the only nights there were shootings were nights when Frank was on duty."

"So he could cover Cal, and vice versa."

"That's the theory."

"So where are they now?"

"Being interrogated by IA."

"Incredible." Mallory shook her head. "What do you hear about Regina? Is she going to make it?"

"She didn't make it out of surgery." He studied her face as she took in the news.

"Shit." She frowned. "You never like to think about killing another human being, but it's hard to work up too much sympathy for someone like her. Still . . ."

"There is no 'still.' You did what you had to do, Mal. Regina Girard was a one-woman killing machine. Whenever you start feeling sorry for Regina, just think about Sally."

"Good point." She nodded.

"Your turn. How was your day?"

Mallory told him about her meeting with Robert Magellan.

"Interesting proposition," he said. "Why you?"

"Magellan was paying the freight for the investigation. His cousin is the parish priest at Our Lady of Angels."

"And Mary Corcoran is the parish secretary."

"Right. Father Burch asked Robert to pay for the investigator, and he agreed, on the condition I not tell anyone he was involved. Sorry I didn't tell you sooner, but . . ."

"Hey, a deal's a deal. You gave your word. Besides, it's not as if it would have made a difference in the outcome."

"True." She thought for a moment. "He overpaid me. I think I should split it with you."

"The city's paying me." Charlie waved her off. "So what did you tell Magellan?"

"I told him I'd think about it. But I'll probably do it, if he's serious. I've made good progress on the book I was working on, but frankly, it just isn't doing it for me. I think maybe the idea appealed to me because it kept me connected to my years as a cop, and when I left the force, I really needed that connection. I had enough money saved to keep me going until I sold my book." She smiled wryly. "It never occurred to me that it wouldn't sell. And I wouldn't be the first ex-cop to write a book about an infamous case she—or he—solved. But I miss working on cases, I'd be lying if I said I didn't. I wasn't even aware of how much until the past few weeks." She grinned. "Robert wants to know if you'd be interested in signing on."

"As tempting as it sounds, I'd have to say no. I like being a cop. I probably will always be a cop. But I'm flattered that he thought of me. It's a really unusual idea, but a great one. A lot of people like the Corcorans and the Bauers could benefit from it." He reached across the table and took her hand. "Besides, this way, we don't have to worry about breaking the rule."

"Which rule is that?"

"The one about not seeing someone you work with."

"Is that what we're going to be doing, Charlie? Seeing each other?"

"Every chance we get."

THIRTY

This has been some week, hasn't it?" Robert said as Susanna walked past on her way to the back door.

"I'll say." She leaned her briefcase on the kitchen counter. "I left some checks on your desk for you to sign. Also, there are some letters you need to look over. They can wait until Monday to go out, but if you want to make any changes, just handwrite on the letter and I'll take care of it when I get in."

"Thanks. I'll take a look." He glanced up at the clock. It was almost seven on Saturday evening. "I appreciate you coming in today, but it looks like we shot your weekend."

"It's fine. I don't mind at all."

"So, what are you going to do with the rest of the weekend?"

"Oh, the usual."

"Nothing exciting?"

"Nope. How about you?" she asked.

"Golf, I think." He walked to the back window. "I'm thinking of having a few holes put in out there on the back couple of acres. I'm not using them for anything else."

"Good idea." She paused at the door. "Well, if there's nothing else . . ."

"Nothing else." He shrugged. "Have a good one."

"You too. Tell Trula I said the same."

"Will do." He followed her out the door. "Oh, hey . . ."

She turned around. "*Hey* what?"

"Hey, I owe you dinner." He smiled. "In Paris, I believe the bet was. Transportation provided."

"I don't know that either of us really won," she pointed out. "The bet was, that Mallory wouldn't pad her bill."

"And she didn't. So you won." He leaned against the doorjamb. "What day's good for you?"

"You tell me. You're the boss."

"Wednesday." He smiled. "Let's go on Wednesday."

"I'll make a note. Wednesday. Paris." She saluted and continued walking down the hall.

She had a lot of road to cover over the next twenty-four hours. Ever since Robert had decided to start up his foundation to find lost souls—as Trula had dubbed it—she'd been on edge. She couldn't wait to get back out to the mountain roads. She knew her theory could be wrong, but until Beth and Ian turned up somewhere else—dead or alive—she would keep looking down every ravine, around every mountain curve. She wanted to be the one to find them. It meant everything to her.

Where they would go from there, she couldn't know. All she knew on this early summer night was that if anyone was going to give him that gift, bring him the peace he was so in need of, it was going to be her.

Susanna turned on her GPS, put a Faith Hill CD in the player, and set off to resume her weekly search.

ABOUT THE AUTHOR

MARIAH STEWART is the award-winning, *New York Times* bestselling author of twenty-three novels. A native of Hightstown, New Jersey, she lives in Chester County, Pennsylvania, with her husband and their two daughters.

ABOUT THE TYPE

This book was set in Minion, a 1990 Adobe Originals typeface by Robert Slimbach. Minion is inspired by classical, old-style typefaces of the late Renaissance, a period of elegant, beautiful, and highly readable type designs. Created primarily for text setting, Minion combines the aesthetic and functional qualities that make text type highly readable with the versatility of digital technology.